AFTERNOONS
WITH
HARVEY
BEAM

Carrie Cox is a journalist, author, tutor, mother and timid surfer, never all at once and not in that order. She grew up in Mackay, Queensland, and has also lived in Sydney, Brisbane and, since 2010, Perth. She has written and subedited for many publications, including *The Sunday Telegraph*, *Encore*, *Practical Parenting*, *Brisbane News*, *Woman's Day*, *TV Week* and *The Weekend West*. Carrie penned a weekly satirical column, 'Carrie On', that was syndicated to six newspapers over ten years until she ran out of things to say. She has also authored two non-fiction books, *Coal, Crisis, Challenge* and *You Take The High Road and I'll Take The Bus*. This is her first novel.

**Published with support from the
Fremantle Press Champions of Literature**

AFTERNOONS
WITH
HARVEY
BEAM

CARRIE COX

 FREMANTLE PRESS

For those who stay, those who leave and those caught between.

1

Harvey Beam looks at the boiling tarmac and mentally crosses himself. God only beckons when he is sitting on a plane and only in those tortuous moments before take-off when everything that is about to happen seems hopelessly naive and poorly thought out. It's in these moments, fingers gouged deep into the armrests, that he silently prays a benevolent onlooker not only exists but will also forgive once again the sheer arrogance of humans, of people who think it reasonable to launch two hundred tonnes (he has looked this up) of bent metal and loosening rivets into the sky on the strength of — please — a run-up. A run-up that frankly never feels sufficiently fast or purposeful to impress gravity. The rattling, the swaying, the sheer blind hope of it all — it's as embarrassing as it is terrifying.

Harvey glimpses at his phone — five new messages — and shuts it down. The woman beside him takes his cue, checks her phone is dutifully compliant.

'It probably makes no difference,' Harvey says to her with a shrug. 'If a phone could actually bring down a plane, I'm pretty sure we wouldn't be allowed to bring them on.'

He laughs to indicate jocularity rather than the look of someone who has actually given this a lot of thought.

'I mean,' he says, 'I doubt the aviation authorities are counting on human conformity to keep us aloft, ha-ha.'

The woman manages a polite smile and Harvey wills himself to shut up.

Finally the aircraft pulls off another miracle and Harvey hopes the pre-midday flight time doesn't give the hosties any big ideas about parking up the drinks trolley. They are not, he reasons, entitled to make any judgement about what help a person may or may not need to cope with flying, with entrapment, with life. He would very much like a drink, thanks.

He wonders about the messages. One will be from Trudi Rice — shit, all five might be from her, such is the unmitigated relentlessness of the head of HR. She has been riding him for weeks: take the payout, Harvey, fill out the forms, see a counsellor — it's on us. But he doesn't want to leave like this, and nor do his listeners want that for him. *I think I know our listeners a little better than you, Trudi. I think I know human relations a little better than you.*

He had long hoped HR managers would go the way of quality assurance consultants and organisational change facilitators and other such experimental workplace creations fired in the kiln of corporate wankery. But like its equally unproductive cousin, IT Support, HR doesn't seem to be going anywhere. Its 'people people' keep employing each other. Always the last left standing.

Beam is bitter, of course he is. Fuck. No denial on that front. He's also sad and worried and incredibly bloody angry, all of which makes him uncooperative. He didn't even tell Trudi Rice he was flying out, taking his own brand of leave in the midst of his 'official' leave.

Anyway, his father is dying, and for some people — plenty of people, he imagines — that's a big deal.

He thinks about this as the hostie edges toward him, trolley contents rattling down the skinny passage dividing the plane in half. His father. Now dying. Dying in the final sense and not just ambling towards oblivion with no fresh ideas. He thought it would be the liver that would get him, get them all in fact, every last true Beam. Or the bowel. Maybe the kidney. An ill-timed stumble down the stairs in the very early morn.

Something that would help those in the church pews nod with a sense of knowing satisfaction, a little smugness. But it is lung cancer that has Lionel Beam, has him in the grip of something apparently horrid. And he never even smoked.

'Coffee, sir?'

Harvey attempts to adjust his feet, as though making a decision. But there is no room for either. He says, 'Are you serving wine?'

'We can. Yes, that's fine.'

'I'll have a red, thanks.'

'Of course.'

The air hostess, a tall woman with red hair, a fine spray of freckles and an oddly playful expression, pulls out a heartbreakingly tiny plastic bottle, screws off the cap and passes it to Harvey across the chest of the woman beside him. *Yes*, he thinks, *both of you, go right ahead and judge me*. But the woman beside him pulls up straight and says, 'Why not? I guess I'll have one too.'

'Bless you,' he says. 'No fun drinking alone.' *Although it is, actually.*

The hostie pulls out another little bottle and Beam hamfists a quip.

'More solid than liquid, hey?'

The woman half smiles, but Beam isn't sure she got it.

'All that plastic? For so little wine. There's more bottle than wine, mass-wise.' *Stop.*

He never usually talks like this in public: light and unwieldy. It's the plane that has him off course, out of character. The plane, the destination, those unheard messages. He looks at his aisle-side companion, serene by comparison. She looks, he decides, like a younger version of that actress who was married to that guy in that early 90s TV show, that comedy, about the self-involved married couple living in New York. *What was it called?*

'Where are you travelling to?' he blusters on, and quickly

realises there is no destination beyond the one they're heading to: Shorton. Town of ninety thousand. Regional epicentre of nowhere. Place of his birth, growth and spiritual death.

Helen something.

'I've got four weeks work at the hospital,' she says. 'They're desperate for casual nurses. You?'

'My father died. Is dying.'

She looks at him and quickly drops her eyes to the armrest between them. 'I'm sorry.'

'It's all good. I'm not close to him. Just going to say goodbye, really.'

Helen Hunt. Bam.

'Oh. Well, that's still very sad.'

'It's fine. I mean, yes ... sad.'

'Death calls us all home in the end,' she says, possibly quoting someone, and Beam is not sure whether she means him or his father.

'I also just need a break. So it's as good a time as any.'

He instantly knows this sounds callous, can't undo it. Wants to say, *I'm really not a prick.*

But instead, somehow warming to the heartless theme, he says: 'You don't have to love your family. It's not an obligation. Some families are poisonous and it's just stupid to keep sucking on that teat.'

'I guess so,' she says, looking past him to the tiny frame of clouds scudding by. 'Why do you need a break?'

'I work in radio, talkback, and it's just ... you can't keep doing it. After eighteen years I just woke up and thought, shit, I need to breathe out.'

'Oh, you're Harvey Beam,' she says, suddenly turning around to have a proper look at him. 'I know you.'

He gets the familiar rush. Recognition, warmth, then the quick correction: how does she know me? Which thing? It's not always his career, not anymore. Sometimes it's the ACRA event, sometimes his divorce, sometimes ... he glances out the plane and focuses on a wing rivet about to lose its mooring.

'My mum rang you once when you were talking about private schools. She's a teacher in Auburn. She said you cut her off mid-sentence.'

'I don't think so. People think that, that's what it sounds like, but it's not like that. There are producers ...'

'Well, she never rang in again. But plenty of people do, which is the main thing, I guess. I'm Grace.' And she smiles at him, and Harvey thinks it's been some time since he saw a real smile up close.

'Hi Grace. I'm Harvey.'

Dickhead.

'So how long are you staying for? I mean, how advanced is your dad's condition?'

'I don't know where he's at. My sisters speak in riddles. I think I'll just stay a week, maybe ten days.' *Ten days sounds solid.*

'My father took three years to die.'

'Three years. I definitely don't have three years. I mean, that's awful.' *Fuck.*

The hostie is back. *Now we're talking*, thinks Beam. *Another wine, please.* But she's here on other business.

'Harvey Beam. You don't remember me, do you?'

He looks up at the whirl of hair and lipstick and rouge. No, he doesn't.

'Jacinta Gold,' she says. 'Shorton High? Same maths class. English too, I think.'

'Jacinta! God, I'm sorry. It's been a while.' *It'll come, it'll come.*

'You took my twin sister to the formal and let her drive home with that idiot footballer. Do you remember that?'

'Yes. Yes I do.' He glances at Grace, who quickly shifts her gaze to her tray table. Harvey attempts a laugh. 'We were all so young,' he says.

'So what brings you home?' Jacinta says. 'Lose your job?'

'No, Jacinta,' Harvey says and takes a long pause to reel in the moral high ground. 'My father is dying.'

'I heard you lost your job.'

'I'm taking a break.'

'Maybe you could have your old job back at 95.3?'

God, Shorton Radio. 'I don't think so,' he says.

'But you can't go back, anyway,' Jacinta says with a theatrical flick of her fringe. 'No-one ever really goes back.'

It's an absurd statement from someone who clearly never left anything in the first place.

'So you're still in Shorton, then, Jacinta?'

Grace drains her plastic glass.

'Yep, why would you leave? It's the best place to raise kids. We just got a Nando's, you know. And David Jones. You won't recognise it. How long since you've been back?'

'About eight years. The high school reunion,' he says, wincing at something, the light through the silly little window. *Had she been there?*

'Mad night,' she says. 'Mad night.' Beam barely remembers.

'Well, I'd better keep going.' Jacinta opens and shuts the overhead locker for effect. 'Have to check on First.'

And there's an odd pause as Jacinta assembles a thought. 'Shouldn't you be up there?' she says, hinting towards the front of the plane.

The seatbelt sign dings back on.

'Great to see you,' Harvey says, deciding not to ask her for another wine.

Jacinta looks at Grace and then at Harvey. 'Good to see you, too, Harvey Beam. Hope the job sitch works out. See you in Shorton!'

Harvey turns to Grace, spots a wry grin pushing at the confines of her mouth. 'I won't be surprised if my luggage goes missing,' he says.

'Because of her twin sister?' Grace responds, smoothing the folds of her dress. She turns to him and Beam sees that she has a lovely nose. So often he is thrown by noses.

'No,' he says. 'Because Shorton people hate people who leave Shorton. It's an act of treachery.'

'Well, it *is* beautiful apparently,' Grace says. 'I've been googling. Lovely beaches, rainforest, gateway to the islands.'

Beam snorts. 'Gateway to the islands! Bloody long gate. They're about three hours' drive away.'

Suddenly he feels ungracious. 'It is nice,' he says. 'But it's not the town it once was. Now it's an industrial town with everything that goes with that.'

'How do you know?' she says. 'If you hardly ever go there?'

'I'm still in touch with people,' he says, thinking of the fifty or so Shorton folk who are friends with him on Facebook. That's enough.

Harvey slides his empty bottle into the pocket in front of him, puts the tray up and stares out the window. *This is why people don't talk on planes. There's no let-up unless you want to seem rude.* He just wants to look out the window now.

Half an hour later they begin their descent. It's been a while since he's looked at Shorton from the air, at its geography rather than its history. It looks like so many regional towns in this state: tin-roofed houses standing their ground at the graph-paper centre, a couple of controversial 'high-rises', a winding river clinging to muddy banks, a proper footy ground now with lights, two public pools and thousands of private ones, industry snaking its way around new housing estates, acres of rendered brick, and eventually, on the outskirts, pushed to limitless boundaries, the town's raison d'être — wheat. Sugarcane. Wine. Beef. Whatever. Pick your town.

But this was his town. And he can still see charm here through the portal window. Charm and memories. The things we are given before we can choose otherwise and compare. He can see these things but doesn't feel them, not anymore. Shorton is just a place, a landmark on his timeline, and he won't be drawn into wistful discussions about the way hometowns shape you, hold you and ultimately pull you back. *No-one ever really goes back.*

Everything seems more peaceful from the air, Beam thinks, as Grace reaches for the inflight magazine.

His luggage does not arrive.

2

Gemma isn't the quickest producer he's ever had and certainly not the brightest, but she's a nice kid who rarely weeps over spilt ideas and who has, on more than one occasion, come up with something that has legs. But not today.

'There's a climate change summit happening in Tokyo this week,' she says, flicking through the dailies Harvey binned more than four hours ago. 'I could see which of our academics are there.'

'It's stale, Gemma. It's just the same rhetoric being recycled. They don't get the science.'

She shrugs. 'You could link it to the bushfires.'

'And ask the bloke with the laptop under his arm running away from his newly renovated pile of ashes how he feels about rising sea levels? I don't think so.'

'It wouldn't have to be ... doesn't matter. *Okaaay.*' She sighs, flicking, flicking. 'It's a slow news day, Harvey.'

'No such thing, Gemma, no such thing.' He resists the predictable slide into 'And here's another pithy vignette I picked up from a career in radio' because he feels he's better than that these days. Harvey Beam is not a dickhead, however close he may have come to tripping down the face of that ravine in the past. And he has learned, albeit aboard a parenting treadmill he spends little time on, that young people have certain perspectives on life that are fresher and truer than anything harvested in older paddocks. If only they knew.

'Aren't university places published this week?' he asks Gemma, and immediately chastens himself because he should know this. His eldest, Cate, is sweating to get into environmental science at UTS, or so her mother has informed him.

'Let's get a breakdown on where demand is and compare it with where the jobs are,' Harvey says, crushing his fourth styrofoam cup for the day, aware he's just consigned Gemma to at least an hour's worth of soulless trawling through the Bureau of Stats website. 'I'm going to grab some lunch and let's meet back here at two.'

Beam lopes down to the bowels of the building where a gym shares space with a coffee shop. The two animals have morphed into one such that the whole floor smells of coffee beans brewed in perspiration.

He doesn't like this body, this body delivered by forty, and he actively looks at it even less often than anyone else these days. Not being in possession of the radical overhaul gene, however, Beam looks upon the office gym less as salvation than simple distraction. He doesn't plan on giving up booze, bread or chicken schnitzels anytime soon, but he can at least attempt to crowd them out a little while watching film clips on the defensible side of porn.

Today he walks briskly on the treadmill while framing his missive for this afternoon's show. Even before the benefit of Gemma's research, he knows what the picture will be: more and more university students competing for fewer jobs. Especially in the arts, he figures, from where thousands of young people wander hopefully into the light each year armed with little more than a working definition of irony, only to discover that grown-ups want skills, tickets, tangible productivity. So they panic and sign up as a postgrad.

The graduates who want *his* job come with their arts degrees, their social media profiles, a sense of entitlement and often little else. What they need — a modicum of natural intelligence, listening skills, adaptive reflexes and a work ethic that doesn't explode upon entry — are either part of their DNA or they're not. They can't be taught, although they can certainly be crushed by endless text deconstruction and postmodernist theorising.

The best thing he, Harvey Beam, ever did was drop out of an arts degree within its first twelve months, even if the act of defiance did invite the barely concealed disappointment of his father, a professor of history. Within four months Beam had his first job in radio and fortnightly fuck-you-dad payslips.

Yes, it's criminal, he thinks, buttoning the machine back to 6.5, that so many kids today are being duped by universities, skinned of cash and profit potential in exchange for a few old classrooms, neolithic teachers and an utterly worthless degree. Graduate a handful of doctors and dentists each year and yet hundreds of thousands of arts students — why? Because arts degrees cost jack shit to supply. *Fucking criminal.*

He hops off the treadmill, grabs his gear and marches back upstairs, now with far more energy to burn than he had a little while ago.

'How'd you go?' he says to Gemma, stuffing a rancid towel into the bottom drawer of an empty filing cabinet.

She hands him a wad of printouts, runs back to the printer for the most important bit — her summary, the 'Gemma Sting', but it's needless because the plucky redhead has it all in her head.

'Fewer graduate jobs than ever before,' she says, 'and far more graduates too.' She unleashes a barrage of figures, then continues. 'There are loads of tertiary-qualified kids working at Cash Converters and Petbarn and just *shit* jobs, up to fifty hours a week, leaving just enough time to apply for jobs that don't even exist anymore. And now the government wants them to pay their HECS debt immediately — have you heard about that?'

He stops her. Doesn't want this to be about uni fees — dull radio. Says, 'What's the proportion of arts graduates versus the rest?'

Gemma looks at her pile of instant research. 'Ah, not sure,' she says, 'but there's also this: one in four secondary students now don't have a job or a course of study within a year of leaving school, so maybe this should be about the broader issue of youth unemployment and the need for transition programs ...'

'No, it's about arts degrees,' Harvey says, swinging into his chair and firing up the panel. The kindling has caught. The endless courting and flirting with this thing that he loves.

Gemma looks wearily at him in full flush. She may never understand what happens in the tunnel between Beam at 12pm and Beam at 4pm; 'twixt sleepy rumination and the hot-wired bulldozer. But he knows what he's doing – at least, he's been doing it a while. Today's mission is Annihilation of the Arts Degree and implicitly the salvation of all young people via the prime-time assassination of Humanities Department overlords.

By 4.30pm however, just half an hour into it, the show is not going to plan, not that it ever does. The beauty of talkback is of course its ugliness – the chaos and terror of faceless humans colliding, listeners empowered by the hermetic security of their drive home, verbal stoushes in which the mediator is also one of the combatants.

But Beam hasn't counted on calls from Jeremy Kayne, a hardware engineer running a Forbes-listed software company who *only* employs people who've first done a liberal arts degree. 'If you teach students one skill,' he says, 'it'll be obsolete within two years on current form, but if you teach them how to look at lots of information and make meaningful connections within it, and only a classic liberal education does that, then you will have taught them adaptive skills for life. That's who I want.'

He hasn't counted on Professor Genny Story, who runs the drama program at a top-100 university and cites an eighty-five percent industry employment rate for her graduates compared to a thirty percent rate for the same university's engineering school.

He hasn't counted on Arthur Vivian, a curmudgeonly

newspaper journalist of thirty years' experience, who says he often feels like a fraud mentoring today's journalism graduates as they seem to know far more than he does about defamation law, background research and 'some waffly but probably important faff about a Code of Ethics'.

It's good radio, good talent, but it's quickly blooming at Beam's expense. The argument he has framed is being dismantled, assumption by assumption, and his statistics mask discrepancies. Many of the law graduates he cites as having far better employment prospects than arts graduates are in fact arts graduates who then topped up with law. More and more arts graduates are taking up overseas volunteer postings for needy NGOs, so they're employed, just not according to the narrow defines of Australia's census data.

Beam's only allies arrive in the form of wounded meatheads; guys (and they're all guys) who say that university is a time-wasting crock of shit for people who can read books but can't build the bookcase to stick them in. And then someone called Hamish calls in to say that not only has he read all the books in the bookcase he built himself, but that the bookcase he built himself rests within the million-dollar eco-house he built himself that recently featured on *Grand Designs Australia*. 'Did you see it?' asks Hamish. Beam: 'No, I didn't.' Hamish: 'It's a show about architecture.' Beam: 'Yes, I know that.' *Fuck.*

But mostly Harvey hasn't counted on university students ringing in. Ringing in, texting, emailing, facebooking and tweeting their download accounts off. *Aren't you meant to be studying?* Beam thinks. *Or fixing a basket to a bike?* They're not even remotely located in his demographic. Arts students, medical students, international students, postgrads ... they've all got an opinion and it isn't his.

Beam doesn't mind being challenged, doesn't even mind being wrong occasionally, but he hates when the show jumps track completely and starts gaining a speed that he can't control.

He makes a time-call at 5.29, just before headlines, and warily looks up through the glass at Gemma. She is impassive; he can't read her mood. It might just be the girl's most marketable skill that she can so convincingly hide being pissed off.

Then his eyes adjust and Beam sees that Gemma is not alone. Behind her stands the station manager, Ron Ibbotsen. Ribbot. He has his arms folded, hands gripping his cuffs. Simultaneously subdued and seething, it would appear, and it looks like he's settled in. This isn't just a friendly tour of the facilities.

Gemma throws Harvey a bone. She phones a guy who had called the morning presenter that day about the dying art of reading. A measured old fellow, he had discussed the economic benefits of self-education; said he'd read more than five hundred books in the last three years — far more than any he might in any university degree. He wasn't boasting, merely saying, 'Why pay university fees? Libraries are free.' Gemma gets him on the phone and encourages him to add some levity to Beam's conversation, which he happily does.

'Thanks', Beam types into the studio monitor for Gemma's viewing on the other side. He shoots a thumb in the air.

'Welcome', she types back. 'How were you to know Ribbot's wife is an arts professor at Deakin, his kids are all studying arts, and the station proprietor has just joined the Senate at his alma mater, UTS?'

Jesus.

So soon after the awards dinner debacle and on the back of last week's shitstorm, when Beam had inadvertently outed a retired Catholic priest, prompting a legal letter from the office of Cardinal George Pell and all sorts of hellfire from the gay community (whom he *thought* would be happy), today's show is not what Harvey needs. He's had a bad run. Is either fading to black or spinning towards implosion. Willing failure to give him a leave pass.

He feels it, the loosening. Something has become untethered. Something, somehow has got lost.

3

Beam leaves his mother's address details with an airport clerk who has vowed through lips trained to smile to locate his luggage as soon as possible. He ends up directly behind Grace in the taxi line and sees now that she is the slightest bit taller than him and is wearing one of those long flowy dresses that have somehow become fashionable. They each shuffle forward while reuniting with their phones — Grace checking messages, Beam playing Candy Crush to avoid checking messages. When a taxi pulls in as Grace reaches the front of the line, Harvey wishes her all the best for her nursing stint.

'Thanks,' she says, and turns to smile at him. *That nose.* 'I hope things work out okay. You know, with your dad.'

'Yes,' Harvey says with a what-do-you-do half-shrug. 'But thanks for the company, Grace. I usually hate flying.'

'Take-offs?' she says, sliding her bag into the car's back seat.

Beam nods, a little bewildered.

Grace smiles at him one last time. 'Me too,' she says.

And she's gone. And not for the first time lately Harvey Beam briefly wonders if there might be a more eloquent plan to life than the one he has so far understood. A plan that is out of his hands. One that puts him in the path of people he is meant to meet, delivers him unlikely lessons and fresh possibilities. Maybe it's like this for everyone and he's just late to catch on. He also knows this sort of hippie thinking is a sign of an ageing brain that has lost its edge.

Beam waits a good while for the next cab. He realises there

is probably still only one taxi company in town and not a lot of competition for jobs. *No rush, fellas.*

Twenty minutes later a cab pulls up and Harvey hops in the back. He is instantly disconsolate and weary. Most of his wearable clothes and shoes were in that bag. It's a pain in the arse, complicating a trip that feels like hard enough work already.

Beam looks at the back of the driver's head. It's familiar. He has always recognised people from the back more readily than the front. He thinks it might be Tony Finetti, in the same year as him at high school, possibly going back to primary school. They played in the same rugby league team, billeted together on at least one trip. Back then Finetti didn't have tattoos all over his hands and an earring resembling a bone, so Beam might be wrong about this. It certainly looks like the back of his head.

Harvey gives the address and sits in silence. Had thought briefly about going straight to the hospital but now thinks he would like to see his mother first. Needs a calmer port.

He's not sure who will be at Lynn's house. She's lived on her own for years now (since Ken, since Richard, and before that his father), but he knows, he imagines, her place is still the spill zone for his siblings — that place to which they can escape the families they've created themselves and come back to what they better understand. Which is not each other.

56 Upton St, Shorton. Emotional space station.

The taxi moves from the south to the north side via the centre of town. Beam feels ready to check his messages now but can't resist a visual appraisal of Shorton's piecemeal aesthetic evolution. The town is wilting, it seems, on this igneous summer day. Few people test their nerve outside of cars and shops and he guesses the air-conditioned local shopping centres will be heaving. He spies old haunts — pubs, nightclubs, cafes, rebadged over and over. Fresh colours that quickly fade. Naff names. Chalked specials. Hanging racks on footpaths.

A 'rejuvenation plan' is underway in Town Central — or so he recently read on the local newspaper's website, a place his fingers sometimes wander to for no clear reason except the prospect of some exceptionally bad and amusing junior reportage. It looks as though rejuvenation means the planting of immature trees and the installation of parking meters.

The cab crosses the bridge and he looks down at the river, still paint-swatch blue, still calling out to him and criminally underutilised. As a boy Harvey had thought this was his river, for no-one else seemed particularly interested in it. He had spent countless hours digging for yabbies in the mudflats. Entire school holidays had disappeared in a sun-blistered haze of wriggling, dying crustaceans. It had always seemed very important to Harvey that his fisherman's basket — his mother's old peg basket, in fact — was filled to the lip with tangled claws and tails before he even contemplated rigging up a handline. And then he would fish, fish all afternoon, full of hope and fresh resolve, until the tide changed or the sun went down.

Once, he had caught a whiting big enough to keep. He couldn't believe his luck. It hadn't even been a big yabby on the end of his hook. The fish had given Harvey a decent fight, a real to-and-fro that spoke to Harvey's manhood. He had instinctively known when to let the fish run, give it a little confidence, and then when to pull up hard. Over and over. It had to have been instinct, Harvey told himself, because no-one had ever shown him how to do it. And now he had the spoils, a quickly fading whiting in his sling. A hundred thousand yabbies had not died in vain.

And Harvey wondered as he walked home that evening if instinct too wouldn't show him how to cut up the fish and make it into something his mum could cook for dinner. For the whole family. But Beam's father had made him throw the fish into the big bin behind the shops.

'Disgusting,' Lionel Beam had said. 'Absolutely putrid.'

Harvey catches the driver's eye in the rear-vision mirror

and quickly pulls out his phone. Two of the messages are from Trudi Rice, one is from his sister, and two are from Cate.

Trudi wants to catch up, wants to know why he isn't answering his phone, wants to talk deadlines. Wants *human relations*.

His youngest sister, Naomi, sounds upset but it's hard to tell because she's also whispering. She says their father may only have days. When is Harvey going to *get here*? She says not to listen to anything their other sister, Penny, has to say about *anything* while he's here.

Beam winces, bracing himself for a fresh round of warfare between his fractious sisters.

But it's the final two messages from his eldest daughter that make him want to turn the cab around now, abort this misguided mission and head back to Sydney. She is clearly distressed and very angry. She says she didn't get into environmental science, didn't get her second or third or fourth preferences either, and that her mother believes she has been LYING about the amount of study she's done for the past two years and wasted THOUSANDS of dollars worth of school fees because she's a SELFISH BITCH and that she, Cate, would have *thought* her mother would be sympathetic instead of ATTACKING her because she DID study, Dad, she did.

'And can I please live with you for a while because I'm OUT OF THERE. I mean it. This is emotional ABUSE.'

Message two from Cate: 'Dad, I'm at your place. Where ARE you?'

It's been a long time since one of his daughters asked him for anything besides money or use of his station-sponsored cinema card and Harvey feels both elated and sick. He hadn't even told Cate and Jayne he was heading to Shorton; had briefly thought about bringing them along to see the grandfather they barely knew but their mother quickly shut down that idea.

'There's nothing in that town for them to do, Harvey,' Suze had said in an email. 'Your father wouldn't even recognise them anymore. But do say goodbye to him from me, I mean, for what it's worth.'

Sure. *Suze says bye!*

Beam finds Cate's mobile in his contacts. It goes straight to her voice message — a cavalier and no doubt much-practised 'So yeah, leave some words' — and he tells her to get his spare key from his neighbour to the right and make herself at home.

'I'm sorry about the uni place,' he says, 'but it's really not the end of the world. There are plenty of ways to skin a cat. Everything happens for a reason.' *Any more clichés, Beam? Done?*

Suze is right on this. He's never known what children need to hear.

The cab pulls in to his mother's driveway and Harvey passes forty dollars over the centre console to the guy who may or may not be Tony Finetti.

'Keep the change,' he says, and hears, 'Yeah, thanks Beam,' as he shuts the door.

Honestly, what could he have discussed with Finetti?

Harvey takes a minute to consider his first words to Lynn. He marvels at families that don't have to do this; those for whom constant engagement is the most natural thing in the world. The only thing. He sometimes watches these families — at barbecues, the beach, on TV — and regards them as the most fascinating social experiment. An unlikely hypothesis that returns a positive result.

He decides he will give Lynn a hug and gauge things from there.

The first thing he notices at his mother's front door is that her gardening phase has clearly ended. The pavers are overrun with runaway buffalo grass and the pot plants lining the porch are all dead. The next thing he notices is that she's taken up smoking because all the late plants have been squashed out with cigarette butts. Finally he notices a Eureka flag taped to one of the front windows and he no longer thinks he should knock on the door.

Beam dials his mother's mobile.

'Harvey! Are you here?'

'I'm at Upton Street. Where are you?'

'I'm at your sister's, remember? I moved into Naomi's place. I told you that.'

Harvey starts walking quickly down the driveway and into the street.

'No, Mum, you didn't tell me that,' he says, nervously looking back at the house over his shoulder. 'That's why I'm at Upton.'

'Well, I definitely thought your sisters had told you. Hang on. Naomi?' she yells, and then Lynn's voice becomes hand-over-phone muffled: 'Didn't you tell Harvey I was here?'

There is a solid minute of radio silence as Harvey decides he might as well walk to the tavern at the end of the adjoining street, if it's still there.

'Harvey, stay where you are and Naomi will come and pick you up now.'

'I can't stay *here*,' Harvey says, exasperated at how obvious that should be. 'Tell Naomi I'll walk to the Rosewood and meet her there.'

Beam walks quickly in the direction of the tavern until the midday humidity overwhelms him and he slows to a beaten shuffle. Why does his mother always assume that important information will automatically find him one way or another, if not via her in their sparse phone chats, then somehow via the osmotic process of 'family'? Why does she place faith in something that has never worked the way it's meant to?

He remembers once looking at an electricity pole in central Bangkok that was completely swamped in a writhing, sparking mountain of tangled wires and broken cords pointing nowhere and ripe for disaster, and his first thought had been: behold the Beam communications model.

He can't believe he's here again.

4

The Australian Commercial Radio Awards is a suitably boozy affair where egos and logos can swill around for a good four hours until it's time to steal the centrepieces and flee. At least, that's how it's gone down for the last twenty-six years. This year the organisers have taken the advice of a new boutique events company that won the job with a pitch that promised 'a new era, new focus, new possibilities'. Subtext: less alcohol, no sit-down meal.

The new venue, a heritage-style room within Sydney Museum, is adorned with sepia prints of radio's golden era (no-one is quite sure when this was) and about twenty rows of linked chairs. The stage is backlit by a large screen spooling through the monikers and frequencies of all the major stations and their sponsors. What looks like a card table holds aloft a small cityscape of trophies.

Harvey takes one look at the scaled-down affair and decides a drink is in order.

But they're few and far between on the balcony adjacent to the main room, where advertising executives, senior managers, promotions girls and his fellow metro presenters have dutifully gathered to pool their anxieties. Harvey spots just two drinks waiters moving at an indolent pace among the three hundred or so guests and makes a snap decision to take his pre-event activity elsewhere.

He heads for 99 On York where earlier in the day Beam had met up with Penny. His sister was in town for the annual gift fair that keeps her Shorton knick-knack shop perennially brimming with useless shiny things and books about friendship that will only ever be opened after the apocalypse when it's all about making fires. Inevitably Penny had used the occasion to talk about their sister and the many ways Naomi had let Penny down of late. Unanswered invitations, misconstrued text messages, subverted agendas ... most of which, he interpreted, had occurred via the apparently benign conduit that is their mother, Lynn. Benign in the manner of early-stage skin cancer.

Penny felt more passionately about this topic — her toxic sister — than anything else. When she wasn't pointing out Naomi's many inconsistencies and deficiencies, Penny was cast-netting for sympathy over something Naomi had said, or not said, or probably said, or allegedly said. Attack, retreat, repeat. Beam found himself thinking, not for the first time, that if these two women weren't so intent on convincing imagined juries of the other's flaws, they might both be infinitely happier. Though with much less to talk about.

But then nothing about sharing genetic material is that simple (although simply walking away is highly underrated, in his opinion). Beam hadn't spoken to his brother since he'd left Shorton.

As if on cue, Penny switched the subject from Naomi to Bryan.

'You know Bryan is taking Dad's sickness really hard,' she said. 'He's given up his job to care for him.'

Beam flinched. 'That seems like an absurd reaction in the circumstances,' he said.

'Why?'

'Just ... delusional. As if he's pining for the man Dad wasn't rather than who he is.'

'That's actually horrible, Harvey.'

He shrugged. 'It is what it is.'

'I hate that saying,' Penny grimaced. 'Naomi says it all the time.'

And back we are.

'How long has he got?' Harvey asked, making this the first official question he'd asked about Lionel Beam's condition.

Penny didn't know. 'But he's refusing chemo, so ...'

'Well, that's just stupid.' *And stubborn and arrogant and typical.*

'He's nearly seventy, Harvey. You can't blame him for not wanting his body poked around and filled with chemicals.'

'No. His choice, I suppose.'

They talked a little more about their father, Beam's least studied subject, and about the benefits and otherwise of knowing one's approximate end date. Penny said she'd rather not know or at least have very little warning.

'I often picture myself in a plane plunging to the ground,' she said. 'It's scary but it's also not. No time for regrets or plans or apologies, nothing. Just enough time to say, alright, let's fucking *do* this.'

'You *often* picture this?' Harvey said.

'Don't judge me, Harvey,' Penny said. 'I'm not the nutbag that Naomi would have you all believe I am.'

Beam looked at his watch. It had been a three-wine catch-up and he had a show to do in forty-five minutes. He wrapped things up by giving his sister a bumpy hug and telling her to say hi to his nephews, James and ... *shit. What's the little one called? It'll come, it'll come.*

'Come visit,' Penny said. 'Don't leave it too long.'

'Okay.' *It's unlikely.*

And now he's back here on York St, wine number five for the day in hand, though it feels like number three, and thinking absently about a guy in the industry who two years ago had thrown it all away, sold all his stuff, moved to Phuket and bought a tuk-tuk. *I bet he's happy*, thinks Beam. *Stripped back and happy as a bingo caller.*

It's 7.30. The mingling would have finished now but Beam reasons he can afford to miss a few early speeches by CEOs and industry stalwarts, all united in their confidence that the commercial radio industry is in its Best Shape Ever, primed for the digital age and ready to snare a whole new generation of listeners through 'interactivity' and 'engagement'. Loosely translated: we've managed to make it through another year in which no-one has invented a way to surf the internet and drive a car at the same time and *thank God.*

None of the awards are for Beam this year, as Trudi Rice had made a point of telling him in the faux warm manner of an ageing air hostess, but fortunately none of them are for John Jackson either. That result Beam could not have handled, not again.

The presenter of mornings is the radio industry's Bali knock-off, a cheap and poorly constructed imitation of something with far more structural integrity if no greater purpose. He's an arsehole, and also a pretender. He got the gig because a hit-and-miss career in corporate MCing had landed him at an event attended by the station CEO. The pair had mainlined bourbon until the wee hours, during which time Jackson was offered the chance to host a few weekend spots.

Jackson had quickly become a daily fixture at the station, fawning over the billboard presenters (except Beam, who steadfastly diverted his gaze as though Jackson were an inconvenient eclipse), gleaning their pithy insights and later regurgitating them to HR and ad reps during the many long lunches to which he unashamedly tagged along. Jackson seemed to understand everything about radio without ever actually having been a part of it, which can certainly look like genius through the right filter.

It was only a matter of time, *because arseholes and receptionists shall inherit the earth*, before Jackson was offered the mornings gig to 'give Harvey Beam a well-earned sleep-in'. A sleep-in that Beam had neither asked for nor wanted. It was a risky decision for the station, and one played out in the pages of *Sydney Confidential* where 'Darlinghurst dynamo' Jackson was reported to be 'fielding multiple offers'.

Bullshit.

But no-one in the media could apparently argue with (nor adequately interrogate, question or challenge *because why would you?*) early figures that showed Jackson had delivered a ratings windfall to the station. Listeners loved his comic timing and all those cheeky asides, much of which Jackson lifted daily from every MC speech he'd ever made.

Beam knew it couldn't last, had faith that Jackson's gravitational pull toward celebrity at the expense of garden-variety listeners and their sometimes mundane anecdotes, would unwind his spool. 'You can fool some of the people some of the time,' his father had often said, 'but you can't fool all the people all the time.'

Moreover, Jackson was a *true* arsehole. And his inner core was leaching out. He would greet new producers with wild enthusiasm, fist-pump their ideas, accept their friend invitations on Facebook, and then suddenly relegate them to tedious coffee-comparison missions, arduous post-show dress-downs and long hours of arctic indifference. He just couldn't trust them to mess with the Jackson juggernaut, with the delicate chemical equation of his brilliance. His confidence glowed brightest in a dark room.

'Silence is golden, except mine,' Jackson had once said to Gemma with no hint of mirth.

She had shared this quote with Beam on the occasion of Jackson's first Golden Mic award. Since then he'd won two more, done a season on *Dancing with the Stars* and guest-edited an edition of *Men's Health* (he'd left a copy on Beam's desk).

But Jackson's form of late had been patchy: aborted inter-views, disgruntled guests unhappy with his lack of preparation, misapplied statistics and stunts gone wrong. Listeners crave consistency, but Jackson's short-term memory couldn't always deliver it. He frequently contradicted his own previously asserted views and triumphantly joined dots that had long ago been joined by others. The chrome was rusting.

Beam had heard a rumour that Jackson was now pressing management to give him the afternoon slot; the early mornings were catching up with him. *But fuck you, Jackson. Not going to happen.*

Taking one last look at the pokies-inspired decor of 99 On York, Harvey finishes his red, restores his suit jacket and walks slowly back to Sydney Museum.

It's a bewitching night. Iridescent sky. Flirty breeze. He loves this city, and not just in the Whitlams way. He really loves it. For all its sharp edges and pointy arguments, Sydney has a soft motherly embrace. It took him in twenty years ago, asked no questions and easily let him be. Let him become something with the flimsiest of résumés.

In the early years he had been enraptured by the pace of the inner city, loved placing himself in the middle of that hyperactive throng each day. Thousands of people making infinite split-second decisions to thread a clear path from A to B. Disengaged engagement. It had taken him a long time to get over the thrilling shock of there being so many people in the world beyond Shorton; so many people he was yet to meet. Potential interviewees, listeners, callers ... stories everywhere! Time may have tempered his green enthusiasm — he's fairly certain now that he's actually been meeting the same four people over and over — but Beam remains grateful to Sydney for cracking open his world.

Harvey climbs the museum steps, which diplomatically inform him that he's on his way to drunk, though not yet beyond the magic tipping point. He reaches the heritage room, hears applause through the closed doors and realises it won't be possible to make a surreptitious late entry. No matter. He heads for the mingling balcony, which is still blessedly open via a side door and rejoins the night air.

A museum staffer is setting up glasses for the post-event debrief and offers Beam a drink. He has time for two more before the doors behind him abruptly open and the awards event breaks like a dam.

Shit. He's not up for this.

Beam heads for the side door — *why the fuck did I come back?* — but is intercepted by Trudi Rice and John Jackson.

'Where have you *been*?' Rice glares at him, managing to look both stunning and furious in fuchsia.

'Emergency,' Beam says.

'What do you *mean*?' she says, because in Rice's world everything is expressed in code. When Harvey had been demoted to afternoons, she announced it on the station intranet as 'an exciting skills-mix adjustment'. When they sacked half the sales team, Rice gushed that the company was 'optimising outplacement potential'.

'Kids,' Beam says. 'A kid emergency.'

Beam detests people who use their children as screens, but here it is.

'I didn't know you had kids,' says Jackson, adjusting his cufflinks to catch the light. He smooths down his hair in deference to the two-knot breeze. 'Who would have thought you had children?'

Rice doesn't let the jibe land. She says, 'You look like you've been on it, Beam. You missed the entire event.'

'But you didn't miss much,' laughs Jackson, and Beam belatedly realises the dickhead's emphasis had been on *you*.

'Harvey, maybe you should go home now,' Rice says, switching her look now from seething fury to responsible concern, a swift chapter-flick in the HR manual.

'Why should I go home, Trudi?' *And just how far up the food chain do you think you fucking are?*

'Yeah, the kids might be needing you,' Jackson says and attempts to laugh convincingly while grabbing a Corona from a passing tray.

'Has anybody ever told you what a colossal knob you are, John?'

Rice grabs Beam's arm and attempts to pull him towards the door he'd previously had in his sights. But his flight response has flown.

'No, Beam, they haven't,' Jackson says. 'But I assume people like you would say it behind my back. As though it counts for something.'

Harvey breathes in. Stumbles slightly. He sees Jackson so clearly now, as though he'd never been looking at him straight on before, always from the side. He is a counterfeit note, a slick detail job masking a bad chassis. Beam's anger rides up his torso like a childhood fever.

'I know you're trying to take afternoons off me, Jackson, but you're not having it. You've fucked up mornings and now you can just piss off. Go back to where you came from.'

For a moment Jackson says nothing and Beam suddenly notices a few semi-familiar faces looking in their direction. He gathers himself, is not one for scenes. Regrets everything. The wine at lunch. The pokies decor. Wishes he were home now.

Jackson squares his shoulders, flaunts his closer proximity to sober. 'I don't have to *try* to do anything, Beam,' he says. 'Things just happen as they should. The old move on and the new move in. It's a shame you fight that. Self-delusion is a lonely game.'

'Is that a line from one of your corporate speeches, John? Do you actually read anything besides your old material?'

'What does that even *mean*, Beam? Sorry, but I don't speak fluent drunk.'

Rice has a hand on each of their arms now. Harvey can't be sure whether she's terrified or excited. Things are happening too fast and a part of him is on his way home in a cab and a part of him is still standing here and maybe he's imagining this exchange because it does seem somehow familiar.

Jackson takes a step closer to Beam. There's no air left between them.

'Beam,' he says, 'the only colossal knob around here is you. It's you for thinking that anyone is still listening to your crap. It's you for thinking that producers *like* you — they pity you. It's you for still even being here. Anyone can do what you do — this shit is *easy*. Why do you think it's anything better than it is? Because *you're* the dickhead, mate, that's why. And —'

Beam thumps him.

5

With each new structural addition over the years, the Rosewood Hotel has sunk deeper into the marshy grounds beneath. Bottle shop, bistro, beer garden, function room, all Legoed haphazardly around a public bar that refuses to either budge or evolve. The latest tack-on, a sprawling gaming room screaming with light and sound, is actually bigger than the sum of all the other parts, a twenty-four-hour dispenser of hope to the overlooked and depressed.

It's here that Harvey sits waiting for his sister, distractedly pressing dollar coins into a game themed around ancient Egypt, possibly the Roman Empire. The occasional penguin motif confuses things. He wants to feel incredulous that his mother failed to tell him she'd moved house but his heart isn't in it. Lynn stopped apologising for her actions (and inaction) years ago, and somehow everyone has blithely accepted this permanent state of absolution.

No, his present anxiety is pointed towards Cate, who still hasn't called him back.

He decides to phone Suze, never a flippant course of action and especially so in light of Cate's version of events and her chosen place of refuge. He is confident Cate has not exaggerated Suze's rage — the woman has a hell of a temper when the plastic film is pierced — but he also regards his ex-wife as a decent mother. A very good mother, if a little prone to martyrdom.

'Harvey,' she answers after the requisite four rings to gather

her thoughts. 'I suppose you've heard from Cate. You know she's at your place?'

'Yes, I got a message. She hasn't called me back. I told her where the spare key is.'

'She's out of control, Harvey,' Suze says at a pitch that flags she won't be taking a breath anytime soon. 'She completely fucked up her exams and didn't get into anything. Not a thing. I didn't even know that was possible. She hasn't got a fallback. But the thing is — she's been *lying* about studying. She goes up there and she's just been pretending, like I'm fucking stupid or something. Which I am! I'm stupid, Harvey, because I thought she was going okay. Stupid Mum. Stupid dumb *Mum* who pays the bills and does the washing and makes all the food and packs the lunches and drives her everywhere and ... are you at a casino?'

Harvey politely waves away a young waitress handing around free glasses of something bubbly to the parched patrons.

'No,' he says, 'a pub in Shorton. I'm waiting for Naomi to pick me up. Mum's moved into her place and ... anyway, I'm happy for Cate to stay at my place if you think she'll be okay there. It's pretty safe and it's handy to everything.'

'And so we just *condone* running away? Is that what we do, Harvey?' Suze says as Beam tries to wave the waitress back. 'We just send the message that when the going gets tough, she can play us off each other like, like, I don't know ... some sports analogy, fucking whatever.'

Harvey smiles in spite of himself. This is the Suze he likes best, flailing and uncertain.

'Suze, it'll be okay. She just needs to blow off some steam. She's embarrassed. She knows you're right. Let her calm down for a few days. I'll be home soon.'

'Soon? How's your father?'

'I haven't seen him yet.'

'Well.'

'Yeah.'

'Well, I hope that goes okay.'

'Yeah.'

'Okay. Can you text me when you hear from Cate?'

'I will. Gotta go. Naomi's here.'

And there she is, Beam's youngest sister, whirling manically across the gaming room floor, more animated, if it's possible, than the bleating rows of heat-seeking poker machines. Beautiful in the tidy, cropped manner of the effortlessly petite, ungiven to long lunches and ponderous vacations, Naomi is both a picture of restraint and impossible to restrain.

'Pencil!' his sister yells across the gaming room (it's her primary school spin on his initials and Harvey's always quietly loved it). Naomi seems happy and irritated and impatient all at once, none of which surprises Beam.

'Took you long enough to get here,' she says, then *woompa!* The full force of a Naomi hug, every emotion open for business.

'Kids are in the car,' she says. 'Like the bloody casino, ha! Let's go.'

Beam follows her out to the parking lot where Naomi has commandeered a handicapped bay.

'Don't judge,' she says before Harvey can mouth a word. 'We've all got our special issues. Mine is parenting these buggers.'

These buggers are the three boys now arranged haphazardly in the back seat. Toby, Finn and Jamie. Beam has no idea what ages they've reached, but he mentally high-fives himself for the full name recall. Toby looks as though he might be in early high school, the kid's furious acne instantly reminding Beam of his two most hellish years at Shorton High.

'I'm sorry we forgot to tell you about Mum's move,' Naomi says, checking her mobile phone and reversing the car at the same time. Beam isn't sure who she means by 'we'. It could be Naomi and their mother, or Penny might be thrown in too, or even Bryan. It could be all of Shorton for all Beam understands about the current military deployment.

'No worries,' he says. 'I just felt a bit stupid rocking up to someone else's house. Lucky no-one opened the door.'

'Yeah,' says Naomi, nudging the car's nose into a tiny traffic gap that inspires a flurry of wild arm thrashing in the rear-vision mirror. 'Well, she had to move because of the stairs. She fell down those stairs one night and nearly died.'

Beam automatically adjusts 'nearly died' to 'had an accident'. Naomi only ever speaks of full-scale drama.

'The doctor said it was the worst case of concussion he'd ever seen and could have led to long-term brain damage,' Naomi continues. 'It was just lucky she landed on Boner. I just said, you're out of there, Mum. Come and live with us. We've got a spare room. There's no need to be all on her own at her age. That's what trans-generational living is all about.'

Beam grips the door handle. Naomi drives as though manoeuvred by cosmic malevolent forces.

'Trans-generational living,' he says. 'Is that a thing?'

'Penny says it's a huge overreaction,' Naomi goes on.

Beam wonders when he'll get a chance to turn around and say a proper hi to the kids.

'She says I've made Mum feel far more old and vulnerable than she needs to; that I've just made a problem where there wasn't one. But she nearly died, Pencil. I don't think that's something you can overreact to, do you?'

'No, death is pretty serious,' he says.

'I think she's just jealous that Mum is at our place now and not hers. I mean, I think that's where she's actually coming from. Whether or not she can admit that to herself, I don't know.'

Harvey glances briefly at the empty cow paddocks flying past. *What is Boner?*

'We're not even speaking at the moment,' Naomi says, now reaching for something in the glove box that opens with an abrupt thwack on Harvey's knees. 'At all. So it's a bit awkward — sorry about that. But I'm not going to apologise, Pencil. I haven't done anything wrong bar care about Mum. And you know Penny won't apologise. As if. So you know ... it just is what it is.'

At a red light that can't present itself too soon, Beam turns around and smiles at the kids, who seem completely tuned out to this possibly familiar rant. Apart from Toby, who seems vaguely interested and angrily disinterested at the same time.

'I can't believe you're still fighting over our mother,' Beam says to his sister when the car again launches into the breach. He immediately regrets articulating the observation.

'I'm not fighting over Mum!' Naomi yells, turning the car viciously into her street.

Shit, too far.

'It's nothing like that at all. God, there is so much you don't know, so many things you haven't seen. Penny is such a bitch to me. She's constantly talking about me behind my back. It's taken me a long time to work this out, and I know you think I'm not very bright but I do get there in the end, but Pencil, Penny is a poison in my bloodstream. I heard that on a show the other day and I thought, that's exactly it. That's what my sister is to me. Poison. I don't know why, I don't know how, and I can't fix it. I'm sick of trying, Pencil. It just ...'

'It is what it is,' he says.

'*Exactly*,' Naomi says, visibly thrilled with Harvey's conclusion. 'This is what happens in families where there isn't enough love to go around in the first place.'

Wow.

Harvey suddenly realises he should have bought Naomi's kids a present. And Penny's kids too. He is hopelessly unprepared for this trip, in every sense.

'Hi guys,' he says to the three boys as Naomi pulls up on her front verge.

'Hi Uncle Pencil,' says Finn, giggling. Toby mutters something indecipherable and the three boys fall over each other getting out of the hot car.

Harvey opens his door to get out too but Naomi hurriedly explains that their mother will mind the boys now while she and Harvey go straight to the hospital.

'He doesn't have long,' Naomi says. I just think it's best you see him straight away and it's so much easier without the kids. Last visit Jamie punctured a lady's IV bag with a Transformer. Hey, where are your bags?'

Harvey looks around as though his luggage had been here a minute ago, then he remembers.

'Might be on the next flight or lost somewhere out the back,' he says. 'They're going to send it to Mum's. Shit. I gave them the Upton Street address.'

'Oh well, just ring and give them mine.'

'Or should I stay at Penny's?' Harvey says, thinking only now that this might be the better option. 'Seeing as you've got a full house now?'

Naomi flicks on the radio. Shorton Radio. His first job in the industry.

'Do what you like,' she says.

Oops.

It's a more subdued drive to the hospital and Beam can see his sister is now deep in thought about something. He suddenly feels sorry for her because she's never been able to relax; can't sit still long enough to enjoy anything properly. Add three young boys to the mix and you're talking enough constant cerebral activity to power the town's grid.

He quietly checks his messages — nothing — and turns his eyes fixedly to the road ahead.

The emotional by-product of a career spent in radio is that Beam only tends to think about two shows at a time: the one he's doing and the next one. His anxiety span is forcibly short and therefore manageable. So now he's thinking about the next show.

Seeing Lionel Beam.

6

If true love is being understood by someone, really understood, then Harvey Beam is in love. Suze (short-for-nothing) Myer understands him in a way that's almost unsettling, except it's not. It's wondrous.

This woman, this person altogether removed from anything he has ever known, peers into Beam's soul on a daily basis, reminding him it's there. She knows when he is disconnected and soon after knows why, and she knows when his heart is light because usually she's the one who made it so. And yes he knows, but somehow doesn't care, that this is the stuff that brings the world unstuck.

Within six months of going out together, Suze had insisted Harvey take her home to Shorton to meet his family.

'I know who you are,' she'd said to him with a sex-sated sigh one afternoon, 'but I want to know *why* you are.'

And so they'd travelled back to his hometown, his radio star on the rise, his confidence soaring, and Beam had introduced Suze to all of his family members in various arrangements over the course of a week. She had dived into it all, his childhood, his siblings, his old haunts, picking up every last item to inspect underneath, looking far too hard for riddle endings and connections. She had observed the time-bomb rivalry between Penny and Naomi, the silent anger that inhabited Bryan, the different version of herself that his mother presented for each child. And despite Harvey's best attempts to obscure any close examination of his father, Suze saw immediately that the answer to Harvey was here, in the space occupied by the tight-jawed man called Lionel Beam.

It was her most triumphant observation and one he vehemently, angrily rejected. The woman was exhausting him. But Harvey had also been humbled by Suze's interest in him, for the clear sincerity and comprehensiveness of her love. He knew he could never love like that; he didn't know how it was done. How does anyone actually understand anyone?

When the trip was over, on the flight back to Sydney, Suze had looked at him earnestly and put a hand on his arm. She'd said: 'He doesn't have to define you.'

And Harvey had looked past her, out of the small window, and smiled at the clouds disappearing beneath them.

And now here they are, their first child in their tangled arms, a curious shiny pile of limbs whom Suze has named Cate. The King George V Memorial Hospital room is awash with flowers. This bed that's not meant for two, let alone three, is the centre of Beam's universe and he didn't know, just had no idea, that all of this was part of the same world he'd been inhabiting.

'She's so beautiful,' Beam says.

Suze says, 'She's us.'

Beam stares at this something that has changed everything and knows instinctively that he could do it forever. How could anyone not love their own child?

'And so it begins,' says Suze. 'The most important thing.'

He looks at her. Pale, tired, beautiful. Says, 'Being a parent?'

'No,' she says. 'The family you create yourself.'

And Beam thinks, *Yes*. And also, with a rising sense of panic, *Shit*.

7

The Charles Addison Private Hospital, named after one of Shorton's first measurably rich people, is a small collection of buildings abutting the river and offering the sick and dying serene water views. It's a new addition to the town with no history to speak of and so he wonders why his father would wish to be here instead of the town's main hospital, which at least has a solid grip on the soil. 'In history,' his father used to say, quoting Churchill, 'lies all the secrets of statecraft.'

Naomi parks in a restricted area, informing Harvey, before he dares point out the transgression, that no parking inspector is going to work on Australia Day. Harvey had completely forgotten the day, the best one of the year to live near Sydney Harbour.

His sister is her own GPS, leading Harvey at a trot out of the car park, through the foyer and around an L-shaped corridor. They are at their father's room in way too short a time. He is definitely not ready for this. It's Australia Day, for God's sake. Naomi pushes the door open and Beam sees an old man in a bed, his father, not awake, and nearby his brother having what appears to be a fervent conversation with a nurse.

The bed is not quite central. The curtains are drawn. A medical machine hums or maybe it's the air-conditioning.

Thank God Naomi is here because Beam has no idea what to do right now; no idea where things are at or how long they've looked like this. He'd felt an obligation to come here, and a sense of entitlement too, but right now he feels absurdly out of place.

Bryan sees him, pretends not to, and refocuses on his conversation with the nurse, which Beam quickly ascertains is about pain relief. Morphine levels. And something about a shower.

Naomi begins fussing over the flowers in the room, emptying vases, replacing water, consolidating small bouquets and unashamedly reading all the card messages. Beam stands there, motionless. His younger daughter Jayne had recently shown him a film clip in which a guy stands fixed to a spot on a road and the whole world swirls nauseatingly around him on hyper-speed, and this is how he feels now. Cannot move.

As is the way with cancer patients, bodies cruelly divided as cells multiply, Lionel Beam is a shrunken version of himself. Once a tall man, wide-shouldered and handsome in the manner of a peppery academic, he now looks like a small sculpture, a generic representation of an old person, resigned to bed, disappearing into the sheets and slowly retreating from the world.

'He sleeps a lot now,' Naomi says as if reading her brother's thoughts. 'But sometimes he only looks like he's sleeping though he's still listening. It's hard to know. You should still say hello.'

At this Bryan turns and looks dimly at his brother. 'He's asleep now,' Bryan says. 'He won't hear you.'

'Hello Bryan,' Harvey says, and somehow it sounds provocative, and it might be. 'It's great that you're, you know — *what?* — doing this.'

'Some of us don't have a choice,' Bryan says. 'And some of us want to.'

And some people say what they fucking mean.

'Well, anyway, thank you,' Harvey says. 'For everything. Naomi says you've quit work.'

'He needed proper care. It's what people do.'

Jesus.

'Well, what can I do to help now?' Harvey says, patting his

sides as though ready to jump on in. 'Now that I'm here?'

Bryan wipes a wet flannel across their father's freckled brow, a brow once given to fits of fury, stormy sermons and tortuous indifference. 'Nothing really,' he says. 'It's all taken care of. I hear you're only here for a few days anyway.'

And which one of them told you that? And in what context?

'I might stay longer,' Beam says. 'I haven't booked a flight home yet. And I've got leave from work.'

Instantly Harvey pictures the face of Trudi Rice and feels a little sick.

'Well,' Bryan says, 'if you'd asked me two days ago how long he had to go, I would have said five days tops. But he sort of rallied yesterday and he's kept down food this morning and he just looks better in himself.'

He looks shit.

Naomi fixes their father's pillow. 'It's day-to-day, isn't it, Bryan,' she says. 'Like everything.'

Harvey feels a sense of solidarity here, a solidarity that he's not part of and not entitled to claim. And he honestly can't remember feeling any other way.

Beam steps closer to the bed. 'Hi Dad,' he says. 'I don't know if you can hear me but it's Harvey. I just wanted to say that I've come here to see you and I'm sorry that you're sick. I just ... yeah. You look ... it's hard. I'm sorry. I flew here this morning. Suze and the girls say hi.'

And bye. They say bye.

And he needs to go outside now, needs air. Harvey pulls the door open and walks quickly into the corridor, back through the foyer and out the glass doors to the scorching concrete circle of the ambulance bay and the fitful blue of Shorton's sky.

8

Naomi drives Harvey to Penny's house on the other side of town. Pulling out of the driveway, she beeps the horn three times with gusto and Harvey is pretty sure it's an 'I saw him first!' message for Penny, for it seems completely unnecessary.

The sister born just eleven months after him looks nothing like Beam and very much like their father. Or how their father used to look. She is statuesque, almost masculine in build, with a savage blonde bob-cut that hasn't changed since late high school. Yet there is a softness in Penny, not hidden but readily visible in her face; eyes that move quickly to smiling and a blush that is never far away.

Naomi is undoubtedly the more attractive Beam sister — Harvey's schoolmates long ago made that abundantly clear to him — but what they didn't see, and weren't looking for, was Penny's relative safety and what a beauty that is in itself. After the last few hours in the company of Naomi, Beam is quickly reminded that he has always felt more at ease with his first sister.

Penny has been briefed on his arrival, he doesn't know how, and gives him a warm hug at the door, a child astride her hip.

'Hello ... little one,' Harvey says. *Why can I never remember this kid's name?*

'Javyn's got a cold.' *Ah, that's why. Because it's ridiculous.* 'He just wants to be held twenty-four seven. It's driving me nuts.'

'Is this okay?' Harvey asks. 'Staying here? I feel like it must be like Grand Central Station over there.'

'God, yes, it's fine,' Penny says, running her free hand down Harvey's arm and then up to his stubbly chin as if to make sure it's him. 'It's great. You know Simon's up on site for another three weeks — he only left yesterday, so it's perfect. I can use the adult stimulation.'

'I'm sorry I missed Simon,' Harvey says, although he most definitely isn't because Beam has no idea how to speak to men who can change the tyres on giant trucks and crawl into manholes. He hates it when these guys call into the show, can instinctively sense their evolutionary superiority goading him down the phone line.

'Actually you can use his car while he's away,' Penny says, 'so you don't have to rely on ... I mean, be restricted by us. You must have loads of people to catch up with.'

'Not that many, actually,' says Beam. *None.*

She pulls out a chair at the dining room table for him, pats it gently to encourage him to sit down. Says, 'Where are your bags?'

'Long story,' Harvey sighs. 'Not that long, but boring. Actually do you mind if I call the airport and give them your address? What's the number here?'

'Twenty-seven. Okay, you do that while I bath the ferals.'

Penny disappears towards the back of her home, a once-beige affair now exploding with the kaleidoscopic entrails of her giftware store. Beam calls the airport, which helpfully knows nothing about the missing bag but is 'looking into it', and then he calls Cate, who uncharacteristically answers.

'So you got in okay?' Beam asks.

'No, I *told* you, Dad, I didn't get into *anything*. I picked all the wrong preferences. Stupid guidance counsellor, she said that —'

'Not uni, Cate, into my apartment. Did you get the key off Bill?'

'Oh, yes. He's a dude. We talked for *ages*. He said university is just like a hiding place for people afraid of hard work. He said I can borrow his Wilbur Smith collection any time, and I was like, *thanks SO much*, but now I'm not sure whether that's, like, books or music or guns.'

Beam has had little more than two-minute conversations with his elderly neighbour for the past six years, although he sometimes suspects Bill calls into his show.

'Look, make yourself at home,' Harvey says. 'There isn't much in the way of food, sorry, but —'

'I *know*, right? Unless you count the grapes in all this wine.'

'They're mostly gifts from advertisers,' Beam says quickly.

He imagines Cate checking out every corner of his apartment as she is talking.

'I've never actually stayed on my own before,' she says. 'This is going to be so cool. Jayne wants to sleep over one night too.'

'God, your mother will love that.'

There's a pause and Harvey can hear his balcony door slide open and a rush of Sydney fill his ear.

'Hey,' Cate says, 'can I use the pool down there?'

'Well, I guess so, but don't be too obvious because I'm really meant to be there with any guests.'

'So no skinny-dipping? No Borat mankinis? Ha-ha.'

Beam thinks Cate is sounding way too sunny for someone who just blew her final year of high school and ran away from home, but frankly he's also enjoying this experience of talking to one of his children about something other than drop-off and pick-up times.

'You need to keep in touch with your mum,' he says, 'even if it's just texting her your whereabouts each day. And I'll be checking in too.'

'Tevs.'

'Tevs?'

'Whatevs. Whatever. Okay.'

'Your generation is destroying the language I love.'

'We're not destroying it, Dad. We're dragging it into a more efficient age. Touring the facilities and picking up slack.'

'That's from a song.'

'I saw it on Tumblr.'

Beam decides not to embarrass himself by asking what that is.

'Okay, well, love you, Cate. Be good and ... yeah.'

'When will you be home?'

'I'm not sure yet but it won't be long,' Beam says, fingering a copy of *Marie Claire* on Penny's table. *Someone actually reads this?* 'There's not much I can do here except get in the way.'

'And it's a pity more people your age don't think like that, Dad.'

Beam smiles. *Smartarse.*

After Cate's call and because he no longer knows how to simply put down his phone with any sense of finality, Beam checks the headlines on his ABC app and then the cricket scores and then his new favourite distraction, BuzzFeed. He briefly considers heading to the noisy part of the house to give Penny a hand with bathtime, but there was a time when middle-aged men could towel down a young nephew without feeling like a creep and that time has passed. Instead, he wanders about the house looking at the many photos Penny has placed in novelty frames — events, birthdays, Christmases. Beam is in none of them. His fault, he knows that. But still.

He flicks through the stack of *Shorton Standard*s on Penny's dining table. This is the newspaper from which Beam used to pilfer most of the headlines for his early-career radio bulletins. Cut-and-pasting from young journos who likely got it wrong in the first place. There's more colour in the rag now but the stories are the same: snakebites, croc sightings, repeat drink-driving charges, business closures. If it can kill you or embarrass you, the *Standard* is all over it, spelling errors notwithstanding.

Penny emerges from the dimly lit hallway, sets up the boys in front of the TV and heads for the kitchen, an armful of dirty clothes on her hip and dinner on her mind. Beam is suddenly reminded of Suze's common refrain during those early child-raising years: *It's not hard, Harvey, it's just relentless.* Suze had been a good mum but those groundhog years, with no extended family help in Sydney, no lifelines, had just about felled them.

'You want some leftover lasagne?' Penny asks, looking deep into the fridge for answers. Beam thinks about saying no; his sister hadn't been expecting him a couple of hours ago, but he's ravenous.

'That'd be great.'

Penny lets the microwave work its worrisome magic and she feeds the boys and then she dishes up to Harvey and puts on a load of washing and supervises teeth brushing and reads a bedtime story and finally she turns to Harvey, having not yet eaten anything herself, and says, 'Hey. Wanna get drunk?'

And Harvey says, 'God, yes.'

Penny fetches two glasses, a bottle of something wine-ish from the fridge and then dumps a plastic bowl of chips on the table between them. It's hot in here and the ceiling fan's heart isn't in it.

'So what did you think about Dad?' Penny says. 'What was that like for you?'

'I ... well, it's horrible obviously,' Beam says, realising he hadn't really had time to think about what he had felt this afternoon with his father, how it might best be described. 'I mean, it's that look, isn't it. So much is gone and it's hard to know what's left. What you're really talking to. But I think, you know, I kind of wasn't shocked. And I don't know why because it is shocking, but standing there I just felt, um ...'

'Sad?'

'I guess so,' he says, grabbing a handful of chips. 'Maybe.' *Not really.* 'But also just sort of powerless in the face of inevitability. Cancer's a cunt.'

Penny laughs. 'Yeah, and I don't know why the Cancer Council hasn't embraced that rousing motto.'

'Sorry. I'm a bit tired, I think.' And Harvey had been feeling tired but now he suspects the wine is giving him a fresh round of fuel. His first glass is gone in minutes.

'What's Bryan's story, anyway?' Harvey says. 'I thought women were supposed to take on the martyr role in these situations.'

'I don't know,' Penny says, topping them both up. 'In a way I think it's given him a sense of purpose. You know he didn't so much give up his job as lose it. He doesn't know that I know this so don't say anything but the bank tried to offer him a voluntary redundancy last year and he didn't take it, didn't take the hint or whatever, and they've been trying to manage him out ever since. He's not the right fit anymore, apparently. So now Dad is his job.'

Take the payout, Harvey, fill out the forms, see a counsellor — it's on us.

'Poor bastard,' Beam says, and wonders if he means it.

'I mean, it's been great in a way,' Penny goes on, 'because, honestly, Naomi and I both have families to run and I have the business and Bryan has just handled all the stuff we wouldn't have had time for.'

'Yeah, but it's not a life, is it? It's just avoiding life.'

Penny shrugs. 'Well, we all do that.'

And then Beam puts it out there before working through the many reasons why he shouldn't: 'Do you think Bryan is gay?'

Penny looks at him hard, puts her glass down and then throws her head back in contrived hysterics.

'*What?*' says Beam incredulously. 'I mean, he doesn't necessarily come across that way, but it's just something... you know, no girlfriends, no kids... the shoes.'

'The shoes?' Penny is really laughing hard now. 'What about his shoes?'

'The shoes he wears,' Harvey says. 'They're ... I mean, I saw them today and they're not *regional* shoes. I think he must buy them online.'

'So in the midst of seeing your father on his deathbed, you've looked at Bryan's shoes and thought, yep, gay?'

Beam throws his hands up in mock theatrics, partly to remove them from the chips and the wine, if only briefly. 'No, I mean it *has* occurred to me before,' he says. 'Not that it's a big deal or anything. But maybe if he's been living this sort of false life for so many years, that's why he's so ... you know, uptight.'

'No, I think Bryan is just Bryan,' Penny says confidently. 'I don't think he's gay. Asexual if anything.'

Yeah, right, Harvey thinks. *Because that's a thing.* 'I still don't understand why he hates me.'

'He doesn't *hate* you, Harvey,' Penny says but her voice falters a little and they both know the truth lies elsewhere.

'Well, maybe he does,' she adds finally. 'To be honest, I think he's never forgiven you for leaving him behind.'

'Leaving him behind!' Harvey's hands fly up to his temples as if to prevent a sudden brain explosion. He pushes back on his chair, considers getting up, doesn't. 'Shit, Penny. I mean, *he* was the one Dad picked to live with him. Not me, not you, not Naomi. *We're* the ones who were left behind.'

'Look, you can't overthink that decision, Harvey,' Penny says, bringing her voice down to remind Harvey of the sleeping children up the hallway. 'Dad picked the easiest option for him. Mum couldn't handle all four of us, he had a two-bedroom house, we were girls, and you were ... you wouldn't have gone with him anyway.'

'Well, I don't think you can *underthink* that decision, Penny,' Harvey says. 'At least not as much as he clearly did. You can't just make a decision like that with no explanation and let everyone else spend the rest of their lives trying to work out what it really meant.'

Beam is now looking at an empty chair because Penny has gone to get another bottle from the outside fridge. He hates himself for this, ripping out this old weed and holding it aloft like a petulant child. The truth is he never thinks about this anymore, never has any reason to. It's being back here that does it to him. This fucking town. This quagmire of owed apologies and frayed endings and stupefying bullshit. He could have been on a boat on Sydney Harbour today.

'Have you seen Mum yet?' Penny says, coming from behind him and giving Harvey's shoulder a squeeze on the way past.

'No. Tomorrow I think.'

'Yeah, we'll visit Dad in the morning — I do mornings, Naomi does arvos — and then I'll drop you at their place, if you like.'

Their place. Beam picks up the chance to shift the topic from their father.

'And what do you think about Mum moving into Naomi's?'

'I think it's stupid, Harvey,' Penny says as though she'd been waiting for the question for several hours. 'I think Naomi's natural gravitation towards complication has peaked. Mum is sixty-seven, not eighty-seven, and so what has Naomi signed up for here? Having Mum under her roof for the next twenty years? For what? Company?'

'She said Mum nearly died.'

'And that's bullshit obviously, Harvey. She had mild concussion, that's all. Nothing broke ... except Boner.' Penny pours another wine. 'RIP Boner,' she says.

'Oh God,' Harvey says mid-gulp. 'Please tell me Mum didn't accidentally kill a dog.'

'Nope, a cat. The neighbour's cat.'

'Oh shit, that's horrible.'

'I know ... it's ...'

Penny covers her mouth and Beam thinks she's about to cry, thinks *shit,* but there is a sudden snort and an explosion of wine. His sister is laughing.

'I'm sorry,' she says, waving her hands in front of her face. 'I'm just ... it's ... oh God.'

Instantly Harvey warms to the new theme. 'Is it because of the name? Penny, be honest. If Mum had landed very hard, virtually impaled herself, on a Megsie or a Snow, would you be having this reaction?'

'Stop it, Harvey,' she says, now almost weeping and indicating she may need to wee. Or just did. Beam is really enjoying himself now.

'Fluffy? Smoky? Tom? Would these work better for you, Penny? Engender a little more sympathy for the cat squashed by our falling mother?'

And Penny is gone, fleeing to the bathroom, and Harvey sits back and smiles to himself. *Here is a moment.* He is happy right now, and five minutes ago he wasn't. And this, he thinks to himself and not for the first time, this is what is *good* about alcohol. Its rare amplification of aggression notwithstanding, its preference for addiction and the steady erosion of vital organs aside, alcohol can at least make the sheer gnawing inexplicability of life seem very funny indeed.

When she returns, Penny is chastened, if still grinning and crimson, and wants to make it clear that she feels very sorry for *any* animal killed by a falling neighbour or indeed via any means of misadventure.

'And I'm so glad you're here, Harvey,' she says, 'because I haven't laughed like that in ages.'

'Glad to be of service,' he says, offering up his glass to be chinked.

And then they talk a little about work, although Beam reveals nothing about his current positional hiatus, and about kids, their interests and personality quirks, and Beam is proud that his descriptions of Cate and Jayne don't seem to be too short on detail given how little time he spends with them.

'And do they get on well?' Penny asks. 'Cate and Jayne?'

'Um, I think so,' he says, and realises he has no idea. 'I mean, I don't hear of any major fights. I think they're probably like most siblings — they have their moments.'

'Then Suze has done a good job,' Penny says. 'And you have too.'

'Thanks. It's all Suze, really. But um, you and Naomi. How long has this current battle been raging?'

Penny looks down at the table and flips *Marie Claire* over as though suddenly embarrassed by it. 'Well, it's actually not raging anymore, not as far as I'm concerned,' she says. 'I mean, we don't really speak anymore, but that's probably a good thing and a safe thing. No more open hostility. It's just ...'

'It is what it is?' Harvey says attempting a Naomi hair flick that doesn't quite work.

Penny replenishes both their glasses. *God bless the Beam bladder*, Harvey thinks. *Big, if not entirely robust.*

'I'll tell you why I hate that phrase, Harvey. Because nothing just is what it is. Everything is how we make it, or what brought us here. Things happen, shit happens, stuff is said and can't be unsaid. Mistakes are made that can't be unmade. And that is why things are the way they are. Thinking that it's all just chance and kismet — that's crap.'

Harvey loves that she knows the word 'kismet'.

'You love that I just used that word, don't you?' Penny smiles and she touches Beam's hand. 'You and your words. You and your books.'

And out of nowhere Harvey thinks, *We shared a childhood. We are still sharing a childhood.*

'Look,' Penny says. 'Honestly? Naomi needs it more than I do. Mum. She needs Mum and the attention and the validation and all that stuff. There's not enough to go around, there never was, and so Naomi can have it. I have learnt ... *am* learning ... to get that stuff from friends. If you can't have a functional family, just have great friends.'

And Harvey winces at the statement, because he suspects he has neither.

'Well, that's great, Penny. So *you're* all sorted then.'

'What does that mean?'

'Well, I just think ... I mean, they're just words, aren't they?' *Careful, Beam.* 'Admirable words, but not ... I just don't think it's possible to sidestep family when you're still standing in it.'

'And you think running away, what you did — that's the answer?'

'I think it's fucking brilliant. Seriously, Penny, I do. I'm back here one day and already I'm up to my neck in all this shit.

Stuff I don't even think about in Sydney. I mean, it's not all bad stuff but it's still ... headfuckery.'

'I think you overrate geography, Harvey. No matter where you go, there you are.'

'That's a very misused saying, Penny. And you know I love my sayings. A little respect, please.'

Penny laughs, and Harvey does too. They have drunk a lot of bad wine in a short amount of time and this conversation wouldn't have happened otherwise. That's how it works in the Beam family. *It is, yes, what it is.*

There's a loud knock at the front door and Harvey looks at his phone — 11pm.

He hears Penny discussing something with a male voice on the other end, then a pause, a thank you, and the door being shut, locked. His sister re-emerges into the dining room holding aloft Beam's Adidas sports bag, triumphant.

'Hey Harvey,' she says, smiling. 'Your emotional baggage arrived.'

9

ON AIR

'And it's just gone ten minutes after nine and the sun is smiling down on your city today, perhaps a little too brightly in the west where the fire danger is high again, but on the balance of things you wouldn't want to be anywhere else.'

Beam nods affirmation through the glass: *The PM is on the line.*

'You certainly wouldn't want to be in Canberra, anyway, where a bunch of thinkers and talkers — I think "movers and shakers" would be stretching it — have gathered together to discuss that most unsexy of topics: the Australian Constitution. Yes, it's day four of the 1998 Constitutional Convention, the talkfest that should ultimately deliver you, the Australian people, well, what? That's the real question, isn't it? Is this exercise, this staggeringly expensive exercise, about genuinely exploring the possibility of an Australia that isn't bound to the British monarchy — and that's an awful lot of coins to be re-minted, folks — or is it about drowning the republican debate in so much waffle that it'll never resurface again? Mr Howard, you'd probably prefer the latter result, would that be fair to say?'

And it's a great interview. Beam is flying and Howard comes along with him, reluctant at first but gradually brought around by Harvey at his most charming. Beam has never been one for full-frontal attack, not even now when it's the height of broadcasting fashion. He leaves the stinging barbs and militant retorts for his callers, who seldom disappoint, and instead he wins over guests with a measured intellect that is neither dominant nor intimidating. Beam is *good* at what he does, is getting better period after period, and he fucking loves it.

The red light on the studio's second phone is flashing, has been for the last twenty minutes, and he can't understand why his producer hasn't intercepted it. It's time for headlines and Beam thanks the Prime Minister for his generosity, politely on air and then much more profusely off. Makes loose arrangements to have lunch when John is next in Sydney.

And that's who Harvey Beam is now: a man who lunches with prime ministers. At the very least, makes plans to.

When finally he picks up the persistent phone, Beam learns from the station receptionist, a resolutely impassive matron he's consistently failed to win over, that his wife has gone into labour. She's in hospital. *Now.*

Shit. Suze has at least eight weeks to go.

The receptionist haughtily arranges a car for him and a fully charged Harvey, the 'High Beam' they now speak of in the dailies, explains the situation to his family of listeners, begs off early, asks for their prayers, makes a passing joke about hoping for a boy. It's great radio and even in that moment he thinks it and knows it.

And when Beam arrives at North Shore Private Hospital, he finds that his second daughter, Jayne, is little, far too little, and he is late. And Suze is crying because of so many things.

10

'Not the best idea I've had lately,' Penny says, passing two Panadol tabs across the kitchen bench to Harvey. 'Getting smashed on a weeknight. Today is going to hurt like a bastard.'

Beam declines the tablets, has always quietly regarded a hangover as a thing unworthy of mercy, and honestly, as he stands here now in the chaos of Penny's breakfast rush, he doesn't actually feel that bad. God knows he's felt much worse.

'I'm alright,' he says. 'Seasoned professional.'

Beam helps get Penny's boys sorted for day care, which is to say that he ties a pair of shoelaces and finds a missing hat under a bed, while domesticity flings Penny about the house like a trained dancer. Harvey is enjoying this, being on the periphery of things, a step removed from primary responsibility but still close enough to observe the bewitching alchemy of family life. The endless race to stand still.

Penny drops the boys at their centre and Beam makes a mental note to add its title, 'Jumping Jolly Bears', to his long private list of Inane Childcare Centre Names, the most recent additions being 'Cuddlewumps', 'Tippy Tots', 'Dashing Ducks' and 'Beautiful Tiny Minds'. How he yearns to meet the industry rogue who one day calls his centre 'Lunch Nap Home'.

They drive over the bridge to the main shopping centre, which houses Penny's store. Beam stands outside the entrance as his sister opens up and gets things ready for her singular staff member, a level-headed teenage girl who Penny says has risen admirably to the challenge of managing Just The Thing on her own each morning while Penny visits their father.

Harvey stands back and regards what his sister has created here, a lovingly curated small business in a fickle regional economy, and he is at once in awe and envious. Beam has never created anything significant; can't manage money or people for the life of him.

She has always done this, he thinks, letting his mind wander back to the endless art shows and concerts and second-hand stalls arranged by Penny in the Beam rumpus room when they were young. Everything had been so well organised and expertly presented, tickets prepared for parents and the neighbours, exact starting times, price tags, two-for-one deals. And then Naomi and Harvey would inevitably bowl in and spoil things, not to be mean of course, not necessarily, but simply because that was their thing, their only thing, to be funny and mocking.

And Bryan. Where had Bryan been when all this was going on?

Beam's thoughts are interrupted by a tap on the shoulder and he twists around to see a familiar face, at least a face that was once very familiar: Hugh Traynor, his first boss at Shorton Radio. More latterly, about fifteen years ago, Hugh had broken off his engagement with Naomi and sent Beam's youngest sister running into the ample arms of her now husband, a man Harvey inwardly refers to as 'Impressionism' because he knows absolutely nothing about him.

'God, Beam,' Hugh says. 'What are you *doing* here? Someone died?'

Traynor is twice the man he used to be, Harvey notes, self-consciously patting his own insistent paunch. The grey sideburns — *sideburns, Traynor, really?* — and trademark gold chain advertise a man who once had reason to strut. Now a strut might be physiologically impossible.

'Ah, well, not quite,' Beam says. 'But my father is very sick, so ... yeah.'

Traynor grins, looking more like an audience member welcoming a fresh plot twist than someone who just put their foot in it. 'Well, how long are you here for?' he says. 'I bet the station wouldn't give you long. Can't let the ratings slide in the Sydney game. We're still not even counting them here, ha!'

'Actually I've got extended leave so I'm just going to play it as it goes.'

'Really? How's your sister?'

'Which one?'

'The nutter.'

'I'm still going to need more clues, Hugh.'

And Hugh Traynor explodes with mirth and slaps Harvey on the back like an old rug with a stick.

The former colleagues exchange a few rib-poking observations about time's treatment of their young men's bodies, about the defiant survival of radio in the face of unthinkable technology and, finally, and perhaps most honestly, about the weather.

Then Hugh's face opens up like an unexpected letter.

'Mate, why don't you do a shift while you're here? Old times'. Shorton's finest export returns to the microphone that launched his stellar career. Seriously, if you're keen, let's do it. But give me a few days to promo it first.'

'I don't think so, Hugh,' Beam answers, 'but thanks. This trip is really about family.'

'And that cannot end well,' Traynor laughs. 'When you need a sanity break, call me. Shorton would love to hear you again, rattle some cages, groove the move.'

What the what?

Hugh rifles through his wallet for a business card and has an absurdly long glance at it — as though he hasn't held one for years — before handing it over.

Beam thanks his old boss, tells him to look him up if he's ever in Sydney, and watches him walk away. Feels a little sorry for the guy — *What is he even doing in a shopping centre at 8.30am on a weekday?* — but isn't entirely sure he's entitled to bestow pity on a man whose career hasn't moved a single place on the board in almost twenty years. Better the steady ride, even the spectacular crash, than the cowardly withering, Beam thinks.

And he knows he has to call Trudi Rice. But first he will visit his father.

Penny drives slowly to Charles Addison. So slowly Beam can't stand it. He breathes the pace of Sydney these days — even in gridlock, things still *feel* like they're moving — and he hates this apathetic dawdling. The long slow shrug of small-town life. He would offer to drive if it didn't risk causing a hungover Penny any offence.

'Was that Hugh Traynor you were talking to?' she says, slowing down for a traffic light that still has a decent stab of orange in it.

'It was indeed,' Beam says. 'He hasn't changed a bit. Apart from losing most of his hair and getting fat and forgetting how to dress.'

Penny nods, checks both mirrors, nods again. Time stands still. 'I see him all the time. He comes into the shop, loves a chat.'

'Really? What does he talk about? Does he ask about me?' *Beam, you dick.*

'Is there any other topic?' Penny says. 'No, Princess. We talk about local stuff, sometimes about Naomi.'

'Bit late now to be hung up on her,' Beam says. Even though he'd left Shorton by the time Hugh left Naomi, Harvey knew his youngest sister had been utterly devastated by the event, her grief inspiring a local caterwaul of outrage and sympathy.

But Penny says, 'He's not hung up on her. People still judge him for hurting "innocent little" Naomi,' Penny makes the marks in the air, hands briefly off the wheel, 'and he feels the wrath of that in this town. I think he feels I'm a safe harbour, like we both know the real Naomi. Everything isn't always black and white. There was fault on both sides.'

'God, it was forever ago, Penny.'

Harvey looks purposefully out the car window, willing his eyes to focus on something familiar. He pictures Penny and Hugh slouched across the gift store counter, bitching about Naomi to their mutual satisfaction. Then he thinks about a book he finished reading not long ago, about a band of Australian POWs stuck on the Thai–Burma Railway in WWII, laying their own deaths stake by stake, peg by peg, flogged and starved by Japanese overlords, their only salvation, the one thing that saved some of them but not nearly enough of them, being solidarity. Mateship. That most cloying of clichés, but maybe so because it's true. Brothers in arms.

And Beam thinks to himself: there is no mateship among sisters. No implicit loyalty. Only love and destruction.

***

Bryan is conspicuously absent when Penny and Beam walk into their father's hospital room, and soon Penny is too, excusing herself to get some restorative coffee from the cafe.

All too quickly it's just Harvey and his sick father again, this time alone, in a pale room wafting with dust motes, a bed, a chair, a tall table of books. And it is just as Beam had pictured things and also nothing like he might have prepared himself for.

For he has, if he's honest, imagined such scenes in the odd reflective moment. Or because a saccharine movie scene led him there. He's imagined deathbed conversations with his father, not in any morbid literal sense but mostly out of curiosity. Would there be, Beam has wondered over the years, some utterances of regret? Explanation? Justification? Latent frightened softness that is almost like love? When there is nowhere left to hide, and no reason to, would there be something other than still more wilful indifference?

Lionel Beam is sleeping, his face turned to the sunny

window, eyelids pitched in two dark grottos. Harvey feels somehow guilty just looking at him like this, as though the act should require permission of sorts. And then he realises that this strangeness is because he has never actually viewed his father sleeping. Had there ever been an opportunity? Had he seen his father do anything bar read books and walk out doors?

Harvey shifts his gaze to the books on the side table. *A Distant Mirror: The Calamitous 14th Century, The Experts Speak: The Definitive Compendium of Authoritative Misinformation, Breaking the Mirror of Heaven: The Conspiracy to Suppress the Voice of Ancient Egypt.*

Jesus Christ, Beam thinks. *Surely a Max Walker could do no harm at this point.*

He realises these and the many other books piled around them have likely been placed here by Bryan, taken from his own or their father's bookshelves, for the two men shared — apparently — a reverence for forgotten worlds and buried civilisations. Ancient history. Harvey is not without his own interest in the past but nothing before people invented cars and picked up the pace a little.

A few years ago Beam had found his father's PhD dissertation, the thing that became for Lynn Beam a rival worse than any mistress, and which finally led her to end their marriage. It wasn't just the writing of it, the ceaseless days of single-minded research, the thump-thumping of books on the office floor at night, the ignorance of bedtimes and birthdays, years and years of that, but later the book tours, the symposiums, the guest lectures and, inevitably, but unforgivably to Lynn, talk of the next book. Lionel Beam and his big historic brain had walked into a world that was so removed from his old one, and so much more welcoming and sensible, that his own personal history, in the face of millennia of far more significant history, could simply no longer be accommodated. At least, that was Lynn's hypothesis and also her final conclusion based on the available evidence.

Harvey had not merely stumbled across this digital tome; rather he had gone looking for it, scouring academic sites for one that he didn't have to join and subscribe to, even though that would have been a far less embarrassing online footprint than his recent porn activity.

And he had struggled admirably through this thing, something about the Edwardian Reformation of the 1500s and its shaping of the Church of England, looking for ... what? Beam still isn't sure but it probably smells like insight. Clues to a closed mind. But what he actually learned from that tedious few days of reading and re-reading was frankly nothing about his father and rather a great deal about the essence of academia itself: criticism. The art, the apparent measured joy, in picking holes in every piece of work that doesn't support one's own and applauding those few that do.

So maybe it was about his father.

The door opens abruptly behind Beam and a woman walks in and he sees it's not Penny returned but a nurse. A nurse with a ponytail and a nose that he knows.

11

Grace.

Harvey's heart shifts. How unexpectedly pleased he is to see this barely familiar face. And he's about to say 'Hey, what are the chances?' when Penny, refuelled, and a grim-faced Bryan file through the door behind her. A new nurse attending to their father: Bryan is all over this.

Grace looks briefly at Harvey but gives nothing away. She picks up Lionel's chart from the end of the bed and turns to address the room's small crowd.

'He might not wake up for quite a while today,' she says. 'The notes here say he had a rough night and the doctor administered extra morphine this morning, so we'll just see how he goes with that.'

Grace checks Lionel's drip line and adjusts his bed linen. The room is heavy with silence and misplaced sunlight.

'I've had words with the head doctor about the morphine levels,' says Bryan. 'I hope that's in your notes too.'

'Yep,' says Grace calmly. 'It is, absolutely. I've had a comprehensive handover.'

'That sounds better than a comprehensive hangover,' Penny says, and Harvey smiles at his sister and her efforts to blunt the Bryan effect.

Oblivious, Grace begins busying herself with small tasks, the three siblings looking on, seeing many different things.

For his part, Harvey is confused. Grace is moving about as though she doesn't know him, a model of gentle efficiency.

He wants to claim her somehow, climb a fortuitously placed ladder in this game of scene-ownership currently dominated by Bryan and his sisters. *I know the nurse, guys, so ... yeah.* But Grace is not playing and Harvey can suddenly see, in the way she carefully notes his father's temperature and listens intently to his heartbeat, that the stakes are too high. His father is very sick.

And soon he excuses himself to stand outside in the corridor, because there are just too many people in the room now, too much of everything and of nothing. And his father might not wake up for hours. *What's the point?* Harvey has no idea where he should be. Where he wants to be. And he feels a little ill. How does anyone not feel sick in a hospital?

Maybe he is hungover, after all.

The hospital car park beckons and beyond that a barren plot of dirt pegged out for some new development. Beam thinks this must be about where he used to ride a mate's trail bike almost three decades ago, along the cane furrows for speed and across them for laughs and spills. He walks and walks until he feels sufficiently removed from everything. New ground. Old ground. The right spot to ring Trudi Rice and get this shit over with.

She is predictably curt and clipped, doesn't like being kept waiting when she's only trying to help him.

'I'm on *your* side here, Harvey. But you make it so difficult.'

And the situation she sets out is this: the payout already offered to Beam will not be on the table beyond Friday. If he doesn't accept it, there'll be a far more standard offer made, a month's notice if he's lucky. It's been noted that Harvey hasn't taken advantage of the counselling provided for him — 'and arranged at great effort and expense' — and so management has no reason to feel any confidence in Beam's future performance and behaviour.

'You've become a risky proposition,' Trudi says, 'in a market where there is just no room for error.'

'That's bullshit,' Harvey says, kicking the coarse dirt at his feet. 'My ratings have taken no bigger a hit than anyone else's. This is about John Jackson getting afternoons and some bizarre new experiment taking over mornings. I'm not *risky*, I'm just in the way.'

Trudi's tone is as clipped as a Point Piper poodle. 'Harvey, the station is moving in directions that you have no interest in. We've had four strategic planning days in the last twelve months and you haven't attended a single one.'

'Strategic planning days,' Harvey spits out. *Fuck, don't get me started.* 'Trudi, with great respect, I think a day spent locked in the boot of a car is a more productive use of time than a strategic planning day. Unless talkback radio has secretly turned into something that doesn't involve a presenter talking to people and them talking back, I fail to see where new strategies might be helpful. It's a complete waste of time, and those of us who work twelve hours a day in the studio, those of us who keep the people listening and the sponsors happy and the money coming in to pay for *your* wages and *your* lunches at Level 41, well, we don't have much of that to spare.'

He's gone too far, Beam knows it, but there was nowhere to go anyway.

'Harvey,' she says, 'I don't expect you to understand my job, but let me assure you that I do understand yours. And what I see is a man no longer making connections, a man who is not happy in himself, a man who is not playing nicely with the other kids, and all of that equals bad radio.'

'Who's taking afternoons, Trudi?'

'That's not my call, Harvey. I'm not part of that decision-making process.'

'Is it Jackson?'

'As I said —'

'Trudi, cut the crap. Is it John Jackson?'

'I've heard something along those lines, but of course nothing is —'

'So maybe *that* was my biggest mistake, Trudi. Not sleeping with the head of HR.'

There is a slight pause, just long enough for an exasperated HR Department sigh.

'I've emailed you the forms, Harvey. Friday is the deadline.'

And she hangs up.

Harvey pulls a wooden stake out of the ground beside him and hurls it into the abyss.

12

Beam's marriage to Suze didn't so much end as gently devolve into something still identifiable but missing several important parts. Like a car without seats and a steering wheel. Still technically a car.

At the height of his most successful ratings arc, a glorious sunbeam spanning the spring and summer of 2005, Suze had asked Harvey to move out for an unspecified period of time — a sports bag's worth — so that he could honestly and without distraction decide if there was still space in his life for a wife and two kids.

'Because, seriously, Harvey,' Suze had said, 'all I'm getting out of you these days is washing.'

Harvey had stayed at a friend's place, the ex-husband of one of Suze's girlfriends, until it felt odd and uncomfortable and he ran out of shirts. He loved his wife, he knew that, and he would work harder to show her.

And Beam did work harder — there were flowers, lunch dates, demonstrative efforts — but something in Suze had already hardened. A resolve had set in, inched gradually forward like a neap tide, but there were no screaming arguments, no accusations of infidelity, and Harvey wasn't sure that any other marriage he'd observed was any different to theirs after ten years and two kids.

It's not hard to be a good husband, but it's easier to be an average one. And the pace and pressure of Beam's position, the constant vacillation between the top and second spots in the survey results, led him to take the easy option in all other parts of his life. He didn't exercise, he didn't ring his mother, he didn't foster friendships and he didn't give his wife and kids any worthwhile part of his diminishing soul. There was nothing left of Beam outside of his job. But he owed it so much. This was the thing that separated him from his past, defined him in ways his old teachers, his father, might never have imagined. It demanded everything of him and he gave it everything. What else did he know? How did other men do it?

On Suze's insistence, he moved out twice again, twice returning, twice willing himself to find something inside him that didn't look like obligation and uncertainty. And then a colleague offered him a six-month housesitting opportunity, a studio apartment just a train stop from work, which somehow turned into the last eight years of his life.

Cate and Jayne had tried to establish a rhythm for time spent at their father's but it became harder as their school lives and social lives grew more complicated. He dared not intervene overtly in matters of parenting—that was Suze's closely guarded domain—but he did continue to sub-edit all their school assignments, usually via email, and to attend as many sports carnivals, debating nights and basketball finals as his schedule allowed. Which wasn't many, but more than none. If anything, Harvey considered himself a much better father out of the family home than inside it and he tried not to dwell too often on why that might be.

He struggled when Suze started dating. Well-meaning friends had set her up with their colleagues and cousins and, when news of these occasions came to Beam via his daughters, he outwardly wished her well but something inside him raged. Their marriage had not yet been severed, there were tendrils linking them, they were still part of the same story. He violently hated the thought of Suze in bed with another man; even more he hated the idea of her kissing another man. And that image came to him often and at the worst possible times—in the middle of interviews, during production meetings, on the train, in bed, everywhere, without warning. Beam sometimes wondered if Suze knew how much this would hurt him, and if she didn't ... well, that was the point, wasn't it?

Thank God it was a big city.

Suze's love-life grated upon him less when Harvey began to make a few abortive dating attempts of his own. He was shit at it, hated every cheesy second of it, but it did result in him having sex again, real sex, albeit in often clumsy, short and regrettable encounters. It was a distraction, and one still defined by the memory of Suze's body, Suze's mouth, the lingering space she filled, but it moved him forward somehow, out of no-man's-land and toward the prospect of something else.

And something else had been Belinda, a two-year investment of Beam's time and the awakener of a hitherto unknown romantic seam within him. Theirs had been a relationship of note, remarked upon in the social pages, and a fresh source of surprise and spontaneity for Harvey. It had been fun, and Beam had suddenly realised he needed more fun in his life, and the holiday they shared in Hawaii was among the fondest guilty pleasures he could recall — his first paid leave in years.

He blew it in the end, in some way that he still can't understand, but Harvey Beam knew he was surely evolving.

13

Penny drops Beam at Naomi's place, his mother's new home, and Naomi rushes past him out the front door, en route for her shift at the hospital.

Harvey wanders down the short hallway to the dining room where he finds Lynn Beam feeding Naomi's youngest something that the child wants no part of.

'Harvey,' she sings, and wraps him in an embrace that is warmer and less awkward than he might have expected.

'Look, Jamie,' she says to her grandson, 'this is *my* little boy.'

'Pencil,' says Jamie, and Lynn laughs.

'Looks like that one's stuck,' she says.

Harvey wipes his hands on his sides. It's hot in here. 'You look great, Mum.'

'I do not.'

'You do.'

And she does. His mother looks good for her age, if a little too trusting of her hairdresser. But she was never going to be someone who woke up fat, creased and shocked at age sixty. Lynn Beam had always kept the years at bay with good tailoring, a daily walk and a healthy dose of vanity.

'I look *ancient,*' she says. 'But let me look at you. I hear you had a big night last night.'

Beam thinks, *How does she know this? How does it even work with these Beam women?*

'I've had plenty of practice, Mum,' he says. 'It wasn't that big a night. Maybe for Penny.'

Lynn clears up Jamie's lunch and wipes his vegie-smeared mouth. *Cute kid.*

'Now. I'm going to take this little soldier for a walk in the stroller, get him to nod off. Let's walk and talk.'

Harvey and his mother head off out the door in the direction of the nearby duck ponds, where as a boy he would rip up and toss entire loaves of bread at overfed ducks and geese until they got bored and turned on him. It's far more overgrown now than he remembers it; the trees are taller and the rushes more unkempt. And it has the effect of making Harvey feel smaller than he once was, instead of bigger. It's unsettling and he feels strange.

And what I see is a man no longer making connections, a man who is not happy in himself.

'How does your father look?' Lynn asks, weaving the stroller along the rocky path. 'I was thinking about visiting him myself — of course I'm sad for him, for all of you — but I honestly don't think he'd welcome it. I don't think he'd want to see me now.'

Harvey watches a duck dive in the water, arse confidently in the air. 'I don't think he wants to see me either.'

'Why?' Lynn stops and looks at Harvey. 'What did he say?'

'Nothing. He's been asleep both times. Two strikes.'

'Yes,' his mother says thoughtfully. 'All that morphine. It's not just for pain. The nurses know what they're doing.'

'What do you mean?'

'The long slow goodbye,' she says.

Beam moves this idea around in his head, imagines an unspoken world of winks and nods among medical staff. Dimwitted families looking on.

'Bryan seems to be running the show more than the nurses,' Harvey says.

'Well, that's his thing.'

'I don't see why it has to be his *thing*. Unless that's what Dad asked him to do.'

'Well,' Lynn says. 'That's probably what happened.'

Beam thinks, *Why? Why Bryan over everyone else?*

'But it's not something to be jealous about, Harvey,' Lynn says and rubs her knuckles kindly on his upper arm. 'It is what it is.'

Jesus. The Naomi effect.

Harvey looks at the child in the pram. *Oh to be a child in a pram.* 'I'm with Penny on this, Mum,' he says. 'That's a ridiculous saying. It means nothing. Just writes off whole chunks of reality and history as though they never happened.'

'Well. Maybe we shouldn't get into this now, Harvey,' Lynn says, directing his attention again to Jamie, who seems to be asleep.

'No. Okay,' he says.

They wander right around the main pond and back to the house and Lynn puts Jamie to bed for his nap, though not convincingly. Ten minutes later the kid is pounding on his bedroom wall.

'It's probably too hot to sleep,' Harvey reasons. *Christ, it is hot.*

'If he can just get an hour in before his brothers are home from school, it makes for a much easier night,' Lynn says.

And in this Beam can see that his mother has quickly become part of the sway and thrum of Naomi's daily life.

'So this is permanent?' he says. 'Staying here?'

'I think so. I don't look too far ahead.'

'It must make it hard to see Penny.'

'Harvey, I don't have anything to do with your sisters' issues.'

This sounds very much like a declaration, Harvey thinks, a speech Lynn has delivered a number of times now to various interested parties. She may have been judged harshly by small-town critics for leaving a husband who did nothing worse than completely ignore her for the best part of a decade, but she will not be blamed for any other fissures in the Beam model.

'Honestly,' Lynn says to Harvey, brushing her hand through

the air as if erasing a cobweb. 'They are grown-ups and I just stay out of it. It has nothing to do with me.'

***

Naomi returns to the house a little while later, the two older boys in train, school uniforms wrenched askew by the heat. She advises that their father definitely looked better this afternoon and made a good fist of conversation. Harvey detects an inference that he should have stuck around for the second sitting.

And then, while emptying lunch boxes and rifling notes out of schoolbags, Naomi invites Harvey to stay for dinner, nothing special, and he squares off with her prickly disposition by saying yes.

'And we'll have a few drinks to welcome you back,' she says.

Beam isn't sure whether the drinks quotient is genuinely to welcome him back or to even up the score with Penny. Regardless, he's grateful for a crowd-pleasing liver.

'Absolutely,' he says.

Harvey texts Penny to let her know he won't be back for dinner and may even stay over if it's a late night. Penny replies, 'K. Key under mat', and Beam is pleased to see Shorton's criminal element has still not progressed beyond a locked door.

Shit, Cate. Harvey excuses himself to make the call outside.

The air is ferocious and Naomi's backyard is a scorched minefield of upturned bikes, soccer balls, cricket stumps and squeaky dog toys. Separated from the house next door by a porous hedge, the setting is a still-life chaos of suburban family life, of half-finished projects and constant interruptions. But it is also somehow brimming with aspiration and hope, as though keeping the wheels turning, the grass growing and the toys replenished will amount to something in the end.

Beam wanders down to the rear of the yard and is surprised to see a man sitting in a wooden deckchair in the middle of it all. Underneath the ragged goatee and the dark glasses, he realises it's Naomi's husband, the mystery known as Matt. By his side, a lumpy black dog sits hungry for attention.

'Matt,' Harvey says. 'I didn't realise you were home.'

Matt rises and holds out a hand to Harvey, shakes it roughly.

'Mate,' he says, 'I heard you were coming. I just got off shift. Fucking eight and six knocks you around.'

'Yeah, I'll bet,' Harvey says, figuring that whatever an eight and six is, it's probably something he'll never have to drive or climb or build.

Matt yanks his fluorescent work shirt out of his jeans like it's the most pleasurable thing he's done all week. The dog trots off to another corner of the yard.

'Beer?'

'Sure,' Harvey says, because there is no other answer, and Matt disappears into his shed, returning with a cold Heineken and another chair.

Beam is fairly confident he has never before had a conversation with Naomi's husband. Not one. Not even at the wedding. And no-one ever speaks about him. How does someone exist, he thinks — exist in the quite significant sense of being a provider to a wife and three children — but cast almost no shadow? How often does he hide out here?

Harvey adopts the pose being demonstrated now by Matt, which is to stare ponderously at the abortive vegie patch adjoining the shed. Their chairs are close and parallel, like a plane ready for take-off.

'Tough job growing things in this heat,' Beam says, eyeing a cucumber that looks like an eggplant.

'Fucken oath,' Matt says, sipping thirstily. 'I'd water more but the bloke next door is a nazi about restrictions.'

'Right.'

'And I'm just away too often to get a good go at it,' he says, surveying the rest of the yard.

'That must be hard,' Beam says. 'Being away so much.'

'On the contrary, Harvey,' Matt says and raises his beer to the sky. 'It's the secret to a happy marriage, mate.'

Harvey laughs. 'I wouldn't know, mate.' And the *mate* lingers in the air uncertainly — Beam never uses the term in Sydney and may well have forgotten how to say it properly.

'So you're here to see your old man?' Matt says.

'Yeah, that's the primary objective.'

'Gotta be tough.'

'Well, hard for us all, I suppose.'

Matt stares hard at something that might be a dead animal. 'But I mean, you know, given your history with him.'

And Beam looks across at Matt a little differently now, as though he might not be a man completely removed from the family life flying about around him.

'I guess so,' he says. 'I mean, I don't really know what that history is. It's just kind of nothing.'

'Well, if it makes you feel any better about things, Harvey, I don't reckon I could sit here with your father and have a beer and find anything to talk about. Not one thing.'

And Harvey is taken aback by this. Because for as long as he can remember, no-one has ever ventured an appraisal of Harvey's relationship with his father that found Lionel lacking in any way. The conclusion has always been that Lionel simply *is what he is*, a man with his mind on other eons, and that perhaps Harvey's expectations are patently too high or unfair.

'And I don't think,' continues Matt, 'that it's okay to just *not like* one of your kids. I mean, I don't think that should be an option for parents.'

Fuck, Harvey thinks. *Is this the conversation I was meant to come back here for? Maybe it was this.*

His phone rings and Beam apologises to Matt, sees that it's Cate and wanders a few metres away from their odd little reverie to take the call.

'Cate?'

'Dad.' Her voice is minus its usual ironic lilt and hints at recent tears. 'When are you coming home?'

Harvey looks up at the sky, at other places. 'Is everything okay, Cate? Where are you?'

'I'm at your place,' she says. 'I got really scared last night, Dad. People come home at all hours around here. There are so many noises.'

'There's nothing to be scared of there, Cate. Honestly. It's very secure. They're just noises.'

And a lengthy pause ensues, in which time Matt walks up to Harvey and hands him another beer. *Thanks, mate.*

'Why don't you invite a friend over?' Harvey suggests. 'Invite Jayne over?'

'Mum won't let Jayne stay the night and I'm not even going to ask her. And everyone else is ... away. People are planning their uni accommodation and stuff. Everyone's got stuff on.'

And Cate has nothing on, Harvey thinks, and is instantly awash with sympathy for his daughter because he can remember, even now, how scary *nothing* feels at eighteen. The emptiness, the void. What's everyone else doing? The urge to run. Reinvent.

Beam's next words form even faster than the idea itself.

'Cate, why don't you come here?' he says. 'I'll pay for a flight. Why don't you come here and see everyone and just ... be somewhere else for a while?'

And possibly the idea had already occurred to her because she says, 'Thanks, Dad. I'll book it online.'

***

After another beer with Matt and a quick education about truck cycle times at your average iron ore mine, Beam heads back inside with his new *mate* and into the whorl of the witching hour. Naomi is in full flight, chopping potatoes, rinsing saucepans and issuing orders, while their mother listens to Finn reading on the couch. A headphone-encased

Toby is seated at the breakfast bench flicking through items on a phone, while duelling TVs on either side of the open-plan area pit *Deal Or No Deal* against the Channel Ten news.

'Hey,' says Naomi, looking up from the sink. 'I thought you must have found each other out there. Did he bore you with his bonsai collection?'

Beam laughs, confused.

'I've got this new butterfly bush,' Matt says, 'that a mate spotted online. It's rarely used as bonsai so there's a lot of scope there to create something quite informal or maybe cascading.'

Shit. He's serious.

'How long have you been doing bonsai?' Harvey says. *Doing? Making? Growing?*

'About three years now,' Matt informs him. 'I've got about twenty trees out there in the shed. I'll show you them tomorrow if you're interested.'

Twenty bonsai trees and a beer fridge in the back shed? Even after twenty years in radio and constantly finding the most unlikely and 'ordinary' people to be the most fascinating, Beam is still thrilled when he discovers one of life's genuinely interesting characters. 'Impressionism' has made an impression.

It's an enjoyable evening, if executed in little more than ten-minute reprieves between overtired toddlers, ruminations over burnt lasagne, teeth-brushing disputes, bedtime stories and the sullen protests of a young teenager. Beam and Matt sit and chat at the dining table, aware of and somehow emboldened by their sharing in this most stereotypical of male behaviours — doing nothing in the eye of familial chaos — and Naomi joins them intermittently as Lynn happily takes care of the children's closing arguments.

Beam sees amidst all this that Penny was probably right. Even though she meant it in terms of emotional support rather than practical assistance, Lynn is helping Naomi in a way that is vital to her daughter's survival. If their mother hadn't fallen down the stairs, Harvey reasons, this experiment in 'trans-generational living' would still be occurring. Because one way or another, if the world is working as it should, family has to shift and settle into the cracks that need filling.

For the first time in several hours, Beam remembers that he is now officially unemployed.

14

Two weeks before Harvey's fourteenth birthday, his father moved out of the family home. Lynn Beam had packed up most of Lionel's belongings (apart from his books which she refused to touch and had threatened to give to charity) and given him the address of a small house on the opposite side of the river available for rent. It had all happened while Harvey and his siblings were at school. Most of the neighbourhood had been at work. The lack of drama involved had been particularly unsettling for his sisters, as though nothing this life-changing should cause so small a ripple.

On Harvey's birthday, his father called by the house for the first time since he had left. He arrived in a taxi, the vehicle idling in the front drive. Harvey sat in his room, waiting to be summoned to the front door where his parents were having a discussion. He could make out a few words — his brother's name, his sister's names, something about a bank, something about a car. Finally, from his mother's mouth, Harvey heard his own name spoken. Then nothing for about ten minutes. Then Harvey heard the taxi drive away.

It wasn't until dinnertime that Harvey learned his father had come over not to drop off a birthday present but to pick up Bryan.

Your brother is going to live with Dad, Lynn Beam had told her three remaining children as she moved a knife through Harvey's chocolate birthday cake.

Penny and Naomi had looked wide-eyed at each other, uncharacteristically silent.

Their mother kept moving, flipping pieces of cake onto saucers, dabbing at crumbs on the table, gathering up the dinner plates, moving, moving.

Harvey looked hard at his cake, at one of the tiny holes in the sponge.

At last Naomi spoke. It was the first question of maybe a hundred that she and Penny lobbed at their mother that night, but it was the only one that mattered to Harvey.

'What about Pencil?' she'd asked.

Lynn Beam explained that their father's home had only two bedrooms. Having Bryan would take some of the pressure off Lynn. Lionel thought it was the right thing to do. It's wrong to separate sisters. Bryan had been happy to go.

Harvey quickly registered that he had not been an option in his father's plan. Discussions had been held that didn't involve him, hadn't even required his opinion. Why was it okay to separate brothers but not sisters? How much had Bryan wanted to go? Harvey had a new sense of how much space he really occupied in this family, in the world.

On the outer edge of his thoughts, Harvey could hear yelling.

'Doesn't he even care about us?' Naomi was wailing at their mother, tears spilling down her face.

'Why couldn't he get a bigger house?' Penny demanded.

'Of course he will still see you all,' Lynn Beam assured them. 'Of course he *wants* to see you all. But he also has to finish the next book and ... it will all just ... work out. Things are going to be better than they were, I promise.'

Harvey looked down at the smudged glass tabletop, willing himself not to smash it.

15

Beam wakes up on a mattress in Naomi's media room, an ambitious title for a small darkened room with a flat screen on the wall and a couch. It's the ping of his phone that rouses him and Harvey sees that he has six messages.

Naomi: Letting you sleep in. Going grocery shopping after dropping kids off. Be back around lunch. Help yourself to whatever. Hangover!

Cate: Bkd flights. Arrive Saturday morning. Emailed u deets.

Trudi Rice: Documents emailed. As discussed, tomorrow is the deadline for accepting the original offer.

Penny: Heading off to see Dad now. Call me later. Key still under mat.

Unknown number: Hi Harvey, this is Grace (nurse, fellow plane drinker). Sorry I couldn't talk yesterday but your sister gave me your number. If you want a break from family stuff, we could do coffee or lunch or something. Up to you. Cheers.

Suze: Call me. Now.

Harvey calls Suze. She's in a meeting; she'll call back. She calls back; he's on the toilet. They call each other at the same time; leave brief messages that might never be heard. The marriage of messaging. Finally he gets her, just as Matt walks into the dining room and says, 'Hey, wanna see the bonsai?'

Beam doesn't want to look unenthusiastic — he *does* want to see the bonsai — but the phone is on his ear now and he does a series of interpretive dance gestures at Matt that mean, in no particular order: sorry, have to take this call, *really* want to see the bonsai, and how bloody *hot* is it?

'Harvey,' says Suze, her voice a familiar mix of rage and resignation. 'Honestly, I may never understand you.'

'What?'

'You've invited Cate to come to Shorton. She's booked a ticket.'

'Yes,' he says. 'She seemed upset, she sounds lost. I thought it might be good. Get her mind off things.'

'Her mind has been *off* things for ages, Harvey. That's not the problem. Not by a long shot.'

'Okay. Sorry.'

'The problem is Jayne.'

'Jayne?' *What?*

'So you offer to fly one child to Shorton to ... what? Say goodbye to Lionel, keep you company, be a human shield against your family, whatever. What is the other child meant to think?'

Beam's head hurts. He is not going to drink today.

'But Cate's going through a tough time,' he says. 'I thought this would help. It's not about bringing *everyone* to Shorton. It's not a family reunion, Suze. It's about dealing with *this* situation ... what's happening now.'

'Kids don't understand the choices we make unless we explain them, Harvey.'

'I know.'

And Harvey knows that Suze knows.

'Jayne is upset,' she says. 'She's already fighting with Cate and now she's really upset. It's a fucking shitstorm.'

'Okay,' he says, 'what do you want me to do?'

'Just do what you always do, Harvey. Stick your head in the sand until it all blows over.'

'Fuck, Suze. What do you want me to *do* here? Just say it.'

But Suze is gone. Always and ever queen of the perfectly timed hang-up. How frustrating she must now find it, Harvey has often thought, to just press END instead of throwing a heavy handset against a wall.

How hard it is to do the right thing, he thinks. How much easier it is to do nothing.

Beam looks at his phone for insight. *Shit. Bonsai. Matt.*

Harvey wanders outside and down the back to Matt's shed. He can hear him inside whistling and Harvey isn't sure whether to knock first or walk right in. He once interviewed a self-described expert in 'shed etiquette' whose golden rule was that a man in his shed must *never* be interrupted unless said shed is in the immediate path of an imminent natural disaster. Even then, you need to be *really* sure about the scale of the disaster.

While recalling this, the door opens from the inside and Matt says, 'Come on in, mate.'

Like many sheds, of which Beam has been inside precious few, it feels much bigger inside than it looks from the exterior, as though ideas and plans and projects occupy a different kind of space to mere oxygen. Matt has set up two pedestal fans in opposite corners, a military flanking manoeuvre against the inexorable heat. There is a small bar fridge in another corner, and all around, on every wall, shelves dotted with bonsai plants at various stages of their evolution.

Matt has names for all of them, monikers that bare little obvious resemblance to their botanic titles. *Weeping Angela. Goodbye Sally. Helena Handbasket. Sigrid Thorn.*

'Ghosts of girlfriends past?' asks Beam.

'Ha. Something like that,' Matt says, taking a small set of secateurs to *You Jane.* 'Don't tell Naomi.'

'So,' Harvey says, positioning his sweating back against one of the fans. 'Is this the most popular secret pastime of men who drive trucks bigger than houses?'

Matt smiles and ponders this. 'I think the reasons I got into it and what I get out of it now are different things,' he says. 'My grandfather used to keep bonsai and my dad was really shitty at him for having such a selfish hobby. He thought it was pointless, the complete opposite of kicking a footy around with your kids. And I get that — I mean, it is time-consuming. But I don't know. I think I was probably just curious to explore something that pissed off my dad so much. I was probably just being an arsehole when I started googling bonsai.'

'And now?' Beam is in interview mode: never divert a good source who's on a roll.

'Now,' Matt says, 'well, this is going to sound really wanky, Harvey, so let's keep it in the shed, but I reckon it's about having control over something bigger than yourself. Being able to shrink a whole landscape to a few pots. Keeping things manageable. It's actually pretty blokey when you think about it. Women are happy to look at the big picture, but the big picture frightens the fuck out of me.'

'Me too,' says Harvey.

'Wanna lift to the hospital?'

***

It's a circuitous drive there as, on a whim, Matt decides to show Harvey the recently completed marina development at the town's harbour. Gone entirely is the beach Beam knew as a child, a left-handed break that was mostly good for bodysurfing and occasionally, when big storms loomed, the unsheathing of a rarely used board. Gone is the old surf club, the public loos, the humble kiosk, and in their place a vast and somehow precarious new arrangement of hotels, apartments and restaurants wrapped around a labyrinth of pontoons.

'Shit,' says Harvey.

'I know.'

'Who asked for this?' Beam wonders aloud, noticing how few boats are moored, none of them showroom material. 'There are so many things this town needed before ... this.'

'Progress, mate. Someone's vision. No-one asked me, that's for sure.'

Beam has no beef with progress but this is something else: there is no evidence, not even a hint, of what once existed here, no familiar fence post on which to hang a childhood memory. An entire beach, the place where Shorton families had long gone to escape the heat and each other, has been eliminated. *That's not progress*, thinks Harvey, *that's annihilation*.

They drive slowly along the arched rock wall, one of the artificial limbs holding this watery meccano set together.

'Where did you grow up?' Beam asks of Matt.

'Whole bunch of places. Moved every couple of years. East coast, west coast. Dog's breakfast. Even spent some time in Indonesia.'

'So where is home?'

Matt looks at Harvey strangely. 'Here,' he says.

They drive back through the vast and hideous industrial estate that rims the coastline — hulking silos and monolithic sheds that could house a billion bonsai. There is no way to get to the new marina except through this, like putting a fancy hotel at the edge of a nuclear wasteland. Just close your eyes, folks, we'll be there soon.

'Is that SR95.3?' Harvey asks, pointing to the centre console.

'Not sure,' says Matt. 'Probably.'

'Do you mind if I have a quick listen? I used to work there.'

'Go for it,' Matt says.

And before long the two men are shaking their heads and laughing and groaning at just how *bad* radio can be. The two hosts, a young guy and girl, are talking about their plans for the weekend, but there's no punchline, no helpful information, just a series of flat in-jokes delivered in a manner that is so rough and inarticulate Harvey assumes it's contrived.

'Jesus,' Beam says. 'Is this for real? I mean, is it work-experience day or something?'

'This ain't the big city, Harvey,' Matt says with a good-natured punch into Beam's pillowy upper arm. 'The work experience kid'd be paid a lot more than these two.'

Harvey laughs. 'But they're not even trying to engage the audience,' he says. 'It's like they don't care.'

'Maybe we're not the audience,' Matt says.

And Harvey suddenly remembers what his father used to say about the local radio station, back when Harvey worked there: *Mulch for the masses. Brain extraction via the ears.*

***

When Harvey reaches the door of his father's hospital room, Grace is walking out.

'Hey,' he says, 'I just got your text.' *Three hours ago. Shit.*

He immediately senses that the delayed reply, the apparent lack of reply — honestly, when had he had the chance? — has been interpreted unfavourably.

'What?' Grace says. 'Oh, that was nothing. The second after I sent it I realised I probably don't have time for anything while I'm here. I've taken on extra shifts.'

'Well, I would actually love to catch up,' says Harvey. 'If there's a chance.'

'Probably not,' she says. 'Look, your dad's asleep at the moment. Has been for about an hour. We walked him around the room this morning and he really did his best but I think it took a lot out of him. He's very frail.'

'Thanks, Grace,' Beam says. 'Thanks for the terrific job you're doing.'

Grace looks to the floor, her ponytail resting to one side of her neck.

'You're very different to your brother,' she says.

'I know. I often think the nurses got one of us mixed up.'

He quickly adds, 'Not that nurses ... mix things up. Except in good ways. Caring ways. Good, sensible mix-ups.'

Grace smiles, and Harvey is taken with a small indentation on her cheek, a tiny scar. And to stop focusing on it, he looks at her nose. That lovely small nose. *There is nothing so difficult to marry as a large nose*, Oscar Wilde had said.

'I'd better get going,' she says.

'Okay. I'll see you soon, Grace.'

And Harvey watches her walk away full of purpose and possibly anger, and he thinks that if it's possible to destroy something that doesn't yet exist, he has just managed it. *You're a dick, Beam.*

He finds Penny and Bryan sitting on either side of their father's bed, both making a fist of reading something. The room feels different somehow to how it felt yesterday, warmer and less daunting. A large new bunch of wildflowers dominates the windowsill.

'Hey,' Beam says in a whisper. 'How are we all?'

'Harvey,' Penny says, looking up at Beam and then back down at their father. 'He's okay. Just the same, really. How was your night? Have you been back to my place?'

'No, I came straight here,' he says. 'Matt drove me. Hey, he's a bloody nice bloke. Where have you all been hiding *him*?'

'You live in Sydney, Harvey.'

'Yes, well, there's that,' he says and smiles. Smiles at both of them, but Bryan doesn't look up from his book.

'Have this chair,' Bryan says, abruptly standing up and returning his book to the side table. 'I have to go and speak with the oncologist.'

And he walks out, single-mindedly making no eye contact with his brother, and Harvey watches him go, a less pleasurable rear view than that of Grace.

'Fucking hell,' Harvey says, pulling up the vacated seat. 'That guy has more issues than Israel.'

Penny is not impressed with the comparison. 'Harvey, this is really, really hard on Bryan,' she whispers. 'Don't be horrible about it. You have no idea.'

'No, I *don't* have any idea, Penny,' Beam says in a poor attempt at whispering. 'Not a fucking clue. How and when did this become the poor Bryan show?'

'Shhh,' Penny says. 'Just stop, Harvey.'

And he is instantly ashamed, for everything about his last response was inappropriate but especially the venue.

They sit for a few minutes in silence. Penny reads her magazine, although it doesn't escape Beam that she's been on the same page since their conversation precipitously ended. He picks up the book recently abandoned by Bryan: *A Man's Place: Masculinity and the Middle-Class Home in Victorian England.*

For fuck's sake.

Harvey digs out his phone, puts it on silent and checks his messages. Just the one from Cate confirming her flight time on Saturday.

Beam decides to text Jayne, aware she won't receive his message until school finishes for the day. Writes: Cate is coming to Shorton for a few days — you're most welcome to come too if you like. Love, Dad.

This will either please or infuriate Suze.

And then he texts Grace: How about a bite to eat tonight? I can show you the sights and delights of Shorton if you've got a spare seven minutes. Cheers, Harvey Beam.

And then he changes his wallpaper, and his screensaver, and then works out he can do both and more by changing the phone's 'theme'. Anything to avoid looking at that depressing bed.

'I'm going to head off now, Harvey,' Penny says, standing up and reframing the sheeting around her father's neck. His chest is barely moving. Lionel Beam is very still.

'Okay,' Harvey says, putting away his phone. 'Sorry about before. I just can't ... sorry. I know it's hard for you too. I'm a dick.'

'You really are,' she says and walks around to Harvey's side of the bed and cradles his head roughly in a gesture of affection that doesn't quite work.

'Well, that's going to look weird when we play it back,' Harvey says.

And there is a reply but it's not from Penny. It's a new voice in the room and Harvey soon realises it has come from his father, eyes still closed, body unmoving. The voice is barely reconcilable with the one Beam remembers.

'Is that you, Harvey?' Lionel Beam says, and he seems to be trying to lick his dry and mottled lips.

'Yes, Dad. It's me.'

Penny looks at Harvey, her eyes suddenly wide and wet.

A lawnmower fires up outside the window and their father says, very slowly, 'Well, now I know I'm really dying.'

16

As an up-and-coming voice on radio, a guy from nowhere special with something to prove, Harvey Beam prided himself on being a hard worker. Even when Suze, dripping with toddlers and drowning in tedium, would argue that spending twelve hours a day doing what you're good at and what you *love* is the very opposite of hard work, Harvey had nevertheless retained a measure of satisfaction about the hours he kept. First to arrive, last to leave. Short lunch, non-smoker.

Lately, however, Beam's come to think Suze might have been right: he *does* gravitate towards easy, even if he's not always aware of it.

At nine weeks premature, Jayne had been born in a state of respiratory distress, or as Harvey most easily described it to people, she *couldn't fucking breathe*. Her immature lungs lacked the substance that enables them to expand. Fortunately her arrival was pre-internet and so Harvey was unable to google himself into a paranoid frenzy about the many other complications she was perilously close to: chronic lung disease, heart collapse, brain haemorrhage.

He and Suze had been lucky — the neonatal unit at Sydney's Royal North Shore Hospital is among the best in the country. God help the too-tiny babies born in regional and rural Australia, Beam had postulated on his show when they were finally out of the premmie wilderness.

But maybe one never makes it fully out, for Harvey still believes that Suze was never the same after Jayne was born.

She had always been looking for the next sign of a post-premmie complication: cerebral palsy, impaired vision, hearing problems, psychological scarring. She showered Jayne with love and worry in equal parts, swaddled her in protective anxiety, and grew increasingly impatient with Harvey's well-intentioned refrain: *For God's sake, Suze, she's fine.*

And she was fine, but never to Suze's satisfaction. She would look at Cate and see a robustness that was never present in Jayne, and Harvey — not that he ever admitted it — could see it too. At least, Cate just *felt* easier than Jayne, easier in terms of not being a threat to Beam's patina of calm, to his holding together of this little world containing the lives he'd helped create. Jayne's fragility, her implied neediness, frightened Harvey to his marrow. He distinctly remembers, even now, looking around the ward of the neonatal unit each day for weeks on end, seeing couples in various states of despair and hope, and thinking, *How are any of these people keeping their shit together?*

As his daughters had grown up, Harvey always spent more time with Cate than Jayne, not deliberately and not because he loved her any more — and he'll frankly never understand parents who literally apportion their love via a hierarchy — but basically because Cate was less frightening to him. She was *easier*, and somehow still is.

And now, sitting in this hospital room in Shorton, his father having thirty minutes ago uttered a sentence of acknowledgment that Harvey still can't decide wasn't a clever insult — vintage Lionel Beam — he finds himself thinking about Cate and Jayne and wondering if they will ever find themselves in a similar position to this: looking down on a man they are supposed to love but don't. Can't.

As if summoned, Jayne's name appears on Harvey's phone.

Her message reads: Hey Dad, thanks for that but I have heaps of stuff on and I said yes to extra holiday shifts at work. But THANK YOU. Say hi to everyone. Love you. X

Beam looks up at the ceiling and sighs in relief. *Thank you Suze.* He looks through the window at a man on a ride-on mower, cutting through grass and weeds that will only grow back. Everything is relentless.

Finally he looks back at his father, for all intents and purposes the least threatening Lionel Beam has ever appeared, and Harvey knows he can't stay in this room. For he has nothing to say and nothing he needs to hear.

You can never go back.

17

Grace has chosen the Shorton Hotel, a corner pub in the main street that looks as though it predates the town itself, as the venue to catch up with Beam after her shift. And he's relieved because nothing that ever happens inside the Shorton Hotel could be classified as a date — there is no white-linen pressure, no sense of time stretching too far or running short, but there is more than enough aged timber and cardboard beer coasters to quickly soak up awkward attempts at conversation.

Grace is now twenty minutes late but that's okay, Harvey reasons, because he'd been slack at replying to her original text and now he must be punished, plus she doesn't want to seem too keen. *Oh yes,* Harvey thinks in a deliberate moment of arrogance inspired by his second beer, *I know how women think.*

When Grace finally arrives ten minutes later, still in uniform but with her regulation ponytail gratefully released, and with Beam's third beer perched in front of him (he had asked the barman for a red wine but the look in response made him pretend he was misunderstood), her excuse is solid: she'd been placating an angry Bryan about the dosage management of Lionel's morphine.

'Your brother doesn't seem to trust the hospital at all,' Grace says after Harvey returns from the bar with a gin and tonic for her. 'Has he had some sort of bad previous experience there?'

'Not that I know of,' Harvey says. *Not that I would.* 'But Bryan and Dad both share a belief that they are intellectually superior to most people.'

'Well, the best patient care doesn't come out of books,' Grace says, fingering the rim of her lipstick-smudged tumbler. 'It comes out of experience.'

And Beam is embarrassed that it's his family who are responsible for making a professional have to explain themselves.

'I mean, it's grief too,' Grace adds. 'Watching someone die can make some people very angry with the world. That's not uncommon.'

'Well, if it's any consolation,' Beam says, looking helpfully into Grace's green eyes, 'Bryan thinks I'm a dickhead too.'

Grace looks down at her drink.

'Not that I'm saying you're a dickhead,' Harvey splutters. 'Or that Bryan even thinks that. Shit. I mean —'

'It's okay, she says. 'I know what you mean.' And Grace self-consciously adjusts her uniform, which Harvey presently regards as the classiest outfit in the room.

Then she stares at him, really stares for a few long seconds, and Beam wishes to God he knew what she is looking for in this moment so that he can deliver it. Because he's starting to sense something about Grace that might be larger than random seat allocations on a plane and a sick patient in hospital. But then beer has always made him feel this way — at first revolted and then … hopeful.

'How long have you not gotten along?' she says finally. 'You and Bryan?'

'Since I left town,' Harvey says. 'No, before that. I mean, we've never been "brotherly".' Beam punctuates the air with his fingers. 'Mum put us into all the same sports as kids … tennis, cricket, footy … because we were so close in age. It was just easier for her — two birds with one stone. But it made us natural rivals and not to Bryan's advantage. Sport isn't his thing. Not that it's mine either, but at least I could catch and run without, you know, standing out for the wrong reasons. Bryan was always more focused on his schoolwork.

He's a smart guy.'

'You don't seem stupid,' Grace says.

And even though this meeting has quickly ventured into fairly unsexy terrain, Harvey realises he is enjoying it. Grace is beautiful and fresh and she is sitting right here in front of him and he has nowhere else to be.

'Like your father?' Grace asks. 'I noticed the books beside his bed. They're not the sort of thing you find on the bargain table at Dymocks.'

Beam laughs. 'No,' he says. 'I read the preface of one today and briefly considered hanging myself with Dad's drip line.'

Grace laughs a little too generously.

'But actually, Dad only got into academia later in life,' Beam says, wondering briefly if he's ever had cause to explain this before. Possibly not. 'He was a loans manager at a bank when I was really young and then he decided to go back to university — unfinished business — and he did it all via correspondence and apparently just *got it*. It was like it was his calling and because it came to him late, he threw himself into it as though he was dying.'

Beam bristles a little and Grace fingers one of the spare coasters on their little round table.

'Doesn't Bryan work at a bank too?' she asks.

'Did,' says Beam. 'Same bank. And he's also completing his PhD, I think. So, yeah, *literally* following in our father's footsteps.'

Harvey briefly considers that he and his brother do now share one defining trait and that is unemployment.

'Hey, do you want to get something to eat?' Grace says, placing her hand on her stomach. 'I haven't had anything since breakfast.'

And Beam would actually be satisfied with just another drink — liquid dinners have become a staple for him — but he says, 'Yes, that sounds great. Here or somewhere else?'

'Somewhere else,' Grace says with a smile.

They wander down the main street, a conceivable couple, Harvey thinks, even if he does have maybe ten years on Grace. But the walk might give them away, he decides, the self-conscious, slightly maladroit pairing of two people guessing at each other's pace.

They settle on a Thai restaurant. It had been Shorton's first but there are others now. The once bright-red facade has relaxed into a dull pink and the signage is missing more letters than it contains.

Grace apologises, for the third time, about still being in her nursing garb and Harvey assures her she looks absolutely fine. 'Thursday night with a woman in uniform at a place with one hundred and sixty-seven numbered menu options?' he says. 'I'm the envy of every man I've ever met, Grace.'

They share a pad Thai (#83), some steamed rice that has congealed to pudding status, and a bottle of red wine. Harvey is careful not to let the conversation veer back to their common ground of Lionel Beam and his warring entourage. He wants to get to know Grace and he wants to get there quickly; nail it in one solid interview.

But she's a tricky proposition who insists, because she's not had children or climbed any mountains, physical or proverbial, that her life is barely worth discussing.

'I wish I was better at embellishment,' she says.

Of course she's wrong about her life's ordinariness, as humbler people generally are. Harvey teases out the details of a woman who has nursed sick children in three impoverished countries, and later her own father to a particularly nasty death exacted by pancreatic cancer. She barracks for Collingwood (he will overlook this), hates cooking (this too) and loves Australian cinema. This latter fact alone, Harvey tells her, makes her truly unique.

And this kind woman, incredibly, loves Eskimo Joe, his favourite band.

As he pours them each another glass of wine, Harvey can't

help himself.

'And so, Grace ... love?'

'It's a many splendoured thing, Harvey.'

'Apparently,' he smiles. 'But have you had it? Are you up to three or four ex-husbands now?'

She looks at him quizzically, her brow slightly furrowed, and Harvey wishes he'd used higher numbers to make it clear he was joking.

'Just the one,' she answers finally.

'Oh.' Beam reaches for the bottle and quickly realises he just did so a minute ago. 'Oh right,' he says. 'An ex-husband?'

'Yep. Matthew. Long time ago. Three years from start to finish. No great story there.'

Harvey looks down at Grace's delicate hands, whose fingers are making unconscious figure eights on the paper table cover.

'So,' Beam says, imagining his producer making gestures through the glass ... *Throw to an ad! Don't mention the ex.* 'Was he a former drug baron who couldn't shake the old tails or did you come home one day and find him singing Celine Dion in your underwear?'

Grace laughs a little, but not convincingly. 'No,' she says, 'we just wanted different things. Well, actually we wanted the same thing — kids — but it just wasn't happening. We started to think it would never happen for us. He just sort of gave up.'

'Three years isn't that long,' Harvey says, hoping this doesn't cause offence. 'Sounds like he gave up too easily.'

'Well, I took up an overseas posting with Red Cross for six months. I wanted to get that out of my system and I thought the break would do us both good, but obviously it didn't. It literally broke us. So I kept working overseas and ... that was that. But anyway, old news,' she says and dismisses the past with a wave of her hand. 'Since then I've been dating up a storm.'

'Really?'

'No.'

'It sucks, doesn't it?'

'It really does.'

Beam decides to tell Grace about the date that saw him pull up stumps on set-ups contrived by friends. Her name was Roberta, a tall brunette with siren-red glasses, a friend of a friend of a work colleague. Just after they'd ordered main course at a ridiculously pretentious restaurant of her choosing, Roberta excused herself to go to the toilet and didn't return for fifty minutes. Fifty. Minutes. Beam had naturally, somewhat embarrassedly, assumed that Roberta had simply not warmed to his countenance — perhaps he'd had something poking out of his teeth or nose? — and had done a runner. It happens. But those big-ticket meals weren't going to eat themselves and so Beam, bolstered by self-pity and excellent red wine, hungrily began to consume both plates. And all the bread and her mojito. He was actually quite enjoying himself, thought this might work for a light talkback segment next week: How to salvage a disastrous date. The joys of eating alone. He was just about to order dessert when Roberta returned to the table, looked at her empty plate and then incredulously at Harvey.

'You ate my meal?' she'd said, as though the best part of an hour hadn't just vanished. '*You ate? My meal?*' People in the restaurant had begun to stare. Harvey began to shake his head nervously: 'No, no, your meal, I don't know what happened.' He glanced around nervously: 'Did anyone else see what happened to this poor woman's meal?'

Grace is looking hard at Harvey now, graciously wincing, feeling his mortification.

'And then,' he tells her, 'Roberta picked up the carafe of iced water, poured it onto my lap and turned the whole thing into a Woody Allen scene.'

'Oh my God,' Grace says, covering her eyes and peering at Beam through her fingers. 'What did you do?'

'I said to her, "Roberta, my ninety-two-year-old grandfather doesn't shit for fifty minutes,"' Beam recounts with, he imagines, pitch-perfect comedic timing. "'And your steak was cooked perfectly.'"

A big, rapturous laugh streams out of Grace, and Harvey is quietly thrilled. Lately it's seemed like everyone only says the words 'Ha-ha' now as some sort of acceptable replacement for actually laughing.

'It gets worse,' he says. 'She started as accounts manager at the station two weeks later. I haven't questioned my pay in years.'

Grace's laughter fills the room now, piercing the air with shards of light and uniting the room's diners in a flash of public revelry. It's a perfect moment and Harvey is grateful for it — for fate, Shorton, everything about this moment. Encroaching age and experience have made it harder, not easier, to meet new people, and he grows impatient with the effort required to get past all the preconceived ideas and concrete-set worldviews. Some days he just couldn't be arsed, quite frankly. Perhaps it's why he started losing his edge on air; he'll concede that. But tonight has been effortless and enjoyable and when such things happen, Harvey thinks, when they happen unexpectedly and perhaps undeservedly, it's as though the world has spun back to your side.

Afterwards, Grace drops Beam at Penny's house in the small car she has hired for her stay in Shorton. He invites her in for a coffee, unsure if Penny will still be awake, but Grace politely declines.

'So I'll see you tomorrow?' Beam says. 'At the hospital?'

'Tomorrow's my RDO,' Grace says. 'Think I might check out your local beach if it's sunny.'

'It's always sunny here,' he says. 'Just ask my mole doctor.'

Grace smiles, but Harvey also spies her masking a small yawn.

He moves to get out of the car, thanks her again for the lift, then turns to kiss Grace lightly on the cheek. *Too much? Too ...? Ugh.*

'Watch out for the sharks tomorrow,' he says lightly. 'And the stingers and the crocodiles and the hole in the ozone layer.' *Stop.*

'Thanks Harvey,' she says. 'I will.'

***

Penny is waiting up for Beam, and he realises there was never a chance she wouldn't be. She wants to know all the details — was this a *date* date? How old is she? Any kids? Where is she staying? How long for? What did they eat? What did they talk about? Was she funny? Did she mention their father? Bryan? Where is she from? Why is she single?

'Penny, this is exhausting,' Harvey says after a solid forty minutes of interrogation. 'It was just dinner. She's a nice girl.'

But Penny is thirteen years old again and living life vicariously through her seventeen-year-old brother. She has always looked up to Harvey; thought if anyone was going to unlock the key at Shorton's city gates, it would be him. And even though she had missed him terribly when he did leave, the twenty-one-year-old voice of Shorton Radio headed for the great unknown, Penny had also been grateful that he'd at least demonstrated it was possible.

Beam checks again that it's okay if Cate stays for a few days and Penny says of course. 'Maybe she can even help out in the shop?' she says. 'You know, if she's bored?'

'She'd probably like that,' he says. 'I don't think she's been doing much.'

'So how long do you think she'll stay? Will she go back with you?'

Beam realises this is Penny's way, once again, of trying to get a better sense of her brother's plans. He knows she smells a rat about his job.

'I still don't know, Penny. I'm not thinking too far ahead. I guess a lot depends on Dad.'

'Well,' Penny says, doing something with her fringe in the cloudy mirror of the fridge door. 'I don't think he has long, Harvey.' She turns to him square on. 'I don't. He doesn't.'

Beam shrugs. 'You've been saying that for weeks.' He realises how this sounds and he looks at Penny apologetically.

'I just don't know what sort of role to play with Dad, Penny. Bryan doesn't want me there. I don't think Dad does either, if he even knows what's going on.'

Penny is adamant. 'He recognised your *voice*, Harvey. He knew you were there.'

'Yeah,' says Beam, 'and that apparently reminded him he was dying.'

'He doesn't know what he's saying,' Penny says, ever the Beam family translator. 'Of course he wants you there. You're his son.'

'Penny, I have no relationship with him. I haven't for twenty years. I might as well be visiting the guy in the next room.'

'But you can't leave yet,' she says. 'You have to stay.'

And Harvey knows that he will stay, for now, mainly because he doesn't feel like being anywhere else in particular.

18

There is an odd melancholy that descends upon a person a few days into time spent away from home. Harvey recognises it as a kind of displacement, a forced inspection of lives and choices beyond the familiar terrain. He anticipates it these days, this unsettling; has got better at heading it off at the pass. Which is why he wakes the next morning with a clear head and a fresh sense of purpose.

First things first: sign the forms and email them back to Trudi Rice. For this task he enlists Penny's printer and scanner and afterwards her coffee machine. It is done. It doesn't even hurt.

Next up, he calls up Hugh Traynor, says why not? 'Let's do a show or two for old times' sake. I've got some thoughts about the new marina.'

Then he texts Grace: Hope this finds you in the ocean and that your phone is waterproof. Thanks for a great night. Care to repeat sometime? Cheers, H.

Finally he gathers his things, musters up the courage to drive Simon's beast of a vehicle and heads to the local shopping centre to get some supplies for Cate.

And all of this feels good, for resolve can be its own salve.

***

If there is a space more spiritually barren than Shorton's main shopping centre, Beam is yet to encounter it. Yet this is where the locals spend much of their time (he gathers), escaping the heat and seeing who else is around. There is much aimless wandering, discussions over empty trolleys and comfort taken in franchise signage — evidence of the town's wider connectedness. And there is great pride in visible progress, most notably the new David Jones. Shortonites strut in and out of its Melbournesque entrance with faux aloofness, as though they haven't been talking about this very thing for two decades.

He sees familiar faces. Old faces that seem new and new faces that seem old. He sees a battered man in a wheelchair enthusiastically picking his nose and realises it's his maths teacher from year eight. He sees the boy who used to live next door to his family in Norwich Street, now grown up and wrestling a tribe of young children. He sees a former mayor stockpiling home-brew ingredients into a trolley. He sees a girl he used to covet in his senior years, now barely recognisable amidst large folds of tattooed flesh spilling out of a singlet top.

Tattoos. There are so *many*. Complex sleeves of tribal warfare and children's names and roses and arrows and death by a thousand indecipherable fonts. Punctuating the ink are piercings: metallic full stops, commas and em dashes. Studs in eyebrows and cheeks and chins. And everywhere, *everywhere*, there is the iridescent flash of hi-vis workwear. Shorton's cultural dress: John Deere cap, hi-vis shirt, jeans, no shoes, cigarette, scowl. The men too.

Harvey knows he is being judgemental; he is *choosing* to look across this scene from a high horse of capital-city horror. This could just as easily be a suburban shopping centre in western Sydney, sans mining apparel and with a liberal dousing of ethnicity. His own siblings exhibit none of the stereotypes he has just picked out like an ancient school inspector. In spite of himself, he is behaving in no less elitist fashion than his own father. Still. This is not the town Beam grew up in; these are not the people he remembers. And moreover, no-one seems to remember him.

You can't go back.

***

Beam arrives at the hospital in the one-hour buffer zone between Penny's and Naomi's visits. Bryan is sitting beside their father's bed, head in a book as Lionel sleeps. There is a spare chair on the opposite side of the bed and one in the corner of the room and Harvey opts for the lesser of two evils. He assumes Bryan will soon find a reason to leave, so apparently discomfited is he by these occasional visits from Harvey, but Bryan remains fixed in his Rodin pose, defiant or oblivious or a calculated combination of the two.

Unlike the rupture between Penny and Naomi, which can be fixed to various events and hurtful outbursts and larger-than-life misunderstandings over the years, the chasm between Harvey and Bryan is without an anchor point. Until this visit Beam hadn't even been sure if it still existed, if it ever did — does not having a relationship have to be the opposite of having one? But Bryan's dislike of Harvey is so palpable in this room that it feels even heavier than the dank hospital air, louder than the whispers of grave illness.

He tries to think back to their last encounters. A brief catch-up in the presence of their mother when Beam travelled back for his high school reunion; nothing to report there. Naomi's wedding, at which the whorl of festivities and the cast-of-thousands guest list made virtually any conversational exchange impossible. Penny's wedding, which Beam did not attend because it clashed with Suze's thirtieth (an oversight on Penny's part that Suze never really forgave); he had sent a funny telegram, a poem entitled 'A Penny for our thoughts', and asked Bryan to read it out on the night. As far as he knows, that's what transpired.

So what is this … thing? If he dared ask Bryan — and he wouldn't, he can't — how would his brother respond? Incredulity … *How can you not know, Harvey?* Anger … *How dare you think about yourself at a time like this.* Or surprise …

I have no idea what you're talking about. Any of these answers is possible, and many more besides, and Harvey has no clue how to respond to any of them. Can only ponder and stare at the emotional sphinx that is Bryan Beam.

And as he does so, sitting here in this tiny plastic chair, the unwanted voyeur of something deeply personal and entirely beyond him, Harvey grows steadily angrier. If anyone should have a grudge to bear, it's him. He was the son overlooked by a father who never once considered how his actions, his inaction, might damage a young man's mettle. He, Harvey, was left behind to wonder if it was something as simple as birth order that had denied him his father's interest, or whether it was something else entirely. Something about Harvey being more difficult, more challenging, unpredictable. Unlikely to sit in a corner and read for hours on end.

Harvey has tried to recall, but cannot, instances when Lionel Beam hit his eldest son. It was instead Harvey who had weathered the beatings, felt the thirsty whack of the strap on the back of his thighs, across his middle, around his shoulders, until the crying shut it down. It was Harvey, not Bryan, who had once gone to school with a black eye, the result of an exasperated backhand from his father. He'd told everyone it was the product of a wild bouncer hurled by the kid next door and that he'd gone on to bravely cart him to every corner of the street.

Bryan had done nothing to attract punishment; flew quietly, effortlessly, *cleverly*, beneath the radar. Harvey, on the other hand, inspired a rage inside their father that he latterly suspected scared even Lionel himself. Rage that was only ever countered with ambivalence. He must, Harvey reasons, have seen something in the face of his second-born that was either the very image of himself or the very opposite, whichever caused the greater irritation. And he turned away from it, turned away from it again and again. Because he could. Lionel had options.

Harvey had visited his father's post-marital home, the little house Lionel had magnanimously set up for him and Bryan, just once. He had glanced at Bryan's bedroom off the hallway, had not even walked into it out of curiosity, and quickly eyed the sunroom-cum-study complete with two desks, one large, one small, and a wraparound bookcase. He had stayed for fifteen minutes, just long enough to tell his father that he'd be working over summer at the local radio station, to which Lionel had said, without shifting his gaze from the newspaper, 'Why would you want to do that?' And then Bryan had wanted to show Harvey something, but Harvey had had enough and he walked out the front door and all the way back to his mother's. Across the bridge. Eight kilometres in the angry sun.

Beam looks more closely now at his father's form in the hospital bed. Shrinking beneath sheaths of linen and blankets, Lionel's body barely forms a hillock. The incongruence of space and impact. His hair looks like the strange material Harvey's mother used to affix to his sisters' dance costumes. His skin is tracing paper atop a spider's web. There is so little left of this man, Harvey thinks. What does Bryan see when he stares at him for so long?

And yet, there is something. Lionel's jaw. It is still set in just the way Harvey remembers: pushed forward slightly, daring a question, arrogant, resolute. And Harvey finds himself thinking something new about Bryan's barely concealed hatred of his younger brother.

Maybe he didn't really have a choice.

19

Because he'd caught a cab from Shorton Airport to the house that is no longer his mother's, Beam hadn't then taken stock of the vastness of the facility's car park. In fact, the airport's car park proper can no longer contain the spillover of utes and four-wheel drives stretching in a melange of unspoken grid arrangements across several reclaimed paddocks. Thousands and thousands of vehicles; one airport coffee shop. The FIFO phenomenon had evidently not been anticipated by last decade's town planners.

Beam finally negotiates a parking spot of sorts for his brother-in-law's behemoth, hearing as he does so a promo for the guest spot on SR95.3 on Monday. *Returning to his old chair next week, star of Sydney radio and courter of controversy, Shorton's own Harvey Beam!*

So. No backing out now.

Cate enters the arrivals hall a picture of whimsy, smiling at something on her phone and emphatically removing her scarf.

'Hi Dad,' she says, kissing Beam on the cheek. 'Fuck it's hot.'

'Only between midnight and midnight,' Harvey says. 'Language, Cate. Welcome to Shorton, love.'

Cate has been here only once before, as a seven- or eight-year-old at Naomi's wedding, but she barely remembers it. Now, casting her heavily made-up eyes over the modest arrivals hall and its current inhabitants, Cate looks every bit the haughty city upstart.

'Welcome to Shitsville more like it,' she says.

Harvey hastily guides his daughter to the baggage carousel, hoping no-one heard her first-impressions appraisal. 'You might need to lose the sass,' he says. 'They don't go for it much around here.'

'Okay,' Cate says. 'But only if you promise never to use that word again.'

'Done,' he says.

After an exhaustive walk (Cate: 'Jesus, Dad, Mandela would have given up by now') back to Simon's car ('Why don't we just wait until it shits out a normal-sized car?'), Beam and Cate drive through town and across the bridge to Penny's house.

'Seriously, Dad,' Cate says, surveying the flat and unsurprising landscape, 'what did you do here when you were growing up? Just sit around wondering what a cinema is?'

'It wasn't that bad,' Harvey says, all of a sudden feeling defensive about the first third of his life. 'I spent a lot of time in that river,' he says, pointing to its implausible blueness with a measure of pride. Something like pride. 'And I played a lot of cricket. A *lot* of cricket.'

'How's your dad?' Cate asks, getting to the point of why someone might return to such a clearly uninspiring place. Beam notices she doesn't mention Lionel with reference to herself — *Grandpa* — and he briefly considers the fact that his children have no relationship with their grandfather largely because he doesn't. The sins of the father.

'I've barely seen him,' Harvey says. 'I mean, I've seen him every day but he's never awake.'

'That's sad,' Cate says, and Beam supposes it is.

On a whim Harvey decides to take a few detours. He shows Cate the house he grew up in and the two schools he went to — Shorton Primary and Shorton High — and he senses his daughter's wilful detachment starting to wane.

'Wow, mini-Dad,' she says. 'Weird.' And Harvey recognises in her face that odd feeling, possible to encounter at any age, that accompanies the realisation one's parents were once children too.

Harvey drives past the main shopping centre and towards the town's giant twenty-four-hour McDonald's restaurant — the state's biggest and busiest, he informs Cate, having just learnt this from Matt. He expects Cate to share his revulsion at such junk food largesse, at a town's devotion to eating even more shit than anyone else, but instead she looks wistfully at the red and yellow monolith and declares: 'Cool.'

'So, how's your mother, anyway?' Harvey asks, changing the subject. 'Has she come around?'

'Yeah, she's calmed down a bit,' Cate says. 'I think she's moved on from the disappointment of her firstborn and has decided to focus her hopes and dreams on number two. All eyes on Jayne, race fans.'

'That's ridiculous, Cate. Your mother isn't disappointed in you. She's disappointed for you.'

'Whoa!' Cate says, holding up her hands in mock protest. 'Cliché alert!'

He continues regardless. 'But we both know you'll get through this,' Beam says. 'You're only seventeen, for goodness' sake. You've got a big future ahead of you.'

'Why do futures have to be big?' Cate says.

Beam has no good answer for this.

***

Penny is animatedly thrilled to see her niece in the flesh again and almost swallows her whole with questions and hugs and compliments. James and Javyn look up from their places on the lounge room rug with puzzled interest.

'Oh my *God*, Harvey,' Penny almost yells. 'She's so beautiful. Look at her! You didn't tell me she'd got so beautiful.' His sister runs her hands over Cate's long auburn hair and stands back to admire the unfolding adolescent chrysalis.

'I didn't say she was ugly.'

'Listen to your father,' Penny laughs, rolling her eyes at Cate, who is clearly relishing this avalanche of adoration. 'Now sit down here and tell me everything about *everything*.'

Dismissed by implication, Harvey leaves his sister and daughter to reconnect in the all-consuming way of women. He is happy to see Cate so embraced by Penny and feels a twinge of guilt that his daughters have long lived without the fullness of extended family, of curious aunts and quirky cousins. He has seen it in friends and colleagues – the armour that a big family can provide; the sense of place and comfort that comes from being part of something bigger and pre-written.

Still, it doesn't always work and Beam secretly enjoys encountering exceptions to the rule. Fractious family Christmas disasters shared around the office each January are among his favourite guilty pleasures.

He retreats to the spare room and checks his phone. Trudi Rice has punctiliously acknowledged receipt of Beam's redundancy forms. Hugh Traynor has emailed him some health and safety information for Monday (presumably in case Harvey falls off his chair and decides to take down City Hall). And Grace writes: Amazing day in the water. Miraculously survived. Can do lunch on Sunday?

Sunday, he thinks. Lunch.

Lunch on Sunday.

But Cate is here. Plus it's lunch, which is not dinner. A step back from the cover of night?

Beam lies back on the bed. *What does any of it mean?*

***

On Sunday morning Harvey is on his way to Naomi's house when he remembers he hasn't replied to Grace's text. He had woken the previous evening, foggy and off-kilter due to an unplanned nap, to find Cate and Penny giggling over photo albums and sharing a butcher's paper spread of fish and chips. Before long he had joined in and the night had furtively dissolved in a slew of memories, old and new. Now Naomi and Lynn were set to deliver the show's second act.

'Hey,' Beam says to Cate as they pull into the driveway. 'You go on in and I'll be right behind you. Just have to make a quick call.'

'Dad, are you high? I'm not going in without you. I haven't seen them for years.'

'Okay, *okay*,' he says, and realises he might just have blown it with Grace. Whatever he'd been going for there, it's clearly beyond his life management skills to return messages within an acceptable amount of time.

Unsurprisingly, Naomi has upped the ante on Cate's welcome-back festival, planning a full day of activities, a tour of the town, picnic at the marina and more — poor Cate — photo perusal. Such ambition is only possible, Harvey thinks, because of Lynn's conspiratorial enthusiasm and her practical help with Naomi's boys, and he finds himself feeling a little sorry for Penny and her more solitary parenting effort. You don't have to move two thousand kilometres away to be cast adrift, it seems.

Fortunately there appears to be no expectation that Harvey should be part of today's activities and he gratefully begs off and agrees to return for dinner this evening. He sees that Cate is still happy, greedily inhaling all the activity and attention, filling the void created by her lonely sabbatical in Harvey's apartment, and he is proud of this, this too-rare capacity to make a child of his, however briefly, content.

On his way out, Beam encounters Matt, arms and cheeks covered in something grease-like and carrying a piece of machinery that may or may not belong in a car.

'Hey,' Matt says. 'I hear you went on a date.'

'Something like that,' Harvey laughs.

'I've got room in there for an extra shelf if you need it.'

Harvey laughs and by the time he reaches the hospital car park he has worked out what Matt meant.

***

The hospital is much quieter today than during the week, even if the patients are no less sick. Beam has a coffee in the foyer cafe and drafts ten or more text messages in his head for Grace before angrily ruing the absurd regression of modern communication. He calls her.

'I'm sorry I'm only getting back to you now,' he says when she answers. 'My daughter arrived here yesterday and it's been sort of chaotic ever since. Everyone wants a piece of her.'

'Don't be silly,' Grace says. 'It's absolutely fine. I was just ... I thought ... well, I start at five today and so I thought maybe you'd like to get some lunch. Something that isn't a pie from the hospital cafe.'

'Grace,' he says, 'If you don't love those pies then I don't think we have anything more to discuss.'

Grace laughs. How quickly he has learned to love the sound, its instinctive propulsion from a generous place.

'Seriously?' Beam says. 'A meal that can also stop a car from rolling backwards? That's all kinds of genius.'

He pledges to pick up Grace at midday and have a think about a lunch venue in the meantime. And even though it's an even more casual arrangement than their first meal, it somehow feels less so, as though a more considered investment of time has been brokered. A second viewing of a potential property.

Harvey wanders to his father's ward and finds Penny manning bedside. The room is strewn with shadows. Their father appears to be awake and Penny is reading something to him, her face close to his ear.

She spies Harvey, puts her book down, says, 'Dad, look. It's Harvey here to see you.'

Lionel Beam doesn't respond, and Harvey slides carefully into the chair opposite Penny's.

'Hello, Dad. It's good to see you awake.'

Lionel blinks at his son.

Penny smiles uncertainly at Harvey.

Their father blinks again, his white eyelashes seeming to get enmeshed in the slow gesture.

'Can he speak?' Harvey says from the corner of his mouth, looking up at Penny. He imagines the process of dying as losing something new and precious each day without warning or fanfare. One withered leaf after another.

'Of course he can,' she says.

Oh.

Harvey puts his hand on the side of the bed, fingers the heavy sheet.

'Dad,' he says, and he's going to try harder this time. *This time with feeling.* 'I'm really sorry to see you so sick. I know you must be hating this.'

And Lionel turns his head slightly, away from Harvey and towards Penny but his gaze rests somewhere between the two of them.

'Where ...?' he says with great effort. 'Where is Bryan?'

20

Many things diminish with age, while others — hair in the ears, odd spooling splotches of disgruntled skin on the forearm, midweek funerals, newspaper consumption, weather observations — flourish without watering. Things recede and new things trickle into the cracks, and it all happens so slowly, when no-one is paying attention.

For Beam, what has gone and what has replaced it are, in turn, surprise and inevitability. Nothing surprises him anymore, or at least very little. Most events, the things that might have once elicited an inner *Wow, I didn't see that coming*, seem increasingly predetermined; certain and unalterable. What was once a grudging acceptance of inevitable change, and before that a wilful determination to change *everything*, is now just acceptance on its own. *Of course* governments must lose in order to win again. *Of course* cancer will visit people close to us. *Of course* fortunes shift, love dies, humans self-destruct.

The burgeoning seniors travel industry, Harvey has thought of late, is driven by people unashamedly curious, sometimes desperate, to see if they can still be surprised by something, *anything*, in this world.

And so it is that Beam finds himself laid out and naked in Grace Hamilton's bedroom, her body reclined breathily on his outstretched arm, the ceiling fan tick-ticking overhead, and all around him the ancient scent of something completely unexpected.

He is deliriously, gratefully, surprised.

Of course Harvey had thought about having sex with Grace; what it might be like, how it might be possible. It had first occurred to him at forty thousand feet. He had imagined back then, and again in his father's hospital room and again in the Thai restaurant and in the many hours between, what it might be like to hold a woman so lovely, so unknown. He had imagined it and incredibly, thanks in no small part to their shared hatred of courting and awkward anticipation and Grace's relatively bare fridge and a tour of her apartment that finished at the bedroom, it had happened.

Just now. On this bed. In this room. To him.

The wondrous surprise of it all.

Beam knows that whatever he is about to say now will somehow diminish what has just occurred. What post-coital comment has any hope of a safe landing? But he wants to try anyway, to say something that will stretch a perfect moment to the limit of its expansion.

'Grace,' he says finally. 'Thank you so much.'

And she laughs. Laughs so hard the bed shakes.

'Harvey, you're so very welcome.'

'Sorry,' he says. 'I didn't mean that to sound ... I just mean ... that was so lovely, Grace. So incredibly good, and I —'

'Good?'

'Well, I can only speak for my own performance,' he says, pulling up the bedsheet to cover his middle.

And she laughs again.

'It was rather good,' Grace says.

'Mind you,' Harvey reasons, turning now to face her and gently guiding a skein of loose hair behind her ear. 'I would have been happy with bad sex. I would have been happy with a lame kiss.'

'Really?' she says.

'God, yes, Grace. You have no idea.'

'Well, that's very sweet,' she says, running her fingers along the hairs of his forearm. 'You're a very sweet man, Harvey Beam.'

'That case has never been made before, Grace. I don't think you'll get a lot of support on that front.'

'Well,' she says. '*I* think there is something there. I can see how distant your father is. How difficult Bryan is making things for you, for everyone. Yet there you are at the hospital every day, doing the right thing.'

Grace prods with her finger at a spot close to Harvey's heart. 'There is goodness in there,' she says. 'Sweetness.'

He kisses her. Delights again in the surprise of her mouth. The shape of her.

'Some people,' he says, 'think doing the right thing counts for nothing if you don't really feel it.'

'Hmm,' she says. 'Maybe.'

Because, Beam thinks, he really doesn't feel anything when he looks at his father each day. There is pity, of course, but it's of the sort he'd feel for any person rendered shell-like by cancer. Sometimes there is anger, but it's weak and it's old, the smoky residue of something once much hotter and more dangerous.

He had wanted to feel something bigger, of course. He had wanted to fly to Shorton and walk into that hospital room and be surprised at how he felt. It was that curiosity, that hope, that had got him on the plane. Surely the anger and the love and the disappointment and the joy and the terror that spins at the core of a family can be summoned at any age; wrest us back into our bodies, awaken old bones.

But he had felt nothing. Nothing unsurprising, until now.

Until Grace.

21

ON AIR

'It's bloody hot and the air-con's cracked it but that's not how I know I'm back in Shorton, folks.' *Breathe. Pause.* 'No, I know I'm back home again because the ute that I followed into the station this morning had spotties that could throw shadows onto the moon. I know I'm back home again because there's a bloke on the main drag peddling pies out the back of his van instead of drugs. And I know I'm back home again because this is the same chair I sat in twenty years ago — *pause* — and it's still broken.'

Beam flicks up the sound on the station jingle, checks the time, cues his first tune ('Run To Paradise' for old times' sake) and forward-promotes the morning's talkback topic: What the hell happened to Shorton Beach? It's exhilarating to be working his old console — the very same panel with the addition of a new computer screen that doesn't appear to be connected to anything — and he's quietly surprised that it is coming back to him so readily, as though the information has been stored in his fingers all this time and he just has to keep them moving.

Hugh Traynor knocks on the glass, gives Beam the two thumbs up. The room behind him, crammed with empty desks and boxes, is full of sunlight — it bores through the cracks in this fibrous building, threatening to bust it wide open — and for a minute things are exactly as Beam remembers them:

sunny, simple, safe. He'd wanted none of these things in 1994. Today they seem far less threatening.

'And that was the Choirboys,' he says when the song is over, brushing his hand smoothly down the left volume column as though shushing an orchestra. 'Who were anything but in their day. It's two minutes to news time and after the news I want to hear from you about something that I, well, quite rudely discovered upon flying back home to Shorton this week.' Pause. Breathe. 'My old beach, *your* old beach, is gone. Come on, you remember it, Shortonites? That long wide strip of glorious sand folding under the Pacific Ocean? Those big coconut trees lining the road — did you ever run up the side of one of those and score a coconut and then wonder what the hell to do with it? Do you remember the little kiosk with the ice-creams and the slushies and do you remember the old surf club? There were some ripper parties held in that lunk of a building. To me, and perhaps you, Shorton Beach holds many of the childhood memories that I still retain in this ageing brain and guess what? It's gone. Replaced by, God, a marina. Well, let me tell you, that was a shock, and maybe some of you are still processing the shock of this development actually having gone from a bad idea to a real thing. An ugly thing. Maybe you like it? Maybe you were the one who asked for it? Maybe you thought you wanted it but now secretly miss what once was? Look, I'm not an immediate fan but I'm happy to be convinced otherwise. I want to hear from all of you. 4489 2000 with your calls please or text me on 0418 700 600 or join the conversation on our Facebook page.'

Hugh knocks on the glass, waves his arms.

'Sorry, no Facebook yet, folks. We're going to wait a little longer to see if this whole social media lark has legs. So give me a call. Here's the news.'

Like a hopeful junkie, Beam is thrilled to strike a laden vein. The calls come in quickly, too quickly for the station receptionist, who seems perturbed at this sudden lining up of her activity levels with her job description. The texts come in too (including this one from Grace: You are nailing it, Harvey xx) and Beam juggles it all masterfully and with a smile on his face that would be impossible to subdue at this point. Shortonites have far more opinions on the marina than there are boats inside it and they are diverse and sometimes measured and sometimes articulate and occasionally incomprehensible, but they are each earnest and true, and they fill the airspace with all that makes a small town feel bigger than itself.

And it is great radio. Trudi Rice is wrong, Harvey thinks as he winds up the three-hour show and crosses to the news. He *is* a man still making connections and he is happy within himself. At this moment he's never been fucking happier.

22

'Killer' Rhodes is Harvey's best mate this week. It's not easy making friendships stick when loyalties shift and fray every lunchtime on the school oval, but Killer seems as keen as Harvey is to take this ragged pairing beyond the cricket pitch. They both barrack for the Swans, are stingy with their favourite tombowlers, and share a fervent comic dislike of their year-five teacher, an American woman called Mrs Sass (Harvey prefers the Aussie pronunciation).

It's a blowy Friday afternoon and Harvey orchestrates a stilted conversation between his mother and Killer's in the schoolyard, the goal being to have his mate over for a play. As Killer lives on a farm out of town, it isn't a simple matter of riding a bike over to Harvey's. The two mothers swap addresses, pick-up times and polite discussion while nearby Harvey and Killer kick each other's feet as if to stub out their mounting excitement.

It's a great afternoon and Harvey is secretly thrilled at the spectacle he is providing for his sisters: a kid at their house who's not from the neighbourhood. Harvey has a real friend. Penny and Naomi have each other, Bryan has his books and his microscope, now Harvey has something too. Something even better.

Killer happily launches himself into the neighbourhood cricket game, an almost daily event held in a patch of cleared bush behind Harvey's house. Anywhere from four to twenty kids descend upon the parched turf each afternoon, a silver bin at one end, someone's shoe at the other, and it's an unspoken race to see who will score the first six or hit a passing car.

Killer is an average batsman but a gun bowler with the dramatic crease-marking cred to match. Harvey watches him bowl a near-perfect yorker with a pride that collects around his neck and rises up to his cheeks, turning them red. The kids in his street look on in quiet admiration. It's the best day, and it's still going.

When the game starts to dissipate — the last available ball is lost in the long grass — Harvey suggests a bike ride and Killer is keen. Harvey tells his friend to use Bryan's bike. In his best-day excitement, Harvey forgets — just doesn't even think of it — his father's rule about not riding beyond the end of the block where the Beams' street meets a busier road. The two boys ride another two blocks, crisscrossing each other's paths, one-wheeling it up kerbs and yelling manly jibes at the darkening sky.

Harvey doesn't see his father's car pass them by.

It's the best day.

Out of breath yet somehow still full of energy, Killer and Harvey slide their bikes into the courtyard at the back of the Beam house. Immediately his mother exits the rear screen door and softly, without looking squarely at either boy, tells Harvey that his father wants him inside.

It must be after five, Harvey realises. The best day has flown by, almost gone.

Killer stays behind with Harvey's mum, starts prising an imaginary stone out of his wheel tread. Harvey walks through the screen door. And now, *now* he remembers the rule and his head turns inside out and his gut tightens and his jaw locks and he knows what's coming, knows what's coming, knows what's coming.

Lionel Beam is standing at the end of his bed, leather belt in hand, steel weight swinging by his trouser leg.

'You know the rule about where to ride,' Harvey's father

says. 'Get on the bed.'

Harvey stands, can't move. Lionel pushes him down, the back of his hand on Harvey's head.

Harvey doesn't scream this time, doesn't say stop, doesn't reach his hands behind him, which only makes Lionel go harder. The pain ricochets through his back, down his legs, like being burnt, like stepping on coals and then falling into the campfire. Twenty times. Thirty times. One rule to remember. One friend. His face is jammed tight into the mattress, wet and on fire.

And all Harvey thinks this time is *Killer ... Killer ... Killer. Don't hear this.*

When it is finally over, night has descended and his friend has gone. Harvey's mother is stirring something on the stove. His father tells him to fetch a beer. There are no beginnings or endings to anything, anywhere in the world.

He goes to sleep on his stomach that night, no sheet. His skin is still alight. His brain is banging inside his skull. He wonders what Killer heard, what he will tell the other kids. What he heard, what he heard.

Bryan is in the bed opposite Harvey. He says nothing, still seething no doubt about his bike's role in the afternoon's activities.

Through the wall Harvey can hear his father remove the cap off another beer.

At last, well after all the lights in the house are off and doors to bedrooms closed, he goes to sleep by trying to think about something good. He thinks about those two blocks beyond the end of his street.

23

Frazzled parents refer to the witching hour, that passage at the end of the day when time bends upon itself, children grow horns, boiling pots spill over, and a glass of wine just doesn't seem to cut it. Suze would often rail against Harvey about the witching hour he'd just missed, again, and he was never sympathetic enough because he knew he couldn't make it better. Couldn't fix it.

Besides, Beam has long had a witching hour of his own. Between five and six o'clock each day, give or take half an hour, Harvey Beam's skin seems to crawl. He can't settle, can't focus, can't finish a conversation, doesn't know how he'll get through the long night, how anyone gets through anything, and he aches for a drink to wash it all away.

It took him years to make the connection between his afternoon meltdowns and the hour his father used to get home from work.

Harvey's best bet these days — and he's getting better at it, a rare display of midlife progress — is to crowd out the witching hour with distractions. To outrun it; trick it into disappearing. A busy train carriage, a harried walk through Centennial Park, a beer with a colleague at the Strawberry Hills Hotel. Just don't be sitting alone with your thoughts and a watch.

Today he's crowding it out in the nicest of ways, sitting with his eldest daughter on the edge of a blunted pier overlooking Shorton River. The evening air is fresh and mild, the shorebirds are steadily drifting back to their nests in the mangroves, and the tide seems to be turning.

'Well, this is a bit weird,' pipes up Cate, her legs swaying from side to side like a bored toddler.

'What is?'

'This father–daughter movie moment,' she says. 'Is this where you're meant to tell me something profound about life, or that I'm adopted or something?'

Harvey laughs. 'Cate,' he says, 'you're adopted. And I'm okay with you finding your real parents.'

'God, I hope they're rich,' she says. 'With a boat.'

A man in a silver tinny idles past them, gently lifts his index finger and nods his head. The universal wave of regional Australia.

'Are you enjoying it here?' Harvey asks.

'I am, actually,' Cate says. 'It's like, small, but cool small.'

'There's not much to do, I know,' he says.

Harvey had spent most of the day helping Matt transfer his bonsai plants into a new, larger lawn-locker, a task prolonged by the occasional ponderous beer and the always entertaining philosophical musings of his brother-in-law. He had heard vignettes about more of the women who had inspired his potted projects — *Runaround Sue* (girlfriend #4), *Mother Mary* (his mum), and *Stacked Stella* (his year six teacher). Harvey had found himself intermittently recalling the ghosts of girlfriends past and also smiling about the new and unexpected development that was Grace. A whiff of romance out of step with time and place. A buzz in his chest. He had wanted to see Grace today but she was working a double shift.

'I like helping Penny in the shop,' Cate says. 'Today I redesigned her whole front window. It's now like an Eiffel Tower wedding proposal scene for Valentine's Day.'

'The Eiffel Tower?' Harvey snorts. 'Well, that's *very* Shorton.'

'Good marketing is about aspiration over reality, Dad. People want to buy when their imagination is stretched.'

'Wow. Now who's being profound?'

Cate throws a stone into the water. 'This is the first time I've felt good at something,' she says. 'Penny says I'm a natural.'

'A natural at retail?' Harvey says, not meaning to sound judgemental, *but still*. 'At working in a gift shop?'

'Forget it,' she says, and Harvey realises he has ruined the moment. *Like trying to hold an ice cube between two fingers,* one of Beam's studio guests had once described the act of talking with teenagers.

But Cate is forgiving and changes the subject. 'So,' she says, removing her shoes and settling in. 'I visited your dad ... my grandfather.'

'Today?'

'Yep.'

'And how did that go?'

'Okay. He's pretty sick.'

'He is.'

'It felt weird because I don't really know him. Like, am I meant to cry or ... I don't know. It was just weird.'

Beam gives a good impression of a sigh. 'Well, Cate, if it makes you feel any better, I don't really know him either and I never know what to do in that room.' *That room. Does he have to go back there?*

Cate lies back on the pier, looks up at the mauve sky.

'Why do you hate him?'

Harvey coughs, runs his hand through his thinning hair, searches for the right answer. 'I don't *hate* him, Cate. I'm just ... indifferent to him.'

'God, that's so much worse.'

'No, it isn't.'

'Yeah it is. Like, you don't even care enough to hate him.'

Harvey feels a burning in his chest. 'That's not quite right.'

'What's wrong with him?' Cate says. 'Why can't you love him? The others love him.'

The others?

Harvey rubs his breast bone. 'I don't know that they ...

maybe Bryan ... I don't know, Cate,' he says. 'Maybe they're just better than me at pretending. Lionel is not an easy man to love. I doubt he's ever even used the term.'

'Do you *like* him?'

Harvey thinks about this, about the picture he is painting of himself on Cate's nascent emotional landscape. She is not yet old enough to know that bitterness can set like a stone; a gradual petrification that becomes part of you, immovable.

Finally he says, 'It's a moot point, Cate. My father didn't like me.'

Cate sits up, mildly incredulous. 'Is that even allowed?' she says. 'For a parent?'

Harvey laughs. 'There are no rules for parenting, love. Most of us just do the best we can. The good thing about having two parents is you can get away with having one who's pretty shit at it.'

'Like you?'

Beam looks at his daughter, who has only the smallest hint of a smile in her eyes, and he gently punches her in the arm.

'I'm not that bad, am I?' he says.

'You were pretty shit at it most of the time,' Cate says, but now she offers him a smile to temper the moment.

'I was, wasn't I? Thank goodness you girls had your mum.'

'Who is not having her best year, either.'

'Look,' says Harvey, realising this is probably the longest conversation he has had with Cate in recent years. 'She just wants what she thinks is best for you. She might be wrong about what is best for you, I don't know, but she's being tough because she loves you.'

'Right. Sure. Tough love. Do you love me?'

'Oh for shit's sake, Cate, of course I do.'

'Poetic,' she says.

'More importantly,' Beam says, 'I *like* you.'

'Well,' says Cate, standing up and dusting off her legs. 'What's not to like?'

Beam realises as they drive back to Penny's house, Cate trying desperately to establish a bluetooth connection between her phone and Simon's giant, industrial-looking car stereo, that this fresh connection with his eldest daughter has happened because of Shorton. Something about being here, about disrupting his Sydney existence and letting all the cogs shift and resettle, has brought him closer to his daughter, to one of them at least.

Something good is happening to his life, Beam thinks, and for once he's present enough to notice.

24

Grace feels like a secret — the best kind. Like winning on the first race and carrying around the unclaimed ticket in your pocket all day. Knowing it's there.

Even though his family suspects Harvey has been 'seeing' Grace, whatever that term means, the specifics of their relationship are unknown to the world. Grace has given nothing away when their paths have crossed at the hospital and there have been few opportunities for subsequent get-togethers now that Cate is here. But at night, every night now, they talk to each other on the phone until sleep can be pushed back no further, and throughout each day text messages zing back and forth — playful, funny, bordering on tender.

Harvey can't help but think this ... *thing* with Grace has been tossed into his path (he refuses to say 'cosmically', but whatever) to take up the space and time he would have almost certainly been devoting to mourning his job; to fearing his best days were behind him and trying to make peace with irrelevance.

The days at Shorton Radio have helped too, kept his professional pride ticking along, although the last two stints (rants about the town's neglect of the river and the need for an art gallery) drew more ire from listeners than agreeance. 'You might want to tone down the criticism a tad,' Hugh Traynor had suggested to Beam afterwards. And Harvey had laughed inwardly because if Traynor knew anything about talkback radio, he wouldn't still be in Shorton.

Today Beam is feeling fearless, even happy, and it's this fleeting state that has led him to bring his secret out into the open, sitting with Grace in a coffee shop in Shorton's main street and using every chance to brush his hand over her smooth knee. He just wants to drink her in today, crowd out everything else.

It's been twenty minutes since Beam ordered them both a coffee and while he could happily sit here all morning looking at Grace's delicate features and making her laugh with wry observations about passers-by ('Look, that guy's ironed his hi-vis shirt — must be off to a wedding'), he knows too that Grace is tired and needs sustenance. She's worked double shifts back to back, much of which has involved caring for his father and dealing with Bryan.

'I think it's a matter of days now, Harvey,' Grace says and rests a hand on his. 'You should visit him again. Before it's time.'

'Yes,' he says. 'I should do that.'

'I don't know when Bryan sleeps. He's always there. Naomi has dropped off a little but Penny is there every morning.'

Harvey looks down. He hasn't been there for several days and really can't see the point.

'Matt has gone back to work,' he says, 'so I think things are fairly busy for Naomi when he's gone. I'll go tonight.' *God, where is this coffee?*

Beam looks up at the shop's main counter, devoid of human life. He looks about for their waitress, a young girl with an enormous nose-ring (*why?*) and an odd body odour. Finally he sees her standing to the side of the main glass entrance, a phone to her ear.

Beam notices a sign on the front glass, 'Staff wanted', and suggests to Grace they surreptitiously scrawl 'Dead or alive' underneath it.

Their coffees finally arrive, tepid at best. Grace's is a flat white instead of a cappuccino and they decide not to complain because the people at the next table have already launched a loud protest about the content of their sandwiches. Silently, though, Beam files 'Shorton's dismal customer service' into his mental collection of future talkback topics.

'Let's go back to mine and I'll make you something to eat,' Grace says, and Harvey feels himself stiffen awkwardly underneath the table just at the thought of being alone again together with no-one else around.

But she doesn't prepare anything and they don't eat, don't even enter Grace's kitchen. Instead she leads Harvey into her bedroom, shuts the door, flicks on the fan and gently pushes him down onto the bed. Then Grace casts aside her white blouse and her sandals and she climbs onto him, astride him, wants him. *Good God.* She's still in her jeans and it's the most exciting sight Harvey thinks he's ever witnessed. A beautiful woman above him in tight dark denim, hair tumbling down one shoulder, the ceiling fan above them click, click, clicking.

Grace.

She leans down over him and cradles Harvey's face in her hands, her elbows resting on either side of him. She kisses him gently and soon hungrily and then softly again, and in between these changes of gear Harvey moves with her. There are no words and no awkward moments, not even when Grace removes those no-daylight jeans.

He is inside her now, shadows of muscle memory wildly kicking in. It is that perfect and rare sex, Harvey thinks, when two people are lit from within and want only each other, only this precise moment.

And Harvey surprises himself by lasting significantly longer than he had expected (a good ten or so extra seconds thanks to his trusty mental dampener: Bronwyn Bishop in bathers) and he's fairly certain Grace comes at about the same time.

The noisy ceiling fan is clapping them now, applauding fantastic afternoon sex.

'Don't say it, Harvey,' Grace says, her head on Beam's chest, hair splayed across his arm.

'Say what?'

'Thank you.'

Beam laughs hard, recalling their first encounter. 'Well,' he says, 'can I perhaps express my gratitude in a different way?'

Grace looks up at him, slaps his shoulder flirtatiously. 'It's called foreplay not afterplay,' she says. 'Best think of your heart, old boy.'

'You might be right about that, Grace,' Beam says. 'I'm not getting any younger.'

'You're doing alright,' she says and kisses his cheek.

'Such tenderness I barely deserve but shall wilfully partake of,' he says gratefully.

'Is that a quote?'

'I don't think so. I think I made it up. It's good, though. I hope someone's writing this stuff down.' Beam pretends to look around desperately for a scribe.

Grace laughs warmly and Harvey smiles. He has never, definitely not since Suze, had such an appreciative audience. His radio listeners generally express criticism before gratitude.

But as Grace's laughter fades, the air in the small room shifts. The ceiling fan loses its rhythm. Harvey wants to fall asleep but is wide awake. *How do women not have TVs in their bedrooms?*

'Do you think, Mr Beam,' Grace says after a lengthy pause. A snack-worthy pause. 'Do you think that we only get, you know, one real love in a lifetime?'

She props up her chin with her hand. 'Do you think there is a "one" and everyone after that is "two" or "three" or "eight", never again the "one"?'

'Would it matter?' Harvey answers, not wishing to diminish her question but not really understanding it either.

'Maybe we'd make different decisions if we knew,' she says. 'If we were somehow informed officially by the universe or whatever that this is your "one". This is your best chance.

Blow it at your peril.'

'I don't know,' Beam says. 'Surely life isn't that big of an arsehole to just give us just one chance.'

But then Beam gets it, knows what Grace is thinking. 'Are you worried your husband — *God, what was his name?* — was your one and there can't be another?'

She holds her bare hand in front of her face, fingers splayed, peering through them at the fan above. 'Sometimes. I felt so sure with him, so *certain*, and then, you know, when something falls apart, you lose your confidence in knowing what's good for you anymore. I feel like I've been flailing about for years now. Can't commit to anything. Can't make a decision bigger than what to wear.'

'I like what you've got on now,' Harvey says, running his hand over Grace's naked body. 'This really works for you.'

Grace looks over and smiles at him but doesn't laugh this time.

'And how does this feel then?' Beam says finally, realising the topic is still hanging in the air, refusing to dissipate. 'You and me? Now?'

'It feels nice,' she says. 'It feels ... lovely.'

'Too right it does.' And Harvey shifts his hands behind his head as though life right at this moment is sorted. *Look, Mum, no hands!*

Just when he thinks he could happily stay in this position, in this bed, with this person, somewhere close to forever, Grace sits up and looks down at him, a large tear hanging on her eyelid. 'I'm going to miss you, Harvey Beam,' she says.

He is taken aback. Says, 'Where am I going?'

'Back to Sydney. Probably before me.'

'Well, there's no tearing hurry,' he says. 'Can I at least collect my trousers on the way out?'

'Your father doesn't have long,' Grace says. 'Days at best.'

'I know, I know,' Beam says. 'But since coming back, I think, I don't know, sometimes it feels like there are other reasons

I'm meant to be here.'

Grace throws her hands up theatrically. 'But you hate the place! All you ever do is complain about it.'

'I don't *hate* it,' he says. 'That's just me firing up the locals — it's good radio.'

'This isn't Sydney, Harvey,' she says, lying back down and taking up a spot in the cradle of his wing. 'Small towns don't like big shots from the city pointing out their flaws.'

'They might not like it but it's what they need,' Beam says. And instantly he hears in that sentence the mighty arrogance of a man in a hospital bed not far away. He winces at the realisation and changes the subject.

'Grace, would you like to meet my daughter?'

The air suddenly feels still, ambivalent towards the ambitious fan. *Where did that come from?* Harvey's phone pings in the other room, or possibly it's Grace's. He thinks about retracting the question, turning it into an odd joke. He knows it's unfair to talk like this, about meeting his children, about the future, but right now a future with Grace seems less impossible than everything else in his life.

After a very long pause, and a return to a more cautious Grace than the one who has just seduced him with single-minded purpose, she says: 'Harvey. Let's just see what happens.'

25

Lionel Beam is home late from work and Harvey has spent most of the past hour and a half wrapping and rewrapping insulation tape around one side of a tennis ball. He'd noticed older boys at school doing it to engineer swing, but he can't seem to get it right. The tape keeps folding upon itself.

He jumps when he hears the car door shut and waits for his father's first words, always a sign of where the evening is headed. It sounds as though his father is in a good mood because the first thing he does is summon the whole family into the lounge room.

'I've been at a conference today,' Lionel Beam tells them, 'and we played a really interesting game.'

Harvey looks at his sisters, who are equally puzzled. Their father rarely plays 'games'. He rarely addresses them as a group. The night is already askew.

From behind his back, Lionel reveals a set of rope quoits. He hands one quoit to each of the four children — Harvey hadn't even noticed Bryan enter the room and slide into a chair behind the girls and himself — and he places the wooden pole stand in the centre of the room. Then Lionel walks backwards to the door and instructs the children to have their throw. To toss the quoit on the pole, simple.

Penny is first to speak, characteristically wanting to be very clear about the rules. 'From where?' she says.

'From wherever you like,' Lionel Beam answers in a measured tone.

'But ...?' Penny is clearly rattled and sits down on the carpet. She's going to give this some thought.

Into the breach leaps Naomi, excitedly wanting to get things started. 'I'll go first,' she says, and stands as far back from the pole as the room will allow. She tosses the quoit, which hits the side of the pole and bounces off. Before anyone can comment, Naomi fetches the quoit and lines up her next throw, and misses again. After another eight or so attempts, during which time their father says precisely nothing, Naomi's quoit spins successfully around its target and she runs around the room in a playful victory dance.

'I don't want to play,' Penny says, and walks out of the room, her quoit still on the ground.

Torn between his curiosity and a strong desire to follow Penny's lead, Harvey walks slowly up to the pole. He puts a foot on either side of it — is literally on top of it — and drops the quoit cleanly around the pole.

Harvey gives a clumsy shrug and looks around at his father. Lionel Beam says nothing and steadily shifts his gaze to Bryan.

Bryan begins by removing Harvey's quoit from the pole. Then he silently takes up a position about one metre back from the stand. He takes aim and tosses his quoit, watches it swirl compliantly around the pole and land where Harvey's had been minutes earlier.

'We all win!' yells Naomi, and gathers up the quoits to play again.

'No,' says Lionel Beam. 'Bryan wins.'

'What?' Harvey says, as Penny creeps back into the room.

Naomi is already tossing again, this time from behind a chair with one hand covering her eyes.

'Why does Bryan win?' Penny says, now standing beside Harvey. 'You didn't say where to throw from or how many chances we could have.'

Their father folds his arms and a small grin pulls at the edges of his thin mouth. 'That's right, Penny,' he says. 'There were no rules because this isn't a normal game. It's a character test. It reveals things about us that we can't mask: our ambition, our intellect, our potential.'

At this moment Harvey's mother enters the room, informing them that dinner is ready.

But Harvey wants answers first. 'If it's not a game,' he says, 'then how come Bryan wins?'

'Well,' Lionel says, and he seems happy to labour the point while dinner waits. 'Naomi here (he points at his youngest child who is now attempting to throw four quoits at once) is certainly ambitious but she wants to make things unnecessarily difficult for herself. Her heart overrules her head and that may affect her potential in life.'

'Lionel,' his wife says to him. 'Can't this wait?'

'No, it can't,' he says. 'This is important, Lynn.'

'They're just kids,' she says.

But Lionel is resolute. 'Character flaws are best addressed during childhood,' he says, 'when there is still time to do something about them. Now, Harvey here has a lot of work to do. He is lazy, naturally lazy, and there is no worse character flaw short of dishonesty. Harvey wants things to be quick and easy, and that's not how the world works. The way he stood over that pole ... no-one even did that at the conference. I was frankly shocked.'

'Lionel ...'

'Lynn, I'm nearly done. Bryan, on the other hand, instinctively knew that without rules, one must apply their own boundaries. But they should be realistic — a personal challenge that's also achievable. To think that way without instruction reveals a naturally strong character with excellent potential.'

'It's just a fucking game,' says Harvey, and all the air flies out of the room. Harvey hears in the long ensuing echo a word that has never before been spoken in this house, a word he can't believe he said in front of their father.

Lionel Beam doesn't take Harvey to his bedroom this time,

doesn't push him on his stomach, doesn't remove his belt. For he is far too enraged to wait, to defer for even one minute the violence that must now occur. And so Harvey can't brace himself properly; isn't ready for the bare fists, for the thrashing around his back and sides. Together the father and boy crash into the side of the door as Harvey tries to run. And he can hear his mother screaming, 'Stop it, Lionel! Not like that!'

Harvey covers his head with his hands and shrinks to the ground as his father rails about him, looking for new entry points. And Harvey screams with his mother, tries to make words but can't. Just wants it to stop. *It has to stop.* His father is beating his back like a drum.

'Lionel,' his wife yells, 'we can't go to the ambulance. You have to stop.'

And Lionel does. Much later, he does.

26

Shorton is a taut blister today and Harvey is spraying Naomi's boys with the hose in their backyard.

'How about some cricket?' Harvey says when he suspects the town's water supply has been halved by his efforts. 'Have you got a bat and ball?'

The eldest boy Toby disappears into the garage while little Jamie peers down the eye of the hose, wondering where the water has gone. Lynn Beam walks out of the house and scoops up the toddler with a towel, leaving Harvey to engineer a three-man game with Toby and Finn.

It's not easy talking up cricket to a generation raised on small screens and Harvey has long predicted the test match will not survive Generation Y or Z or whatever lurks beyond it. Yet he perseveres with the boys today, their father having gone back out to work and Naomi putting in a big day at the hospital.

He teaches wiry Toby, whose limbs appear to have outgrown his body in that cruel and ungainly passage of early adolescence, how to deflect the ball when batting and even nick it past the invisible wicket keeper when the opportunity presents itself. It's these subtleties of cricket that Harvey likes best, although Toby seems much keener at this point to hit a six or break a window. Encouragingly Finn shows some promise as a bowler, which is to say that he can generally peg the ball within a four-metre radius of the wheelie bin currently serving as stumps.

Not for the first time, Harvey finds himself wondering how

his experience of fatherhood might have been different if he'd not had two girls. It's a guilty thought, and he feels even guiltier when he reasons that it hadn't been gender inhibiting his connection with Cate and Jayne; it had always been work. Work and a wife who filled every corner of the space left behind.

He would be a much better parent if he started again tomorrow.

As shadows stretch like ghosts across the backyard, Lynn calls them in for an early dinner. 'Naomi's going to stay at the hospital for another couple of hours,' she says, and busies herself with some sort of fishes-and-loaves routine in the kitchen. Harvey had peered in the fridge at lunchtime and saw nothing bar odd-looking wet food in plastic containers. Now Lynn is making it obvious that a well-rounded meal lurked within.

'Hit the showers, boys,' Harvey says to Toby and Finn, who don't appear to get the sporting reference. Then he quietly flicks on the TV in the lounge, hoping to catch the first bit of news he's watched since landing in Shorton. A few weeks ago it was unheard of for Beam to miss a single bulletin or update. He watches it now as though it's all happening in a parallel universe. Anti-austerity protests in Greece. A shopping-centre knife attack in Tokyo. Hurricanes somewhere. Bushfires. Blizzards. A thousand stories reduced to a dozen headlines. A cat that swims laps. So much shit.

'It was nice to see you playing with your nephews today,' Harvey's mother says to him after dinner.

'Yeah, it was good,' he says, still wondering how a two-decade investment in world affairs had dissolved in the space of a few weeks. Had he ever really cared?

Lynn pours them each a glass of red wine. 'You seem content,' she says. 'Happier than when you arrived.'

'Yeah, it's surprised me, this visit,' he says and then pauses, letting the words catch up to the recent equanimity he'd yet to fully inspect himself. 'I'd actually been dreading it, but it's been okay. Better than okay. And I didn't expect Cate to like it here, but she's a different kid. Loves working for Penny in that shop.'

His mother taps her finger gingerly on Harvey's hand. 'Are you sure it's not just a certain nurse who's making you smile?'

'God, Mum,' Beam says, taking a quick gulp from his glass. 'Can we not have this conversation?'

Lynn laughs. 'A holiday romance, Harvey. Who would have thought?'

'Who would have thought I'd start up something while visiting my dying father?'

'Oh, Harvey, no. Not at all. No-one is judging you about that. If anything, I'm impressed that you came back at all. I didn't think you would.'

'Well,' Beam says, 'I'm not sure it's made any real difference to anything, not as far as he's concerned. If your ex-husband has had any deathbed epiphanies about his shortfalls as a parent, I haven't been in the room to hear them.'

Lynn sits back into her chair, breathes in deeply and wearily, as though suddenly rendered helpless by global tragedies out of her control.

'What would you like him to say, Harvey? What do you need to hear?'

Beam has no idea how to answer this. He is suddenly aware that any response will expose his own character flaws more than any of his father's. Lionel Beam has made no obvious mistakes. There's no clear path of destruction. Acts of omission, ambivalence, hitting one of his children with a little too much enjoyment and spite in an era when that made for a good anecdote — they don't easily court apology or explanation. Emptiness, Harvey thinks, just vanishes into itself.

'Nothing,' he says finally. 'There's really nothing to say.'

'Of course there is,' Lynn says, now sitting up straight and drawing Beam's gaze out of his empty glass. 'But you won't hear it from your father, Harvey. Believe me, I know. So how about you let me say some things that might help you a little —'

'No,' Harvey interjects, instinctively rejecting the whiff of pity. 'I don't need help, Mum.' And instantly he feels not just one set of eyes upon him but figuratively those of his sisters too, a quorum of judgement and misunderstanding. Hates this more than anything. None of them know him.

'Harvey,' Lynn says, 'the biggest mistake I ever made was letting Bryan live with your father. I was in a bad place, making bad decisions.'

Harvey gets up from his chair, reaches for the wine bottle on the bench and pours them another glass. 'Mum, you don't need to say anything. It all happened a long time ago.'

But Lynn is resolute and pushes her glass away to the centre of the small dining room table.

'Listen,' she says. 'Look at me. I thought your father needed, I don't know, something. I thought he was empty. Even though I hated him at the time, and I did, I really did, I felt sorry for him too. I know that sounds ridiculous, Harvey. I let him take Bryan, still thinking we'd see your brother every week, have an easy back-and-forth arrangement, people do that, but it was like Bryan disappeared. He became your father's shadow. I don't think he had the confidence to be anything else, not like you. So I lost a son and you all lost a brother. Bryan has no time for me now because your father had no time for me.'

Beam knows he should say something. Can't think what would not be the wrong thing. He'd never really missed Bryan. How did this get to be about his brother?

'And yes, Harvey,' Lynn continues, 'it's the same thing with you. Bryan ignores you because your father ignored you. He treated you very, very badly, Harvey, and I should have left him years earlier because of what he was doing to you. He saw things in you that made him angry. I mean, he was always angry about something, angry and frustrated with the world, but you were like the spare key on the kitchen hook. The thing that unlocked him. Easy to reach for.'

Harvey looks up at his mother in surprise, blindsided by her uncharacteristic use of metaphor.

'But why me?' he says. Hates how that sounds, but there it is. 'Was I that difficult a child?'

'No,' Lynn says, 'but you expected more than the others. You expected more of Lionel and you probably still do. Expectations can feel like unfair demands to someone who just can't deliver. Harvey, don't blame yourself. I did the same thing until I finally gave up.'

And then she says, her hand on Harvey's, the air in the room a billion particles awaiting rearrangement ... she says: 'You were such a smart boy to fly away.'

Harvey sees himself now, from outside himself and this room and this lifetime, a terrified young man on his first ever plane flight, descending over Sydney, the harbour suddenly blinding him with her shiny curves and angles and light. How could so much bigness not swallow all his smallness? He couldn't wait, *couldn't wait.*

Harvey looks at his mother now as if a stranger just sat down in front of him. He has never heard his mother express regret. There was always veneer. Thick, busy veneer and fortnightly phone calls about the weather and his sisters, and generic vouchers at Christmas. It didn't seem to him that she ever stopped long enough to understand the events that propelled them all forward, all in different directions, Harvey the furthest of all. They were her children, part of her story, but not necessarily four individual human beings.

Suze had been the first person to really understand Harvey, and as far as he knew the only person.

But now Lynn Beam is crying, gently weeping in front of her son, and Harvey is moved to stand behind her and hold on to her shoulders and kiss her on the top of her purple-streaked head.

27

Today, Beam says to himself, aware he's feeling something close to happy and uncharacteristically still. *Today I will have the conversation.*

He is sat in the kiosk at the front of the hospital, where the coffee is predictably appalling and scalding, as though brewed in a fire pit, and where a constant movement of people in various states of worry and anticipation and feigned concern inspire an odd sense of calm within him. Peace in the shared terror of getting by. Of just coping. Processing all the scary possibilities, drawing up new deals.

Yes, today, he thinks, his mother's words having given him a rare restful sleep (the truncated wine intake having helped too) and an almost worrying measure of comfort — *You were such a smart boy to fly away* — Harvey will tell his father, conscious or not, that he forgives him. That everything good and bad shapes us and takes us places and most of it all works out in the end. That if he hadn't left Shorton, hadn't raged against Lionel's rejection and disappointment, hadn't taken it all so *personally*, then he wouldn't have met Suze, wouldn't have had his daughters. He almost certainly wouldn't have pursued a mostly successful career carved out of angry opinions.

He will tell his father that parenting is hard. Really fucking hard. So many ill-matched expectations flying at each other like rabid bats in a storm. He gets that. And Harvey hasn't made the best fist of it himself, although he does now intend to spend more time in the nets, getting it right.

He will say that family isn't everything. It is one thing. And maybe it works, and maybe it doesn't. Maybe parts of it work. Maybe it's just people thrown together and there's no magic alchemy to it at all. DNA might mean everything and nothing. Love is arbitrary. It doesn't exist outside of the decisions we make every day, the things we say. The things we don't. Tiny things. Suspicion and expectation. The law of diminishing returns.

I didn't like you either, Harvey also wants to say, but probably won't. He won't. A deathbed is not the right place to indulge the satisfaction of the final word, he thinks, and is instantly relieved that this was the ethical card he randomly selected from today's deck. For he had expected anger at this juncture, stunted boyhood anger, fighting words and parting shots and X-rays of his mangled heart. Far from closure, he had long wondered about busting things wide open if given the chance. *A boy needs his father. Where were you? What was wrong with me?*

Harvey explores the bottom of his cardboard cup. Maybe it's not forgiveness for his father that he's feeling right now. Maybe it's kindness, the base compassion one might feel for anyone pulled up short by imminent death.

Maybe it's regret.

Maybe it's nothing.

Beam's phone lights up with Suze's name and he smiles to himself, for if anyone can offer him an accurate diagnosis at this moment, it's her. She who knows him well enough to have wisely cut him loose.

'Harvey, have you been trying to call me?' Suze says in her signature breathless tone. Always running somewhere. 'Because I think my phone is fucked. It rings people randomly but then I think other calls aren't getting through.'

'No,' Harvey says.

'*Yes!* It's bizarre. Yesterday it rang my aunt, for God's sake. I had to actually *talk* to her. It was like dental work.'

'No, I mean I haven't rung you, Suze.'

'Oh. Well, why not?' And then she laughs.

'Sorry, I've been busy.'

'Really?'

'No.'

'How's the nurse?

'For God's sake, Suze.' *Jesus*. 'How's the fireman?'

'What fireman?'

'There's always a fireman.'

'Right. Okay. Anyway, how is Cate, do you think? She called me yesterday — she called me, get that — and we had a really good talk. She does seem happy there at the moment. I think your sisters have been very good to her. Naomi anyway.' This is unfair of Suze, Harvey thinks but without surprise. Penny's been the one looking out for Cate in Shorton, but Suze favours Naomi and will always line up her evidence to support her first impression.

'Yeah, she is happy. Seems she's got a knack for retail.'

'Good God. I'm bursting with pride.'

'Suze, your own mother runs a shop.'

'No, Harvey, she stands at a counter all day so that she doesn't have to be home watching my father navigate the weather channel.'

'Anyway,' Beam says and wants to say more on this, he *does*, but he missed the window a long time ago to help Suze make sense of her family. He would listen, at various moments over weeks and years, to the abruptly finished phone calls, the meaning-bereft text messages, the forgotten birthdays, and he would look to Suze for cues on how to respond. There were no clear cues. She seemed okay with it all. Mad, yes, always mad, but somehow resigned to the distance between childhood and adulthood, a family of origin that held her at arm's length. All those blind turns to avoid.

'Look,' Suze says. 'I'm actually really happy that Cate's feeling good about everything because I mean, well, that's the point of it all, isn't it? But what happens next, Harvey? What does she *do* after this? You can't let her start thinking that this is her future, because it can't be.'

'Why can't it be?'

'What the fuck, Harvey? She's not staying there.'

'It's not that bad, Suze.'

'Well, I think your own judgement might be a little... compromised at present.'

Beam says nothing and silently indicates to the waitress that he'd like another coffee. *Same again thanks.* Only it's not a waitress. It's a nurse. *And this, Harvey, you dick, is a hospital kiosk, not the lobby of the Ritz-Carlton.*

'Suze, I don't know what you want me to say about Cate. You've always known what's best for the girls. And I don't mean that sarcastically.'

'Well, thank you, Harvey. And I *do* mean that sarcastically.'

'How is Jayne?' he asks.

'It wouldn't hurt to call her. She misses you.'

'I know. I will.'

'Kids don't know you think about them if you don't tell them.'

'Yep, I know.'

'But she's good. And Harvey, she wants to come with me to the funeral.'

'The funeral?'

'I mean, when he goes. Sorry, Harvey. When your father passes. Dies. Shit.'

Harvey lets the moment sit awkwardly. It feels somehow wrong, a little cosmically dangerous, to speak about funeral plans before the requisite death.

There is a belated pause, rare dead air from Suze. 'How is he, anyway? Is he ...'

'Alive? Yes. Just.'

'Sorry. Fuck, you know I'm bad with death, Harvey. Sorry.'

'And weddings.'

'Yes.'

'And reunions.'

Suze laughs.

'And milestone birthdays.' For as long as he's known her, Suze has reacted badly to all the emotional extremities of orchestrated events, often before any extremities have been reached.

'Just all the big things, really,' she agrees. 'But I am coming. To the funeral. Jayne and I will be coming to support you.'

'You don't have to do that, Suze,' Harvey says, but finds a measure of comfort in the idea that she will.

'But Harvey, I'll need some notice so that I can get time off work and book tickets and get the dog minded and I might ask Cherie to stay in the house while we're gone. So, yeah ... keep me in the loop.'

'I'll definitely let you know when he dies.'

'Thank you.'

'And I'll call Jayne.'

'Excellent.'

'And you should try just turning your phone off and turning it on again.'

'Wow, Harvey, I hadn't thought of that. You should work in IT.'

Beam laughs but it comes out wrong, an uncertain gargle. The mention of work has tripped a switch and he's no longer comforted by the human chaos of the coffee shop and the hospital full of stories beyond it. It's a feeling that's been landing rudely upon him of late, unannounced and confused, as though time and place have been separated by a rupture deep below. Not for the first time he wonders if he might be depressed. A single thought removed from a fresh low point. Irrelevance.

The Third Act: Misery.

He ends the call with Suze and wanders out of the kiosk into the white-hot car park at the front of the hospital before remembering that he hadn't just come here for coffee. There'd been a purpose to today.

And though his legs seem entirely unconvinced, Beam turns around and walks back inside, down the stark angled corridors that will lead him to Lionel Beam.

***

Bryan is not in the room when Harvey enters. But Grace is. She is bent over his father, adjusting a monitor attached to his chest. Lionel's face, pinched and dry, seemingly collapsed under the weight of the room's soupy oxygen, is turned away from everything but the window.

Inexplicably, Harvey feels as though he has stood here before, in precisely this spot, looking at this scene. It is not foreign; it is entirely familiar. *Every moment*, a middle-aged rockstar had once told him, stoned and clutching the guest microphone in Beam's studio as though conjuring an engorged penis. *Every moment has been lived before. We just keep doing this shit over and over until we get it right.*

Grace smiles at Harvey, a beautiful smile that mocks the room's ugliness. She says nothing but places a hand on Beam's forearm as she walks around behind him and deposits Lionel's chart back in its metal holder.

'Is he ... can he hear?' Harvey asks her, barely whispering.

Grace looks at Lionel. She sees everything Harvey sees. The grim finality of hospital linen. The end of someone's turn at life. Everyone's turn. Says, 'It's impossible to know, Harvey. Sometimes they are coming in and out, looking for voices, especially towards the end. But I honestly don't know.'

Harvey looks at her. He wants direction. Wants not to do the wrong thing. Not now.

'It doesn't matter, Harvey,' Grace says at last. 'Just sit with him. That's all that matters.'

And Beam does. He sits.

He looks at his father, so pale, so barely present. And he continues looking for a long time, sometimes at the old man's empty face (*Is this what I'll look like on my deathbed? Jesus Christ*) and sometimes out the window, at the river in the distance.

He recognises an emotion from his early radio days — a prickly uncertainty. The pressure to say something meaningful to an audience that might be entirely imagined.

Words form inside him, then pop like bubbles. In the end, after an hour or six of just sitting, of waiting for Bryan to slink in or Cyclone Naomi to bear down, anything to puncture the endless moment, Harvey says nothing at all.

28

ON AIR

'Give up your secrets, Shorton. I need to know if there is a single place in this town where I can buy a decent coffee. You know the kind: not just drinkable but actually *enjoyable*. Hot but not too hot. Quality beans. Robust flavour. Milk that still has life in it. And maybe, if it's not too much to ask, a little finesse about the presentation. At four-fifty a go, I don't want a chipped cup with old lipstick stains on the rim. I want a pleasurable coffee moment — a gold-star start to my day.'

Harvey can taste it now, smell it. The cinnamon aroma of his choice coffee shop in Surry Hills. Cups and glasses full of promise and relief moving between the tables like an endless game of draughts. Strangers in overlapping moments of suspended time, perched over their addiction. Wooden boxes stuffed with coffee beans, cranky baristas in headscarves, bouncy waiters in faux aprons and Birkenstocks. An urban hip-pocket of movement and existence funded by dressed-up caffeine.

'Who's with me, Shortonites? How much better would your day be with a decent coffee or two pushing it along? I want to hear from you this morning. Give me a call and let's talk coffee. When did you have your last decent cup? Where was it? Was it in Shorton or were you on holidays somewhere? Because, folks, if there is good coffee in this town, I haven't tasted it. Maybe I'm wrong. It's happened before, although ... *audible smirk* ... rarely after a decent cup of coffee.'

Beam fades up a track from Powderfinger (their halcyon days when Bernard Fanning was still pretending he wasn't a grass-chewing bumpkin aching to sing about falling leaves and banging screen doors) and he waits for the phone to light up. And it doesn't.

He goes straight into Oasis's 'Wonderwall' (naff, yes, but always guaranteed to inspire a round of mimed riffing among bored drivers) and he wanders out of the booth to check with the receptionist whether calls are getting through. The girl looks about twelve and suspiciously related to Hugh Traynor. She shrugs. No calls.

And so he plays 'MacArthur Park' because surely someone will call in during seven minutes of cake being left out in the rain. And someone does, but it's a taxi driver called Craig who wants to talk about petrol prices rather than coffee and will not be moved from the topic despite Beam's best segue manoeuvres.

Coffee, he decides, might not be Shorton's cup of tea on a humid Monday morning and he opts to throw the conversational net much wider, to the topic of customer service: how bad it is here, how entirely *absent* it is, and what might be done about it. He knows this will run because *everyone* loves to whinge about customer service.

Beam leads the way with a set piece about his last dinner experience with Grace — a thirty-minute wait for an entrée that consisted of three dips and some crackers, a misplaced order at the next table, a steak seared to old-boot status, and an amusing recount (he chuckles when he tells it, though he was inwardly seething at the time) of the waitress talking on her phone for the entire time Harvey was paying the bill and attempting to give helpful feedback.

The first caller is Carly, a restaurant owner who quite possibly recognises the crackers-and-dip menu item as her own for she is bitterly defensive about the pressures of finding young people who will work on weekends.

'And what,' she fires at Harvey, 'would you know about running a small business in a town that is struggling? What would you know about the impact of penalty rates? About how I can grow several ulcers each weekend working out whether I can afford to roster on three staff instead of two when I probably need about five?'

Beam is passive and quietly compassionate. Knows how to play this. Let the anger fully expend itself ... lots of *absolutely*s and *of course, of course* ... until the caller is sated. Happier for having shared.

Tougher to placate is Jenny, who furiously berates him for laying the blame for average food at the feet of wait staff. And she has a point, Beam thinks, and says so, even if her frequent use of *gunna* and *would ya* and *ya think ya top shit* somewhat lower her high horse.

Jenny's tantrum ignites the phones. The young receptionist smacks on the glass and holds up nine fingers to Beam. Nine calls waiting, he interprets. *Fantastic.*

But there is no to-and-fro among them, no alternating of vantage points, no *I have to disagree with your previous caller*, just a mounting attack on Harvey himself, a personal assault on the outsider who dares to complain.

'You're a dick, mate,' says Jim. 'Go back to your wanker friends in the city.'

Karen: 'There's a reason we live here and it's to avoid having to put up with people like you.'

Mick: 'We don't sell poofter coffee here, mate, because there aren't enough poofters around.'

John: 'Shut up and play another song.'

Liam: 'Cock.'

God, the language in this fucking town. Harvey tries to wrest it back, makes a few humble comments about his own cooking. He recounts a (completely made-up) tale about the nicest cup of coffee he ever had: a simple International Roast served with a biscuit by a kind old lady at the blood bank. But today's show is gone and Harvey knows it.

Rob: 'You were a dick at school and you're a dick now. Go back to where you came from.'

This is *where I bloody came from.*

Finally, regrettably, Beam mistimes the seven-second delay that would have prevented Shorton hearing him declared a *pillow-biting fucktard* by a man called Leslie (strangely not 'Les'), an error that brings Hugh Traynor flying to the window, eyebrows leaping for his hairline, arms all *what the hell?*

Harvey looks at him and shrugs. Throws on Counting Crows and walks out of the station into a wall of heat that sears his eyeballs.

29

'Wow, I wish I'd been listening in,' Grace says, perched with Harvey on a too-small love seat on the balcony of her unit. Nothing about this sparsely furnished rent scam has been designed well (Harvey regularly hits his head on the swinging light bulb in the toilet), except for its aspect, a masterful accident no doubt, that affords the balcony both an afternoon sea breeze and cooling shade.

'I'm glad you weren't,' Harvey says, his arms resting across the pair of slender legs recently liberated from stockings and now draped artfully across his lap and against his paunch. He has got to stop eating.

'But I mean, isn't that good radio?' Grace asks. 'When there's conflict and anger?'

'Not when it's all directed at the host,' he says. 'And the profanity could get Hugh fined.'

'But you weren't the one who swore.'

'I inspired it.'

'So,' she says with a kind and slightly uncertain smile, 'you're an inspiration.'

God, this woman.

'Hardly, Grace. But thank you. No, I'm actually a dick, a cock and a poofter, not necessarily in that order.'

She grins. 'And a fucktard.'

Harvey pretends to push her off the chair before pulling her close and kissing her hard.

They watch the sun set blithely behind a motley group of

mangroves. It takes its time tonight, somehow reluctant. Afterwards Grace fetches them both a cider from inside and a candle that smells like an old bookshop.

Harvey wants to ask Grace about her day at work but knows she'll end up talking about his father, or more likely lead with this, and it's a topic he just can't come at today. This morning he had orchestrated the sort of professional failure Lionel Beam had so often predicted for him, as though being back in his father's orbit made defeat somehow inevitable. And this, he thinks, is the irony of what happened – that the audience thought Beam felt emboldened in Shorton, not as it happened, as it had always happened, utterly diminished and lost. Caught in an adolescent black hole.

Tonight he makes love to Grace in the way that couples sometimes do – to disappear. Eyes shut tight, dismissive of time and space, he pours himself into the act, vanishes into sparks and flares and gaps in the air. Sandpaper tenderness. Sex that expels every breath and all the words between two people that in any other setting sound insane. Sex that exacts a deep and grateful sleep. He could be anywhere.

In the morning, after not a single dream he can remember, Harvey wakes to Grace in her hospital uniform, hair damp from the shower, handing him his ringing phone.

It's Naomi and she speaks to Beam in a soft and measured tone that sounds nothing at all like her.

'It was early this morning, Pencil,' she says. 'Maybe two thirty. The nurse checked on him and he had just, you know, stopped breathing.'

Harvey looks at Grace and he can see that she knows what he's hearing.

'Was Bryan there?' Harvey asks.

'No, he was alone. Harvey, he's gone.'

'Yes, I know.'

In his mind, Beam sees books. A ragged pile of books hit by a whirly wind and sending loose pages, thousands and thousands of them, flying into the sky.

Finally, with Grace's hand on his knee and his heart outside of himself, Beam says, 'Are you okay, Naomi?'

And Naomi says, 'I'm okay, Pencil. I mean, sad, but, yeah. Are you okay?'

Harvey thinks about this — *Am I okay? What is this?* — and waits to see what rises from his chest, what reaction comes of its own accord, without summons, without thinking too hard about it. He stares at the patch of carpet beneath his feet and it seems too far away, as though he is looking down from the ceiling, watching himself, curious to witness his own reaction. And there is none for now. Not yet, he thinks. Maybe later.

'Harvey,' says Grace, 'I'm so sorry. Let me drive you to your sister's house, or to your mum's.'

Beam shakes his head.

'Where do you want to go?' Grace asks. 'I'll take you there.'

And the options seem suddenly endless, he thinks, because Lionel Beam is no longer here.

30

The narrowest section of Shorton River flows quickly today, sluiced through two banks that seem destined to touch at some point in the future. Beam is not surprised to find himself here, standing on a small coarse shore, wrongly dressed for the occasion and minus a fishing rod. He needed to buy some time, wasn't ready yet for the Beam family's take on Death Of A Father, the intermingling of grief, real and imagined, the set pieces and positional play.

Until he had a better sense of what his face might convey to sisters who'd be scanning it, and each other, with infra-red precision, Beam knew he needed to be alone and he'd asked Grace to drop him into town on her way to work. Within an hour, his feet had brought him here, to a familiar current and a blue that spilled into everything.

Once on his show he'd trialled a weekly segment called Thrillosophy, an attempt to sex up philosophy by asking listeners to give their take on an ancient riddle or lofty ideological quote. It hadn't really taken off, but one of the better chats prior to the show's quiet disappearance had been sparked by that quote from Greek philosopher Heraclitus about a man not being able to step into a river twice because it's not the same river and he's not the same man. Beam had loved this idea, that he might be continuously evolving, even without trying, that childhood wasn't a mould that couldn't be discarded, and that everything, all of it, keeps flowing and flowing and nothing stands still.

Every mistake disappears, eventually.

It had been this hope, if he's honest with himself, that Harvey had carried back to Shorton on previous occasions: that things might somehow be different with his father. Different then, too, with his whole family because that one relationship had somehow skewed all the others, creating fracture lines and conversational no-go zones too confusing to plot on any map. He'd hoped that old misunderstandings, hurts, transgressions, whatever had led to all the wilful indifference between Harvey and Lionel Beam, all of it would have flowed beneath them by then. Different river, different men.

But Shorton River feels the same today, same water washed back by ancient tides, and the feeling of relief Harvey had long imagined might accompany the death of his father has not yet presented itself. Even Lionel Beam's face, so ravaged and beaten within the folds of the hospital sheets, had looked more like sameness than difference to Harvey. The eyes. Nothing had shifted and clearly nothing benign had flowed beneath them over the years, and so Harvey's words had remained in his chest by his father's bedside, suspended and possibly irrelevant.

This he now understands: something got stuck all those years ago. Something broke in a way that no-one deemed reparable, like one of those old cars left to rust in the outback.

Beam's shoes are beside him and his feet are buried deep in the rough, wet sand. The hairs on his arms look brassy in the sun and the top of his head is burning. He should have worn a hat. Always forgets hats. Lionel Beam had once belted him into a half-open cupboard, his ear splitting on the handle, for forgetting to bring his hat home from school. Like a dog with a practised nose, Lionel had looked only in Harvey's schoolbag, one of four lined up like sandbags near the front door, certain if not hopeful he would be the errant child again. In the hours when some men reached thirstily for a beer, Lionel Beam had looked to Harvey as his transitional activity between the working day and the quiet terror of sleep.

Now he is dead. And this, Beam thinks, is more than he can process today. More than he can process alone anyway, and certainly more than he can make sense of with his family. Not yet.

He lets his head burn. It's going to hurt tomorrow.

'Suze,' Beam says finally, sloppy tears punctuating his voice down the phone line to Sydney. He had promised to call her when it happened, but he is really doing this for himself. Suze doesn't always say the right thing, but it usually becomes the right thing at some point. And she has always been able to bring him back to the present.

'Is he gone?' she says, the roar of inner-west traffic buffeting her clipped syllables.

'Yes,' Beam says. 'Last night.'

'Well. About fucking time.'

31

For someone who shunned levity and coveted order, Lionel
Beam had made surprisingly few stipulations about his funeral
plans. No song requests. No preference or otherwise for a
wake. No dying wish to be ultimately ignored by well-meaning
family members. What few demands he had made resided in
the care of Bryan, or so Bryan makes clear to his siblings as
they sit around Naomi's kitchen table the following morning.

It is a scene, Harvey thinks, surreptitiously touching his
seared scalp, that any other family might assemble every
day when a far-flung sibling visits town: coming together
to reminisce and laugh and jibe and rewrite history as only
people who share a childhood can. But it has taken the death
of their father to put Naomi and Penny in the same room again
and for all of them to witness Bryan in any setting that could
be construed as familial.

Hovering about the edges this morning is Lynn, present only
(she insists) to feed and water the gaggle of cousins gathered
around the Xbox in Naomi's lounge room. 'Seriously, I'm not
even here,' she says, singularly omnipresent with her constant
darting in and out of the kitchen. Possibly, Harvey reasons,
Lynn can't quite believe what she's seeing: all her children
gathered in one place at the same time. It's either warming her
heart or triggering an anxiety attack, he can't be sure.

Matt is here too, bouncing the youngest boy on his leg and
pretending to be engrossed in a magazine about small indoor
flowering plants. Beam muses at the obscurity of the title,

having once fielded a zingy morning of calls about listeners' most niche magazine purchases: *Keeping Goats Happy, Wind Tunnel Monthly* and Harvey's favourite, *Newly Retired Indoor-Outdoor Croquet Enthusiasts.*

Simon is absent, away again at work, his roster being one that works conveniently around nothing, ever. And Penny is unmistakeably miffed and uncomfortable as a result, outnumbered by her sister, no father's knee on which to bounce her children. As far as Harvey can see, his sisters haven't yet made eye contact since they all sat down about thirty minutes ago, each having mastered a hundred or more different eye movements and angles, the likes of which he would secretly love to see drawn up as one of those computerised batting graphics on the cricket.

Just as Harvey considers suggesting an obligatory glass of red wine to lighten the mood, the mood having not yet reached midday status, Cate walks into the room and pulls up sharply at the scene before her.

'Wow,' she says. 'Awkward.'

And Beam loves her for calling it — this room of palpable unease that no-one, except perhaps their mother, really wants to be in.

'Let's continue with the planning,' Bryan says, apparently oblivious to the room's new arrival.

Harvey bristles. 'Remember Cate, Bryan? My daughter. Your niece.'

And Bryan says, 'Well, yes,' and the sides of his mouth quiver awkwardly as though recalling a smile response. But the gesture falls just shy of Cate, who sits down on a stool and shrugs at the universe and all its stupidity.

Matt flashes her a smile and a wink.

Bryan resumes, his brow now deeply furrowed, the pen in his hand at considerable risk of snapping. 'Time is important here, Harvey,' he says. 'The funeral company would like all of our requests by tomorrow.'

'Why the hurry?' Naomi asks. 'Is this like the busy season for death?'

Cate spits out a mouthful of lemonade.

'I'm serious,' Naomi says. 'Shouldn't families have more time to make these decisions?'

'We've had plenty of time to make these decisions,' Penny answers, directing her comment to Bryan.

'What Naomi means,' says Matt, releasing the boy on his knee and pointing him towards the lounge room, 'is that we've never all got together like this and talked about what should happen.'

'There's been no need to,' Bryan says. 'Dad told me what he wanted and it's relatively straightforward. Just a non-religious service in the big church in town. Dark wooden casket. All donations to the National Library of Australia. All we need to decide is —'

'A non-religious service in a church?' Harvey cuts in. 'What? For irony's sake?'

'Because the Edward Street church holds a lot of people,' Bryan says, eyes trained fiercely on the leather-bound notebook in front of him. 'More than the town hall.'

Harvey can't help himself. 'But why was he expecting a lot of people, Bryan? I mean, no offence, but he was hardly Joe Social.'

'You wouldn't really know, Harvey. You weren't here.'

Beam is caught off guard. He hadn't expected this from Penny. Bores his eyes now into the tablecloth, no longer sure where safety resides.

'We all know a different version of Dad,' Penny adds. 'We'll probably be having this same sort of conversation when Mum dies too.'

At this moment, a familiar voice calls out from the lounge. 'I'm still here,' Lynn Beam trills.

Cate laughs broadly again, clearly enjoying herself despite the meeting's purpose. Bryan waits for her to stop, a primary-school-worthy pause to restore quiet.

'The casket has been ordered and paid for,' he continues. 'It will arrive tomorrow. The funeral director recommended an open viewing before the service, but I said no. I didn't think there would be any objections.'

Harvey glances about the table, willing there to be no counter-arguments on this front at least. He had seen his grandmother's body in an open casket several years ago and it was a sight that returned to him with alarming clarity at inexplicable moments. The white horror of those sharp bones scaffolding crepe-paper skin, eye sockets retreating like sinkholes. The indignity of it all, just to show that death had occurred. That a mortician had done their job.

'No argument from me,' says Naomi. Penny shrugs in half-hearted agreement.

An uneasy silence engulfs the room. Harvey pictures himself pushing a button to issue a song, a promo, anything to kill it.

'I've actually never seen a dead body,' Cate says, glancing up at Harvey. 'I mean, I'm not saying I want to, but you know, it's one of those things. Not a bucket list thing. But it's kind of ... something. To talk about. When people say, "Have you ever seen a dead body?", you can say, well, I *have* actually. Like, it might not be weird at all. It might be kind of cool and ... important. I'm just saying.'

Harvey looks back at her, wide-eyed in the manner of *what the actual fuck?*

'Just watch old episodes of *Six Feet Under*, Cate,' says Matt with a sympathetic grin. 'Or that old woman who judges *Dancing with the Stars*. I mean she's sitting there, sure, but I think she actually died a while ago and the other judges are just propping her up, like *Weekend At Bernie's*, until the end of the season.'

Cate feigns a laugh. Harvey looks at Matt gratefully. His daughter is clearly flying well above the gravity of the situation, but then so is he. The entire scene feels as though it's already happened and he's simply revisiting it now to note any missed subtleties. Like flicking back through a complicated part in a movie.

Bryan continues to move through a raft of minor details, not once looking up to notice his audience drifting away, until the matter of music comes up. 'We can choose one or two songs,' he says, 'or just go with the funeral company's recommendations, which I am inclined to do.'

'Didn't he have a favourite song?' asks Naomi. 'Everyone has a favourite song.'

'I can't remember him ever listening to music,' says Penny.

'I think you'll find he enjoys the classics,' says Bryan, as though describing a visiting dignitary they would soon play host to.

'Classic what?' asks Harvey. 'Classic rock? R&B? Australiana? Never-play death metal?'

He is rolling through the playlist categories at his former station, can still see them all as though he's sitting in his old chair, sailing back and forth between screens and panels, master of his soundproof lair.

'Classical music,' deadpans Bryan. 'Dad would listen to it when he was researching.'

Beam looks out the kitchen window to mask a slow roll of his eyes.

'Any particular classical music?' asks Matt. 'Any one symphony or composer?'

Bryan says nothing, and in this Harvey sees an instant resemblance with his father: the use of silence to evoke superiority. *I answer the questions I think worthy.*

'Should we choose a song that reflects his love of study?' suggests Penny. 'Something kind of academic?'

Cate starts typing and scrolling on her phone. 'Let me have a look,' she says. 'I have an app for this.'

'An app for finding relevant funeral songs?' laughs Matt.

'No, for finding songs about a particular theme,' Cate says, her eyes trained on the soft glow of her phone.

'You know,' says Matt, 'I read the other day that there are now more apps available than there are beaded necklaces for sale in Bali.'

'What?' Harvey grins at his brother-in-law, easily the most likeable person in the room right now. 'Are you serious?'

'Absolutely. I read it on the Bizarre Comparisons app.'

'Okay,' announces Cate. 'There's "Education" by Pearl Jam. There's "Don't Stand So Close to Me". No, that would be weird. How about "Mass Nerder" by The Descendents, but you know, "nerd" in a good way?'

Cate keeps scrolling as Penny begins to giggle and Naomi looks nervously at Bryan. Matt's face is a beacon of pure delight.

'"School Boy Heart",' Cate continues. 'That's Jimmy Buffett. "Another Brick in the Wall", Pink Floyd. But I think that might be ironic. "College Man" by someone called Bill Justis.' Cate looks around the table hopefully: 'Well, that's a possibility, right?' she says. 'Okay, there's "Brain Damage" by Eminem. Probably not. "Don't be a Dropout", James Brown. "Fifth Period Massacre" — um, *no*. "One Angry Dwarf and 200 Solemn Faces". Look, I think these are mostly about school, not uni, and they're all pretty negative. Maybe there's another app ...'

'We could always adapt an existing song,' says Harvey, secretly thrilled the conversation has led them to one of his favourite time-wasters. 'So the AC/DC classic "TNT" becomes' — and Harvey begins to sing with gritty emphasis — 'P.H.D. It's dynamite!'

'God, Dad,' says Cate, still swiping her phone screen. 'That is so lame.'

'I think you'll find that's comedy gold, Cate.'

Penny looks hard at the table. Harvey can't decide if she's trying to think of a song or willing the floor to open up beneath them all. Why didn't she just get the hell out of Shorton too, he finds himself thinking.

'"Thesis of Suburbia",' offers Matt. 'You know, from that Green Day song about Jesus?'

'Oh I know!' says Penny, suddenly animated and switching into a Beach Boys lilt. 'Good, good, good ... good *citations*."

Harvey adds the requisite 'bop, bop' at the end and everyone at the table besides Bryan laughs loudly.

'I can't think of one,' says Naomi disappointedly, just as Matt kicks out his chair, throws his hand to his hip theatrically and pouts "I'm Too Texty for My Shirt", then proceeds to swagger about the room like a misunderstood male model.

Harvey is mid rapturous applause when his mother appears conspicuously at the doorway, Naomi's youngest on her hip. She appears to wait for quiet.

'You know,' Lynn Beam announces to the room, 'your father's favourite song when we met was "Groovy Kind of Love".'

Obedient silence, a sea of incredulity, laps before her.

'It really was,' she continues. 'He sang it to me on the night he proposed. It was beautiful. I think he was a little high at the time.'

'High?' chokes Penny.

'He *sang* it?' says Naomi.

Harvey looks at his mother as though for the first time. She seems lost in a moment, her gaze fixed on a point somewhere between the kitchen bench and an entirely different life. Beam has never before seen his mother looking wistful, never heard her speak of a time before children, and he realises with a measure of shame that Lynn Beam is more than entitled to be in this room, discussing this death and this funeral. She knows their father better than any of them.

'Yes, he sang it to me,' Lynn continues. 'He sang it beautifully. He was such a catch, your father. Such a handsome man and so ... unexpected. I see him in each of you all the time. Every day.'

'Gosh, Mum,' says Penny. 'That's ... *wow*.'

'And then,' Lynn Beam says, putting her hands over Jamie's little ears. 'Then your father turned into a complete arsehole.'

32

Beam had once fielded a talkback session about funerals. Prompted by a quirky news story about Sweden having the world's longest waiting periods between death and funeral (twenty-three days on average), listeners had called the station for four manic hours, all desperate to share their own experiences of the gap between checkout and goodbye. Some described the period as being too short, a frenzy of half-formed decisions. They said important things had been overlooked that had ultimately ruined a funeral and compounded grief, like not having wheelchair access for Great Aunt Mavis (who had been forced to sit at the exit of the church where she was stung by heartless bees) and time for the deceased's daughter's giant hickey to fade.

But most people, the vast majority, had felt that the wait for a funeral was interminable. While a handful of people busied themselves with the heady minutiae of event organisation, the rest were left suspended in a slow dance through emotional space dust. Waiting for the end. For the beginning. For permanent grief to show its face. For a green light.

Four days, they said, is right. Five at most. Another couple for significant overseas guests to arrive. But no more. Make it stop, they said. Enough already.

And Harvey feels this now. It's been two days since the family meeting at Naomi's kitchen table. Two days since Bryan marched out of the house without saying a word. Since their mother upgraded her position from 'extra' to 'key protagonist'.

Since Matt made Beam laugh harder than he has in a very long time.

He is lost. Doesn't understand the rules about recent paternal death and doesn't want to. Bryan is presumably making whatever decisions are left to be made, Penny is organising the funeral booklet using stationery from her store, and Naomi is taking care of the wake. That leaves Harvey with nothing to do. Nothing he can even pretend to do. He's an outsider here. The One Who Left. And he would feel punished by this fringe-dweller status if he didn't also feel relieved to be excluded from activities easily buggered up through lack of insider knowledge.

Still, Beam feels obliged to stay close to the light for now, the family bug-zapper of activity. He nods at the right times, makes inappropriate jokes, pitches in money, offers to take his various nephews on walks and park excursions, all the while watching the clock on his phone, those long hours aching by until 10am on Friday when this will all be over. Each day feels like a game of inches.

And really, he just wants to be with Grace.

Achingly, he wants to be with her now, even though she has made it clear he should be with his family at this time. Maybe because of that.

Lost.

The funeral is in two days' time. Two long, long days if he doesn't see Grace. Suze and Jayne arrive in Shorton tomorrow morning and while their presence will help soak up time, he also suspects it will add to the weight of things, for nothing short of a funeral would bring his ex-wife back to Shorton. And Suze will, he knows, infuse the air with the echoes of Beam's own hurt and resentment, and he's not sure he's up for that. Just wants this to be over, for Lionel Beam to be buried, and to know how that feels.

He calls Grace. 'What are you up to? Are you at work? Can I see you?'

Grace says she's finishing work shortly. Would he like to join her at the beach?

His chest tightens. His heart literally races. He is sixteen again. *God, yes.*

They drive to Shorton's most out-of-the-way beach via a dirt track through a mess of bush. And the water is brochure-blue and glass-topped and they are the only people from here to the horizon.

Grace moves into the water and Harvey follows. She throws questions over her shoulder at him, questions about the funeral plans, about Bryan, about how Harvey is feeling. And Beam doesn't answer any of them but instead dives forward and pulls Grace under, wrapping his arms around her and spinning her to face him as they surface together.

Harvey kisses her with what he feels might look like movie-star prowess to an onlooker. He'd forgotten how marvellously different it feels to kiss someone with the aid of water. The glorious smoothness of it. The closeness of their bodies in bathers. The weightless coil of limbs.

Before Grace can ask another question or scan the surface for shark fins, Harvey takes down his shorts and inches Grace's bikini bottom to one side. She looks at him wide-eyed and he smiles and he begins to make love to her there in the ocean, something he hasn't done since maybe his early twenties and it is singularly the best thing he has felt in a very long time. The exquisite wonder of being inside Grace.

She hugs him afterwards, still in the water, her arms around his neck and her mouth near his ear. And she says, 'That was beautiful, Harvey.'

Beam kisses her shoulder, gleaming in the sunlight. 'Why don't we stay here forever?' he says.

'In Shorton?' Grace answers, moving her face to look at Beam's eyes.

'No, here in the ocean, making awesome love.'

And Grace laughs, tilting her head toward the sky. 'Funerals are always too long a wait, aren't they?'

33

With a great measure of discomfort, Beam takes Simon's monster truck to the airport the next morning. It takes him half an hour to find a parking space that will accommodate it. Already cutting it fine, Beam starts jogging towards the terminal only to discover he's forgotten how to run without a treadmill and his left knee seems to be collapsing in on itself. He finds it incredulous that people *start* running marathons at this age.

Fortunately Suze and Jayne are not standing around waiting for him because their flight has been delayed. Harvey decides to wait it out, not wanting to renegotiate that car space. He orders a coffee and finds a seat in the packed airport cafe, the only food and beverage option in a facility that clearly needs about six more. People spill across melamine tables still covered in the plastic rubble of the previous tenants, while children teeter precariously on adult knees and shoulders. The air is a mess of shouted conversations and disappointment.

Harvey does what he swore he wouldn't do, what he has rigorously avoided since his last talk with Trudi Rice. He googles 'Sydney radio' and 'industry news' on his phone and steers willingly into the slipstream of his recent despair.

The new mornings experiment – a top-heavy team of three hosts – is rating poorly (*excellent*), as one might expect of a jaded ex-pollie, a retired footballer and a pompous arts commentator thrown together for the first time. Each of them, Harvey knows, would see themselves as the 'talent', not the listeners and callers, and he inwardly rages against this unnecessary ignorance of the basic premise of good talkback. Common sense undone by strategic planning days.

Less gratifying is the news that John Jackson is faring well in the afternoons, leading the timeslot and 'settling in nicely'. *Arse hat.* Beam tightens his grip on the phone, scrolls violently to find a bad review of Jackson, anything that Trudi Rice hasn't already massaged into something positive. He finds nothing.

All trace, too, of Harvey has been removed from the station website, the site itself bearing no resemblance to the one he last looked at a few weeks ago. *More strategic planning.* And he hates himself for feeling like this, like an overlooked child. He knows that nothing really ends unless it ends badly, but the truth of it bites hard. He had loved his job, loved everything about where it had taken him beyond Shorton, loved that he was good at it. Had any of it mattered?

Not according to the internet.

What now? *What the fuck now?*

Suze leads Jayne through the gate like a front of unexpected weather. They are both dressed in Sydney blacks and greys, Jayne looking rail thin, ever the contrast to her sister's much softer frame. Suze has cut all her hair off, again, and Harvey reads from her approaching expression that she is distinctly unhappy about having been delayed, a fact she confirms by kissing Harvey on the cheek and uttering in his ear at the same time: 'Tiger Air. Can we have it shot?'

He wraps up Jayne in a hug that he hopes doesn't come across as awkward and unsure because he never does this well; always goes in too hard or too soft and gets the angle wrong. It should be easier to be a father when you do actually love your kids, but it's not. Affection is a difficult thing to start with confidence in your twenties.

'Hey, Dad,' says Jayne. 'I'm sorry about your father.'

Like Cate, Harvey notes, Jayne hasn't referenced him as 'Grandad'. He feels a light stab of something that is probably guilt.

'Yes, I'm sorry, too,' Suze says. 'But only in a polite way. I'm not manifestly sorry.'

Harvey smiles at his ex-wife. She who knows him far better than he'd sometimes like. Who makes the best curries he's ever had before or since, who once gave him a head job while driving across the Nullarbor Plain (*Because seriously, what else is there to do, Harvey?*). Who says 'manifestly'.

'Thanks, Suze,' he says, leading them both toward the baggage carousel. 'Thanks for coming. You didn't have to, but I'm really glad you're here.'

'Of course I had to come,' she says, surveying the sea of waiting travellers, a tide of untucked shirts and thongs and sports bags. 'You shouldn't have to do this on your own. Brush up against all the crazy. And the girls should be here anyway, out of respect.'

'I didn't even know him,' says Jayne.

'And that's to be respected,' Harvey says with a laugh that doesn't quite take. Suze briefly glares at him.

'We're going to stay in a hotel,' she says, edging her way through the thrum of people trapped around the carousel like late Christmas shoppers. 'I know you said we could stay with Penny, but I'd prefer not to.'

Harvey wonders how this decision will be interpreted by Penny, who had already made up the spare beds yesterday, but knows there is no changing Suze's course once it's plotted.

'How is school?' he says to Jayne.

'Okay.'

'Friends all good?'

'They're okay.'

'How is netball going?'

'I haven't played netball for two years, Dad.'

'Wow. Really?' *Shit.*

'Really,' she says, but softens her tone with a smile. Though she can be sullen at times, Jayne does not share Cate's passion for biting sarcasm.

'Well, it's great to see you,' Beam says. 'I've missed you.'

'Thanks, Dad.'

And they both stare at the still unmoving carousel, willing it to provide the next thing to talk about.

'So what's Cate been doing?' Jayne says finally.

Harvey pauses to answer, because while he doesn't really understand the shifting sands beneath his daughters' relationship, he knows it is mostly defined by jealousy and far more difference than one might expect of common genes. He suddenly pictures Bryan hunched over his funeral notebook and inwardly winces.

'She's been helping out in Penny's shop, actually,' he says. 'The gift shop. She seems to like it, which surprised me.'

'Hmm,' Jayne says without expression.

'This is taking longer than the flight,' Suze says. 'Honestly, how hard can it be? How has no-one ever come up with a better system for getting bags off a plane?'

Just be happy if they get here at all, Beam thinks.

But they do and Suze's agitation quickly passes, as it usually does once she is extricated from large groups of people she will never need to know. Within the hour the three of them are driving through the centre of Shorton and laughing (hysterically in Jayne's case) at Harvey's attempts to drive a vehicle larger than his apartment.

'There's no way I can park this anywhere here in town,' Beam admits. 'People will be maimed. Let's head out to the marina and find somewhere to have lunch.'

'Marina?' Suze says.

'Don't ask,' Beam replies.

Jayne surprises both parents by asking to be dropped off along the way at Penny's shop. So it's just the two of them about to share lunch, and Beam briefly wonders when such a prospect stopped scaring him and became something rather pleasurable. He can't even remember the last time he and Suze had done something like this post-divorce — possibly never — and he's relieved to feel so at ease about it. There is actually no-one, he thinks, save Grace, who he'd rather be lunching with today than his ex-wife.

They find an Italian pizzeria on the edge of the marina (which Suze agrees is a physical abomination — 'cultural rape') and they are the only customers today. The sole waiter tends to them nervously, as though suspicious of their motives. Suze orders a salad and Beam a large meaty pizza and they agree that a bottle of sauvignon blanc seems mandatory.

It is odd, though not in a bad way, to be looking at Suze up close like this. So much of their relationship in recent years has taken place over the phone. She is ever a voice in his ear, even when they're not physically talking, even when he is going to sleep at night and recalling their last conversation; his conch shell. Suze's voice is omnipresent. He'd forgotten it came attached to a face and a body.

And he can see now, up close like this that, while Suze is still very attractive by most conventional standards, she is now unmistakeably a middle-aged woman. And the inescapable correlation — that he is a middle-aged man — hits him hard in the chest, as it increasingly does these days. Age hasn't just crept up on him; it's tackled him from the side, taken out his legs and his thirties.

Suze talks endlessly about the girls, one sentence running into the next. Harvey marvels at all the things she thinks about, things that never occur to him, stuff about going on the pill and doomed friendships and social media boundaries and apparently stooped posture (Jayne). Suze's brain fizzes like welding sparks.

'You're a great mum, Suze,' he says. 'The girls are doing great. You need to cut yourself some slack.'

At this Suze reels. 'I'm a *shit* mum, Harvey. I feel like I'm doing everything wrong — that's how I feel most days. It's just endless, the pressure of all that responsibility. And it's all so fucking mysterious. Like there's no way of knowing what you're getting right or wrong until it's too late and they hate you and they're completely screwed in the head. Sometimes I think parenting is the worst kind of arrogance, like how do we as mostly fucked-up people ourselves think we can be responsible for other people's lives? What kind of delusion is that? And it never ends, Harvey. *It never ends.* I know I will feel this way until the day I die. Completely fucking confused and exhausted.'

Beam fills Suze glass with wine. He knows he won't say the right thing and so says nothing. Also knows that, for Suze, an expletive-filled rant is less a cry for help than a temporary solution of its own.

Harvey recalls an interview he did last year with a humanitarian refugee from Africa, a man recently resettled in Australia with nine children. Wow, nine children, Beam had said to him. That must keep you busy. The African man had laughed good-naturedly at Harvey's observation and replied: 'No, sir. One child keeps you busy. Two children keep you very busy. I am never busy with nine children.'

Sure, no time to overthink things, Harvey had thought, although he later realised the gentleman had meant that the older kids look out for the younger ones and life works out in a way that transcends 'play dates' and micro-managed birthday parties and the new season's clothing.

'Anyway,' Suze says with a smile, quickly discarding her vented spleen like junk mail. 'Your job, Harvey. It's gone, isn't it? I've been listening most mornings and there's no talk of you returning or any new project. What happened? What's wrong?'

Beam's pizza lands in front of him like a meaty UFO, a Shorton up-yours to nouveau cuisine. 'I'm sorry,' Harvey says to the waiter, 'but I actually ordered a "large".'

Suze laughs. This is one of their old jokes, best enjoyed when a waiter doesn't get it. But this one does and indulges them with a smile. The sort of smile, Harvey thinks, that young people reserve for old farts making bad jokes.

'Yes, the job has gone,' Harvey says. 'I got a redundancy but only just. John Jackson wins again because the world is designed by arseholes.'

'Harvey, I'm so sorry,' Suze says as her salad arrives, two cherry tomatoes crowd-surfing a sea of lettuce. 'That really sucks. It's not fair. I hope you realise it's not fair.'

'Actually,' he says, a geyser of cheese suddenly hitting him in the cheek. 'It feels kind of ... inevitable. Like I was running out of rope. Like I didn't have enough rope in the first place and everyone knew it.'

'That's bullshit, Harvey. You were one of the best. You *are* one of the best. I think you actually got better at it in recent years — you lost all that arrogance. I even enjoyed listening to you sometimes, and I used to hate it. This salad is shit.'

'Have some of my pizza,' Beam says and slides a piece onto Suze's bread plate.

'Harvey, I know you're hiding here at the moment, but you can't hide forever.'

'I don't know, Suze,' he says, reaching for his wine glass. 'Maybe I can.'

Suze puts down her fork abruptly, leans across the table and fills Harvey's field of vision with an incredulous expression.

'You are *not*,' she says, '*seriously* thinking about staying here?'

And Beam pauses, gives in to dead air. Wonders what will come out of his mouth next. Fills it with pizza.

'You cannot stay here, Harvey. You're only considering it because your current response to the situation is self-destruction.'

'Honestly, Suze, I think I've reached the end of my career. About twenty years too early.'

'Oh for fuck's sake, Harvey,' Suze says, whipping a piece of bacon off Beam's pizza like a shameless seagull. 'Do you know what the common denominator is in every midlife crisis?'

Beam shrugs.

'Failure?'

'*Overreaction*,' Suze replies. 'Supreme overreaction.'

'I think that's a bit simplistic, Suze.'

'No, it's not,' she says, damning her serviette into a perfect half and wedging it under a plate. 'This town might have been your beginning, Harvey, but it's not your end. This is not where it ends. Life is not a circle. It's a ... some other sort of fucking shape.'

Beam leans back in his chair, hands interlaced over the gut he plans to resurrect with sit-ups in the next week or so. 'Thanks, Suze, I just ... you know, it's just. Hard. To make a plan. Without a job to wrap it around.'

'This isn't about the nurse, is it?'

'What? No.'

'You're not throwing everything away for a hometown fling?'

'Suze, she's not even from here. She's only here for work. It's nothing to do with Grace.'

'Grace,' Suze says, draining her glass. 'Nice name. Doesn't sound like she's from here.'

He smiles curtly, tries not to look like someone who's definitely been having amazing sex. 'That's a bit harsh.'

'Harvey, you have a skill. You have a profession. There are plenty of radio stations in Sydney. Just because you've finished up at one of them doesn't mean the sky has to fall in. It doesn't mean you have to scamper back home with your tail between your legs.'

Harvey feels a small wave of salami rise to his throat. 'I came back here because my father was dying, Suze. Losing my job at the same time was just a coincidence.'

'But somehow, Harvey, you've wrapped it all up together and you've got stuck. And you can't think clearly because you're having hot nurse sex.'

Beam thinks about this for a minute, stares out the window at the vivid hue of the stagnant marina, and decides: *That's probably about it.*

34

Ten-year-old Harvey sits this morning in the back of his father's Commodore, a slick of wetness between the back of his legs and the vinyl seat. Lionel Beam regards air-conditioning in cars as a reckless indulgence, the world going mad, and he never switches it on, not even on sweltering Shorton days like this.

It feels strange to be the only other person in the car besides his father. Can't remember when this has happened before. Even stranger that the rest of the world is at school right now while he got to leave early for a dentist appointment. A painful hole in his tooth.

His father had picked him up from school at 10am, an unwelcome disruption to Lionel's work day that had caused an argument between his parents the night before. But he seems less cranky now, Harvey notices. Was even friendly to Harvey's teacher, who he had never before met.

He looks at the back of his father's head as he drives, the neat clipping of his dark hair. Harvey could pull a face right now, stick his tongue out and cross his eyes, twirl his finger at the side of his head and point it at his father — he would never know. But Harvey can barely move for the strangeness of this setting.

If he was Penny or Naomi or even Bryan, he would think of something to say in this sticky, silent car (his father doesn't like the radio either — says it pollutes the air with stupidity). But Harvey can think of nothing that might not be the wrong thing, that thing that turns a normal moment into an explosion, and he hopes his thoughts aren't making any noise.

'Why don't you tell me where to go from here?' Harvey's father suddenly says over his shoulder.

Harvey is so taken aback he isn't sure he heard the words correctly. Says, 'What do you mean?'

'You tell me whether to go right or left and we'll see where we end up.'

Harvey's eyes dart about the car as though he's just been shaken awake and has no idea where he is. Doesn't know what to make of this request or how to respond. He looks out the rear window, desperate to recognise something – a shop, a park, a street sign. The right answer. But he has no idea where he is, for the family dentist is on the opposite side of the river to home. It's the side of town he doesn't know, an old swampish chequerboard of little streets, sinking houses and corner shops.

'Left,' Harvey hears himself say.

At the end of the street, Harvey's father turns the car left.

'What next?' his father says.

Harvey shivers with something that is either excitement or encroaching dread, he can't be sure. 'Right,' he says.

The car turns right.

'Left,' Harvey says.

His father turns left. Says, 'I hope you know where you're going, son.'

Harvey laughs nervously. Of course he doesn't know where he's going, but that's the game, isn't it?

A dozen or so more lefts and rights and go-straights and Harvey and his father are well beyond the city gates. The land is agricultural, the houses few and far between.

'Left,' says Harvey, now uncharacteristically jaunty in his father's company. They are both, he thinks, somewhere new here. Somewhere just beyond terror and loathing.

'There are no lefts or rights now, Harvey,' his father says.

'This is a highway. Can you see?'

Abruptly the car pulls to the shoulder of the road and Harvey's father waits for an oncoming road train to pass before he swiftly turns the car around. Looks at his watch, shakes his head, and makes the car go much faster than it was before. Dusty crops whizz by Harvey's window.

He isn't sure if the game has finished. Waits a minute or two, tries to read the silence, the pull of his father's jaw. Then Harvey says, with a hopeful smile in his voice: 'Right!'

Lionel Beam smacks his left hand hard against the top of the steering wheel; yells furiously at the windscreen and the world: 'You've *always* got to take things too far, don't you? You *never* fucking know when to stop. You're just so stupid.'

Harvey drops his head to his chest, looks down at the sweaty hands in his lap and wonders where he made the mistake. Hopes to God there's enough road left to let his father stop being mad.

***

Years later, many years later, on the eve of his father's funeral, Harvey looks back on this day and reads it with fresh eyes and a heart that isn't jumping out of his chest. His tongue finds the gap where his father had pulled the offending tooth out himself with pliers later that night. A new one had never grown through.

That strange car trip had not, he decides, been a botched game or even one of his father's many psychological tests. He hadn't imagined the forced shift in the atmosphere, the tiny gap between kindness and rage.

That day Lionel Beam had consciously made an effort to like the child that he simply, conclusively didn't.

35

St Emmanuel's is a beautiful church, less for what it is than what it isn't. It isn't grand and it isn't pretentious. The pulpit doesn't look like a Charlton Heston movie set. Though large, its dark panelling and original rough-hewn pews evoke a quaint colonial air. There is an authentic sense of modern history about the place, as though the walls have absorbed many a sermon, many desperate prayers, which in other churches merely bounce off the shiny tiles and gilt edges.

Harvey's first girlfriend, Wendy, had once given him a head job in the confessional box and he tries not to think about this as he moves down the centre aisle to take a seat at his father's funeral.

Predictable Beam drama had consumed the day's beginnings. Penny had discovered a spelling error in the funeral booklet and raced into her shop at 6am to redo the entire thing and print off new copies. Harvey had stayed behind at her house to mind the kids, innocently mentioning to Naomi via text message that he was struggling to find appropriate funeral wear in their cupboards. Appalled that Penny was letting the children attend *at all* — A funeral is NO place for kidz!!!!!!!!!!!!!! !!!!!!!!!!!!!!!!!!, she'd texted back (and he'd winced at the spelling and the excessive exclamation) — Naomi had then vented her exasperation to their mother. Lynn had subsequently had words with Penny, who in turn phoned her husband to instruct him, not for the first time, to *find a job in another fucking town.*

At some point in the morning, Naomi had decided that she

needed to speak at the funeral. She would be emotional but she could do it. Harvey had no idea why this had suddenly become a compelling necessity and he didn't dare ask. But it meant that Matt was ordered to get the kids out of the house while Naomi wrote frantically on the home computer, grief pouring out of her in the unedited blur of a late school assignment.

Matt had turned up at Penny's, his three boys in tow, and with Penny absent, the two men had let both sets of children go nuts on the computer while they shared a funereal beer in place of breakfast.

'I don't know why she feels she has to speak at the funeral,' Matt had said to Harvey at Penny's kitchen table. 'And she won't be able to do it. She won't. And she'll tear strips off herself for months and we'll all duck for cover. And then she'll read an inspiring quote somewhere and decide she needs to become a personal trainer for disabled people. And we'll all ride that wave.'

Harvey had laughed. 'But you do love her?' he asked, feeling suddenly protective of his sister and her many aborted plans and wild emotions.

And Matt had put his beer down on the table for emphasis and looked at Beam square on and said: 'God, yes, Harvey. I love your nutty sister an unspeakable amount.'

At this, Harvey had chinked his beer against Matt's and knew that this would probably be the high point of the day.

Within minutes, he was attending to Suze's own funeral drama: a missing shoe. Apparently she'd packed a pair of high-heeled black shoes in her luggage but only one shoe had survived the flight. 'Fucking baggage handlers,' she'd said to Harvey over the phone. 'All criminals.' Harvey had replied, helpfully he thought, that it was more likely that she'd only packed one shoe by mistake because it seemed an odd thing for a baggage handler to pilfer just one shoe and Suze had responded by telling him she had had some *very serious second thoughts* on their wedding day.

Harvey had rung his mother for a suggestion on where Suze might buy a pair of appropriate shoes on short notice and Lynn had responded with undisguised curtness: 'She's going shoe shopping? Before a funeral?' *Unbelievable.*

Beam suddenly turned over the thought in his mind that his own mother really didn't like the mother of his children. That possibly she'd been feigning affection all along and how had this fact never presented itself to him before? They'd always been polite on the phone.

Beam desperately wants today to be over.

In the midst of all this, he had called Grace to ask if she was coming to the funeral. If she'd made up her mind. In recent days she'd said she was undecided and would make a call on the day. She felt weird about Suze being there, about his kids being there, about Bryan, all of it. But she knew Harvey wanted her at the church — he'd made that clear in the ocean and in a dozen text messages since. Even though they wouldn't be sitting together, he would know Grace was there. This person who is not family and who likes Harvey even though she has a choice in the matter. It's a selfish request and he knows that.

But Grace didn't answer her phone this morning and so now, as Beam walks along the church aisle ahead of Suze, Jayne and Cate, and behind someone he suspects is an aunty, he is feeling slightly sick.

St Emmanuel's is about half full — so much for Bryan's standing-room-only expectations. Harvey takes a seat flanked by Cate and Jayne a few rows from the front. Ahead of them are Naomi and Matt with Lynn in between them, and ahead again is Penny, Simon and their boys.

He glances about the front of the church at the other attendees, a few of whom look faintly familiar. A cousin called Tom, a teacher from his old high school called Mrs Dalton (Beam has no idea of her connection with Lionel), Aunty Faye (who is not really his aunty), Hugh Traynor (*What is he thinking?*), and the city librarian with the French surname.

Bryan is at the front of the church, talking earnestly with the priest.

Beam wonders if any of the other guests are 'professional mourners', people who surreptitiously attend funeral services to sate either morbid curiosity or unquenchable pathos. He knows this to be a thing, having done a talkback segment about it a few years ago. An open-casket viewing is the money-shot for these people. Many are even bold enough to attend wakes, counting on clueless mourners to assume their legitimacy. Some with less disturbing intentions are just lonely souls in search of human connection and free hugs from strangers.

Harvey would happily pay any one of them to take his place today.

He glances toward the back of the church (no sign of Grace) and then turns his attention to the priest, a man in his early seventies at best, shiny face sprouting from a swathe of heavy cloth and sashes. He is looking out over the congregation, an ambitious term for this lot, Harvey thinks, and unmistakeably the man looks disappointed. Surely he must see, on days like this, a collection of disconnected people for whom religion is just scaffolding for major life events, nothing more.

Music is playing, he can't tell from where. It sounds like a choir or possibly just the 'choir' button on an organ. *Do organs exist anywhere outside of churches these days?* Beam suddenly recalls that the family who lived beside the Beams for most of his younger years were the proud owners of an organ, and Harvey had got to play it once. He couldn't believe that you could just press a button and a drumbeat started, masking all the imperfections of any attempt at melody. Beam had thought it pure genius and clearly the way of the future — death to the piano! He'd been one of the first people to buy a Beta video recorder too.

And he is thinking about anything now really to avoid thinking about this funeral.

One last look back to the entrance and, yes, he sees her.

Grace in a navy dress takes a seat in a pew behind the last of the gathering. He tries to catch her eye, wants to thank her with a smile, but she is focused on her feet and possibly being invisible.

The service finally begins, fifteen minutes late according to Harvey's phone, which he quickly flicks on 'silent' lest Murphy enacts his law. Maybe Bryan's private words to the priest were to allow some time for additional mourners to arrive. But save for Grace, there are no late arrivals.

Let's just get on with it.

Harvey looks down at his left knee just as Cate puts her hand on it. To his right, Suze has both Jayne's hands wrapped within hers. He is so grateful that they are here, that they know what Harvey needs sometimes better than he. For a second he feels a surge of pride, a heart swell that quickly slips into its more familiar guise: the sense that when it comes to keeping a family, Harvey has somehow got away with it so far. One more child and the odds are one would have hated him.

Father Steven introduces himself over the sound of the organist having a coughing fit and slipping out a side door. In fact, all the church doors are wide open — it's another broiling, airless Shorton day — and the effect is a steady backdrop of cars going past and trucks working through their gears and the occasional cacophony of birds. Reminders, if any were needed, that even when a life ceremoniously ends, the world keeps rolling on and, broadly speaking, doesn't give a shit.

Harvey senses movement to his right and feels a tap on his shoulder. It's Suze reaching behind Jayne to get his attention. She is all mouth-gestures and dancing eyebrows. *Is she here?* he finally understands her as saying. *The nurse?* And Harvey shrugs in a hadn't-even-occurred-to-me way.

Suze glares at him, quickly and all too aware of the circumstances, but still right through his eyeballs to the back of his skull.

Beam thinks, *She will find her.* She will find her and she

will make an immediate appraisal. An appraisal that she will subsequently refine within a relatively short space of time but ultimately come back to because Suze loyally trusts her first instincts and always has.

Harvey looks properly at the casket for the first time. His father in a box with flowers on top. Flowers chosen by whom? Most likely Bryan. Maybe the funeral organisers or maybe the church. He wonders how much organisational minutiae he has been left out of in recent days. He could have formed an opinion on flowers if pressed.

'This is so weird,' Cate whispers to Harvey.

'What is?'

'Everything,' Cate says. 'Funerals. They're just so *weird*.'

'I guess so,' Beam says, not really sure which things are most presenting themselves as odd to his daughter. But he envies it, this third-eye perspective inherent to Cate's generation. He was never one to question rituals and traditions, things presented as part of life by people who had been around longer. Cate, however, and the young radio producers he has worked with in recent years share a cool suspicion about pretty much everything, especially if it predates social media.

Harvey looks about the church, at the audience gathered for a dead host and a sexless man in a dress, at a group of people connected by one person's mortality, quietly shaken by this reminder of their own. He decides Cate's assessment is not unfair: funerals *are* weird.

A truck outside howls to an inelegant stop and Beam realises he is now on his knees and can't remember getting there. Fortunately everyone around him is kneeling too. *At least one person here must know what they're doing,* he thinks.

'The reality of death,' the priest says, 'confronts us all today and it is this collective sorrow that brings us together.'

Father Steven looks out to the congregation and then somewhere well beyond them.

'But there is something else that unites us today,' he says.

Beam whispers quietly to his eldest daughter: 'Obligation.'

'It is faith,' says the priest.

Harvey reaches into his jacket pocket, double-checks that his phone is off.

'Faith opens our minds to the big picture ... life, death, love and forgiveness. It gives us strength. It gives us hope for what lies beyond death. For Lionel's next journey, beyond what we know.'

Harvey looks hard at his father's casket. *Christ. Let this be it. Journey over.*

Father Steven moves on, through retribution, through sin, through grief and unconditional love. Through Serving the Lord and something about sheep. Through walking towards the Light and, Beam thinks to himself, being so blinded by it that you can't see anything else for several minutes at a time.

Finally, having made his best fist at converting at least one of the hapless sinners in these ill-fitting pews, the priest introduces Bryan. And Harvey realises now, with a grinding twist of his gut, that this is what he has been silently dreading about today: a summation of their father by the only son permitted to get close to him. The laying bare of the Beam family's wildly unequal playing field for everyone to publicly question and assess. One version of a dead man that will do nothing to explain the trail marks of Harvey's adolescence.

Because if Beam is honest with himself, and he feels inclined to be today, it's the numbers game that bothers him most. For it's one thing for a father to let loose a child without explanation and certainly without regret, but it's another entirely for a sibling to follow suit, for the two of them to be united in their disinterest. It just, well, it looks bad.

In his more morose moments, usually after too much red wine or on his birthday or both, Harvey again suspects he has given Lionel and Bryan more to jointly criticise than any poorly written thesis, more joy than they would ever wish to unpick in the name of family. Merciless assessments of

Harvey's intellectual failings might represent the ultimate in academic downtime. But then, when he has a clearer head, Beam is embarrassed to realise just how self-important the very idea sounds. And how unfair it is to assume that Bryan is just another version of their father, two peas in the proverbial, when really he doesn't know Bryan at all.

Maybe Bryan's whole life has sucked because he didn't, couldn't, fly away.

Beam's brother steps up to the lectern, all elbows and loose paper. He looks nervous, but Harvey suspects there isn't a 'confident' look in Bryan's repertoire. Not once looking up from his notes, Bryan reads in an unbroken tone details about Lionel Beam's life that, to Harvey (and surely everyone else here, he thinks), sound more like a job application than a eulogy.

Much of it Harvey hadn't known: the multiple research awards, a Distinguished Professor prize, international citations, key speaker invitations and prestigious conferences. His father was undoubtedly an anomaly in a town whose highest educational option remains TAFE. Harvey briefly wonders why his father chose to stay here when he might easily have secured a position at a sandstone university somewhere.

Then, for no clear reason, Bryan reads a quote from Thomas Cromwell, who, as he explains to the presumably unenlightened gathering, was chief minister to King Henry VIII. Harvey briefly recalls his father's PhD dissertation being about the Tudor period. Bryan reads: *My Prayer is that God give me no longer life that I shall be glad to use mine office in edification, and not in destruction.*

Suze catches Harvey's eye and mouths a none-too-subtle *What the?* Beam shrugs back at her.

Bryan continues: 'Before and of course during his rich academic life, the legacy of which will endure to the benefit of generations of historians and students, Lionel raised a family including myself and two daughters, Penny and Naomi, and they themselves have children of their own.'

To Harvey's left, he sees Cate's hands turn upwards in her lap in a *what-the-hell?* fashion.

Bryan's pace now quickens. 'And so,' he says, 'Lionel Beam dies a grandfather and sadly not a great-grandfather, although great he most certainly was. As a father, Lionel believed in discipline, respect and honesty, and we as children are the beneficiaries of that approach. Society is the beneficiary of that approach and all who execute it.'

With that Bryan appears to be finished. He folds his papers in half, nods to the priest, glances at Lionel Beam's casket, and walks off the pulpit.

Harvey's eyes don't work. He blinks and blinks until the focus returns. His throat starts swallowing by itself. Feels as though he's somewhere on either side of this moment, before when it couldn't possibly happen and after when it just did. He feels someone's hand on his shoulder and shakes it off. Briefly considers lifting both his legs onto the pew in front of him and kicking with the full force of his chest.

Cannot fucking believe it. And yet he should and he does and he knows he will. Over and over again, for all the years he has left. Harvey thinks: *This changes everything. And I imagined none of it.* Bryan's final act of devotion to their father was Harvey's humiliation.

Complete omission of his name.

Of his very existence.

In front of his own family.

In front of everyone.

And just as quickly as the fire roared into his head, it stops. And Harvey thinks, in spite of himself, in spite of the injustice that can't be undone, *It doesn't fucking matter.*

And this too: *It never fucking did.*

As he thinks this and wonders if he really means it, if any unbidden emotion can ever be truly trusted, Beam sees Matt clumsily work his way out of the pew in front of him and walk up to the lectern. The priest is there again, talking into his big book, and he looks up sharply at the interloper, at Matt looking certain and uncertain at the same time. And the two men exchange words that no-one else can hear and Father Steven recedes to the side of the pulpit and Matt stands squarely at the lectern. And speaks.

'Hi,' he says. 'I'm Matt. Married to Naomi.'

Matt gestures to the location of his wife with a nod of his head.

'I'm not part of the schedule on your booklet there and I hadn't planned to speak, but Naomi isn't quite feeling up to it, so yeah. Look, I didn't actually know Lionel Beam very well and I don't know that I was ever going to. But I sort of think every life should be celebrated and people should be remembered properly, and I think Bryan did a good job of outlining the many achievements Lionel had in his career. I actually didn't know a lot about all of that academic stuff, so I guess one of Lionel's qualities was that he was a fairly humble man. And I think there's a lot to be said for humility.'

Harvey glances about for Bryan and finally spots him sitting on his own in one of the side pews flanking the stage. He is looking down at his hands, still holding his sheafs of paper.

Matt grips each side of the lectern now. He looks over at Naomi, who is now weeping with full shoulder-shudders.

'I think,' he continues, 'that grief is different for everyone. And not just because some of us are tougher than others or just, you know, wired differently. It's more because we all know different sides of a person.'

Harvey feels movement beside him. Suze is swapping places with Jayne, untidily for her patent efforts to do so unnoticed. She grabs Beam's knee with her hand and squeezes it roughly. Less affection than a prediction of battle. Suze is angry and it's firing out of her pores.

'It's okay,' Harvey whispers to her and diverts her eyes to focus on Matt.

Matt continues: 'Bryan's version of his dad is different to Naomi's, different to Penny's, and vastly different to Harvey's. I'm not sure that Harvey was mentioned in Bryan's speech, but yeah. There was Harvey too and he's a bloody champ.'

Matt now runs his hand, almost violently, through his hair. He might have expected Naomi to back out of speaking, Harvey thinks, but he clearly hadn't planned to do it himself. His discomfort fills the church and Beam is immensely grateful for it.

'Lionel and Lynn had four kids,' he goes on. 'Bryan, Harvey, Penny and Naomi, in that order. I don't think Lynn was mentioned either, but yeah, Lynn was a big help to Lionel when he changed careers and she's a terrific mum to his kids. She's a terrific grandmum too. Because I think, look, I don't know ...'

Matt pauses here. Then says emphatically, 'Shit.' And immediately, 'Sorry Father.'

The priest nods back with a wan smile.

Matt says: 'Parenting is probably the toughest gig of all. I find it really, really hard and I don't even do that much of it. The only easy bit, I think, is loving them. And it's the first and most important thing we owe our kids, every single kid, in exchange for dragging them here. You meet people who didn't get that love and you see that life is different for them. All the little things, they're just ... harder. And they make it harder too, for themselves, because no-one tells them not to.'

A ripple of wind moves through the church, ruffling restless shirtsleeves and Penny's hard-won booklets.

'So anyway,' Matt says, his voice now sounding as if it's about to expire, 'you're probably thinking, what does any of this have to do with Lionel Beam?'

He waits here for an answer from the audience, possibly hoping for something better than the one he has, which is, it transpires: 'I dunno. Whatever you want it to. Just, you know, whatever.'

Then he fiddles nervously with the microphone, as though

just noticing its presence for the first time, and the effect is to issue a violent stab of feedback throughout the hall. '*God!*' Matt says, as frantic hands fly up to assaulted ears and Penny's children squeal. Father Steven drops his head to the floor, to the feet he can't see beneath his robes, exhausted by all of mankind.

But Matt is not apparently finished. 'The more important thing I want to say up here is this,' he continues. 'We're having a wake for Lionel Beam at my place and you're all welcome. I've got stacks of home-brew and my neighbour, the nice one, not the idiot, lent me some chairs. Just follow someone from here who knows the way to my place. Make it around two o-clock-ish, though, or I won't have cleaned out the garage and Naomi will rip me a new one.'

At this, a semi-generous whorl of laughter rises from the floor.

'If you're interested,' Matt says, inhaling the laughter, 'I'll be taking a few tour groups through my bonsai shed from about four when the beer kicks in.'

Matt looks down at Naomi hopefully, and Harvey can't see her response but he hopes that she's proud of her husband. He hopes she understands.

And he hopes Lionel Beam, from his keynote position at the front of the room, heard all of it.

Harvey reaches behind Suze to tap Jayne on the shoulder, not because he wants to tell her something but because he wants to look back at Grace now without it seeming obvious to Suze.

Jayne mouths 'What?' and Harvey says, 'You okay?' and this gives him just enough time to furtively move his gaze to the rear of the church where he sees Grace. He sees the back of Grace leaving the church through the front door. She is walking quickly and with one hand raised to the side of her face. Is it possible she's upset, Harvey thinks, on his behalf? *Embarrassed?*

Instantly he wants to text her but Suze's presence has a

bodyguard feel to it. All personal space has been exhumed.

Father Steven leads them now in a song, a hymn that squeezes twenty-eight lines of scripture into eight lines of music, like every hymn ever written. Nothing rhymes and not a single true note is struck by the collective warblers. Then he says a final prayer, and a grateful group 'Amen' rises to the high ceiling.

And it is done.

It is done.

Harvey checks now to see what he is feeling, just as he's attempted at least once a day for the past five. Whether there's been a change, any change at all from a dim nothingness. From an opaque sense of anti-climax and muted failure at the departure of Lionel Beam. *Anything?*

He isn't sure. Maybe something has shifted, maybe it hasn't. He's starting to suspect that anger is the only emotion he'd readily identify in a line-up these days.

'Right,' says Suze, as the crowd starts to extricate itself from the narrow pews. 'I'm talking to Bryan.'

'No,' says Harvey, tugging her sleeve to sit back down. 'Don't worry about it, Suze. Honestly, what's the point?'

Suze's cheeks flood crimson. 'The point is that he's completely fucked in the head and he made you look *stupid*, Harvey.' She is madder than he's ever seen her, at least in recent years. 'He deliberately hurt you in front of everyone. What a ...' and Suze flounders a little here, momentarily tempered by the expectations of the venue. But she gets there in the end with: 'Cock. Just a right cock.'

Beam is about to try a different tack with his ex-wife, a sideways manoeuvre to prevent her from flying at Bryan like a winged monkey, but he is too late. Suze is off, marching purposefully in the direction of his brother, who is stood now beside their father's coffin.

Harvey hurries after her, noting his mother's worried gaze as he passes her seat. Feeling his sisters' eyes on his back.

Feeling his daughters stumbling behind. He is a step behind Suze as she reaches Bryan.

'What the *hell* was that all about, Bryan?' she says, gesturing manically in the direction of the lectern. 'What *exactly* were you hoping to achieve there?'

Bryan looks oddly at Suze, as though he's trying to place her, and Harvey suddenly remembers that it has been years (and maybe twenty hairstyles on Suze's part) since the two of them have seen each other.

Finally Bryan says: 'I'm sorry, Suzanne. What do you mean?'

'Not including Harvey,' she says, thrusting both hands in the air. 'Not even mentioning that he was a son of Lionel's too. Why would you *do* that?'

Bryan looks down at his shoes, which Harvey once again notices are completely at odds with his otherwise conservative dress code. *Are those tassels?*

'I'm sorry,' Bryan says. 'It's just one perspective.'

Suze's eyes widen, her red lipstick now a slash of fury. 'Perspective is not *fact*,' she says. 'Fact is fact, Bryan. Lionel and Lynn had four kids. Just like I had two. There is no perspective on how many children exit a vagina.'

Of all the words uttered today, 'vagina' seems to ricochet most wildly off the oak panelling. Beam grimaces.

'Suzanne, I didn't write the eulogy,' Bryan says. 'I was just the one to read it out.'

Suze looks at Bryan in confusion, then quickly at Harvey, who is now looking at the casket to their right.

Beam gets it now. Understands what power would motivate Bryan to make himself look mean-spirited, or clearly wrong at the very least.

'He wrote it,' says Harvey, shrugging at the flower-draped box. 'Dad wrote it.'

'He asked me to read it,' Bryan says, looking at Harvey with an uncertain expression that might be guilt or remorse or the absence of both. 'It was the last thing he said to me.'

Beam looks at the creased sheafs of thin paper hanging limply in Bryan's hands. Old man's paper. Says to Bryan: 'Hell of a dying wish.'

'Yes,' Bryan says, and Harvey wonders what it would feel like to punch him out right now, punch him hard. John Jackson style.

Possibly sensing Harvey's unwelcome urge (Suze had once dragged him away from a sightseeing walk along The Gap because she correctly intuited Harvey's silent compulsion to leap into its nothingness), his ex-wife now grabs his elbow to lead him back to their daughters and out of the church. She turns back to Bryan only once but directs her parting comment at Lionel Beam's coffin.

'What a fucker,' she says.

***

A small crowd mills at the front of the church. Back-row attendees retreat on tiptoe to the car park. Streaky clouds cool the air and the footpath. Naomi is sitting on a stone step, Matt beside her, his arm around her shoulders. Penny's husband is cradling their youngest while also appearing to inspect the tyres on a large ute.

Beam's mother is deep in discussion with Penny, but as Harvey approaches it's clear they are waiting for him. Suze peels away from Beam's side just as a conversation with his mother appears unavoidable.

'Harvey,' she says, brushing some small apparent thing off her son's shoulder. 'I just don't understand. What did you say to Bryan in the hospital? Why would he do that?'

And Beam blinks hard at his mother, at this request for an explanation, of all things.

'*Mum*,' Penny barks at Lynn. 'It's not Harvey's fault.'

'I didn't say it was his *fault*, Penny. I'm just trying to understand why it happened.'

Penny throws her gaze upward. Her face looks as though it's done a carnival of funerals today rather than just one. 'Everything doesn't have an explanation, Mum. People do shitty things all the time.'

At this, Cate steps up to her father's side — Harvey hadn't even realised both daughters were standing behind him (a blind spot he'd had since they'd been able to walk) — and she looks at her grandmother and then at Penny. She explains to them that Lionel had written his own eulogy, had asked Bryan to read it. That it was his 'dying wish', quoting her father directly, and in hearing her do so, Harvey is relieved he didn't say many of the other things that had streaked across the windscreen of his forehead just minutes ago.

'He didn't need to do that,' Penny says, shaking her head. 'He shouldn't have done that.'

But Lynn seems unconvinced, shaking her head slightly and glancing left and right to check, it seems, for onlookers. 'Maybe he didn't feel he had a choice,' she says.

The air is abruptly split by the sound of a plane tearing low above their heads and Beam instinctively lifts his gaze to watch until it disappears or plummets without warning.

He can't take it anymore, any of it, not today. Can't have one more conversation like this. Can't listen to the women of the Beam family unpick and rethread versions of reality that best marry with the way they've always seen things. Far from tending to wounds, they are simply reviewing the military strategy.

He leads Cate and Jayne away from the church, from the event he had presciently dreaded, and from Lionel Beam. He'll be buggered if he's going to the cemetery.

Beam has no idea where Suze is now. Or Grace for that matter. But he will not be following any hearse. He will not be filing any additional efforts today under the headings of obligation and respect. He is done with this.

'Let's get a milkshake,' he says to his daughters.

36

ON AIR

'Maybe it was the first thing that occurred to you this morning. Maybe it wasn't until you wrote down the date. September 11. A month and a number that have come to mean so much more. They conjure instantly in our minds pictures of burning towers, of ashen faces craned skyward, of desperate leaps toward an unimaginable death. Perhaps what you most remember — I know it's what I most vividly recall — was that sense of collective disbelief, of sheer incredulity, a sort of numbness. It felt like everything, in a single day, had changed irrevocably. That nothing would or could ever be the same again. The future turned into a giant, terrifying question mark. Would there even be a future? Was this the beginning of the end?' *Pause. Two beats.* 'And here we are. Ten years down the track. Living in the future we doubted might exist. And things *have* changed irrevocably and many changes can easily be pinned to that day. Others have been more subtle, a kind of slow burn.'

Breathe.

'Today I don't want to talk about the political fallout from the September 11 terrorist attacks. In many ways, we talk about that daily on this show, every time we talk about protecting our borders and international security and what sort of immigrants we want and don't want. It's all related in some way to the brand new set of fears we inherited on September

11 and through the subsequent "war on terror". The war on whatever.'

It's a long intro, a little self-indulgent, but Beam figures it's justifiable.

'No, today I want to talk about the human fallout from September 11. Because I read earlier this week that at least ten thousand people in the US — emergency workers, police officers and everyday citizens — have been found to have post-traumatic stress disorder as a result of their exposure to the events of September 11. They have recurrent nightmares, they can't sleep, they jump at every little thing. They no longer trust easily, they love less fully. They self-medicate to devastating effect.

'And,' he continues, 'they're not getting any better. Which is why the US government is now spending at least four billion dollars — that's *billion*, folks — on getting September 11 victims to start talking again. To talk about what they saw, how it made them feel and how they're coping. I'm in the right game, you see, because it turns out that talking about things, really talking about things to people who will listen and attempt to understand, is the best hope for the future of this damaged human race. Whatever pain lurks in your soul, the pathway out is through your mouth.

'Today you're going to hear from a panel of guests who were in various different ways directly exposed to the September 11 attacks. They are all Australians who happened to be in New York at the time, either holidaying or working there. And they've all come home with baggage they've never completely unpacked.

'After you've heard their stories, which I think you'll find both motivating and inspiring, I want you to call in with your own September 11 stories. Do you remember how you felt when you first heard what had happened? Where were you when you saw those unimaginable pictures on the television? Perhaps you were in New York at the time, one of the thousands of

Aussies who live and holiday there on any given day. Perhaps you saw things you'll never forget.

'Perhaps it's time to talk.'

And they do. Listeners dial the station in waves unbroken, many just to share their own where-I-was-when-the-Towers-collapsed-on-TV moments — a caravan park in Ryde, an arrested hangover in Kiama, a final wedding gown fitting that felt like a funeral. Some ring with unrelated tales of trauma (that Beam elegantly deflects in the manner of a batsman who respects the off-form bowler). But many others still — and this is what Harvey and his producer had openly hoped for — call in with first-person accounts of being on the ground in New York at the time. About their instinctive reactions, both immediate and now ten years down the track.

Talkback at its best: compelling pictures painted in the gaps between words, in hollow sighs, faltering breaths and the pure honesty that only hiding behind a voice can provide. The events might have happened yesterday, so vivid are many of the descriptions of smoky calamity and swirling panic. Beam is an untiring fieldsman of the storytelling, covering every position.

It's one of those days on air, so much rarer now than when he started in this game, that finds Beam hearing each word as it's spoken, not just in anticipation of the next question and not only hours later during another pointless attempt at sleep. He is in the moment today, the sweet spot, and he hears not only the human battle cries of loss and despair but beyond that, a clear common thread: *family.*

For almost every caller, every rundown soul, tells a story of a day that ended, inevitably somehow, at Point A. Blood. Family. The origin of the species.

Even those for whom family had come to represent something painful, or dangerous, or simply something so long ago that phone numbers have been erased, photos lost, heirlooms sold at garage sales ... they'd each followed their legs home. Powerless, pained, lost and found. They returned to childhood homes that had long been rebuilt. To grown-up daughters who hadn't spoken to them for twenty years. To ex-husbands, ex-wives, grandparents long forgotten. To whatever, in the face of the unspeakable and the unknown, looked like a sanctuary one might be entitled to or where, amidst the unbearable noise of it all, one mightn't have to say anything at all.

Strip it all back and douse it in fear and all that is left in this world is family. That's the message from today's program. Common noses. Shared bedrooms. Drunken grandpas. Hand-me-downs. Old jokes. Irrevocable damage. Brutality. Joy. Fear. Neglect. Hope.

It all starts and ends with family.

Beam finds it deeply irritating and profoundly concerning.

37

In the darker days after his separation from Suze, before the genuine matter of his singledom had set in and given his flagging libido a fresh and guiltless cause, Beam had contemplated suicide. Not in the very deliberate way of the purposeful, but rather as an abstract idea that swam into his brain on occasion, unbidden and therefore momentarily arresting. It usually coincided with a macabre opportunity, an afternoon's walk at The Gap, wild waves at Avalon, or a long drive down the coast passing oncoming trucks. It was never more than a one-minute thought excursion and he often wondered if this was the tiny window of madness into which most suicides fell. Just a thought, just a jump to the left. A minute's silence, please? Instantly regrettable if that were possible.

But he knew of exceptions too. A second cousin. Not close to Harvey in adulthood but they'd spent many a summer locked in bloodied cricket crusades as children. When Beam learned two years ago that Gerard had taken his life, had overdosed on pills ordered several months earlier, had shored up his family's finances, changed his life insurance policy and penned his beloved wife and four children long earnest letters of explanation, love and absolution, well, he had developed a new respect for suicide. And for Gerard.

Beam's mother had said the funeral had swirled with rumours of sexual abuse by a priest at Gerard's boarding school circa year five. And Harvey remembers thinking, *Fair enough, Gerard. Your call, mate.*

He is grateful, then, that Cate and Jayne are sitting with him here in this sweltering coffee shop, killing the time they would have otherwise have spent watching Lionel Beam's coffin descend into the earth, because he might have gravitated to suicide-lite this afternoon. Might have ventured down to Shorton River, sat too long and started thinking... how? *Now?*

Because even dead, Lionel Beam had managed to wound Harvey. And if there is no end to the race away from his father, if it can't stop here, on this day, then he's not sure if he has the heart to keep going. It's just too fucking exhausting.

But he looks now at his daughters, sitting here today in a town far from their home because of him. For him. Quietly watching him stir his coffee. He remembers Suze's words all those years ago, about the most important family being the one you create yourself. And he knows she was right.

But it's still exhausting.

'Dad, I think I might stay here for a while,' Cate says. 'In Shorton.'

'Really?' Harvey says and looks at Jayne for any sign of surprise. But they've clearly discussed this already.

'I really love working in Penny's shop and I'm getting lots of experience and I thought maybe, like, I could do this for, like, a gap year or maybe six months or nine or eleven months and then come back to Sydney maybe and do... like, something, I don't know. A course. Or go somewhere else even.'

'Sounds like a hell of a plan, Cate,' Harvey says with a playful wink at Jayne. 'Is there a spreadsheet to go with it?'

Cate laughs. Shrugs.

'What about your mother?' Beam says. 'What do you think she'll say about it?'

'I thought,' Cate says sheepishly, 'that maybe you could tell her?'

'Well,' Harvey says, making a pistol out of his right hand and aiming it at his temple. 'I look forward to that conversation, Cate.'

'What about you, Dad?' says Jayne, tucking her too-short fringe habitually and fruitlessly behind her ear. 'When are you coming back home?'

Beam looks for an answer in the dregs of his cold coffee. *Nothing*. 'Don't know,' he says. 'Unlike Cate here, I'm not great with solid plans.'

'I think you should come home with me and Mum,' Jayne says. 'I don't think this place is good for you.'

Beam understands she's talking about the funeral. Of the public portrait of a family with one face heavily pixelated. Jayne is so like her mother, he thinks, when it comes to lining up cause and effect.

'I'm thinking about it, Jayne,' he says. 'There are a few things to weigh up.'

'Yeah, like the nurse he's schtooping,' Cate says to Jayne and loudly slurps the last of her milkshake for effect.

'God, Cate!' Beam exclaims. And at the same time, in that very instant, he sees himself in the ocean, Grace astride him, kissing like teenagers. How that scene would look to his children. Feels his jaw burn, red hot. *God*.

'I'm not *schtooping* anyone,' he says.

Grace aside, Beam had always thought he'd be much better at this: taking to his children about sex. At the very least, fielding a question about it without hiding behind an imagined pillar. As young parents, he and Suze had enjoyed ridiculing their own parents' pathetic attempts to articulate human affection. The mechanics of it. The need for it. They would never leave their children to work it out for themselves. And yet they had, for the most part. Talk of walking about the house naked for the benefit of the children's development had quickly given way to blushing deference to the children's development. Sex was taken care of, quietly, on Sunday mornings. Mostly. Once they had been caught by Cate — she would have been five maybe — and they made up an elaborate story about furniture arranging and a sudden heatwave. The birds-and-the-bees discussion had never happened with either daughter. Despite the best of intentions, Suze and Harvey had both known that by the time they were ready to sit the girls down for the awkward chat, the girls already knew everything. Probably more than Suze and Harvey did. Best not to go there.

'Where *is* your bloody mother?' Beam says finally. 'She just disappeared after the funeral. Is she going to the wake?'

'Are *we* going to the wake?' asks Cate.

Beam isn't sure about this. He wants today to be over. Just ... *done*. But at the same time he feels an urge to thank Matt for his words at the funeral, not to mention a disquieting sense that today isn't yet done with him.

'I suppose so,' Harvey says finally. 'If you girls want to.'

Cate looks at Jayne, who returns a noncommittal shrug.

'Nothing else around here to do,' Cate says. 'Unless you're cool with us getting a couple of tatts each and an early drug habit.'

Jayne laughs, but for once Beam is unimpressed with his elder daughter's sass. 'That's enough,' he says. 'This is where I grew up.'

He has no idea from where that sentiment arose or whether it has any shred of truth about it. White-hot day of madness.

'Anyway, we need to find your mum first,' Beam says, signalling to the waitress for the bill. She signals in return that he needs to get off his arse and pay at the counter. And as he does so, Harvey's back pocket vibrates and he pulls out his phone and sees a message from Suze that reads, inexplicably: I'm with Grace.

He puts his phone on the counter and stares at it for a very long time.

38

As she later recounted to Beam, Suze had sure enough spotted Grace in the church early on, before the first round of mumbled warbling in fact, thanks to Harvey's clunky attempts at the furtive glance. She'd also seen Grace leave the church prematurely and knew at once the nervy walk of a woman upset and keen to disappear.

Suze had known that if Grace was on foot, she would soon find herself on a walking trail into the nearby botanic gardens, an ambitious description for a tangle of unkempt warrens and broken benches. And this is where she'd found Grace, sitting on the edge of a dry fountain and looking into her hands.

'I'm Suzanne,' she'd said to Grace as she approached the fountain, momentarily startling the woman and causing her cheeks and neck to flush like algae bloom.

'Sorry, love. I'm Harvey's wife. Ex-wife. Very ex.'

Grace had looked up at Suze, suitably mystified.

Suze plundered forth, feeling that she was doing good here and would be able to say the right thing once she'd determined the cause of Grace's sadness. It was her gift.

It transpired that in attending a funeral she'd almost not attended and now wished she hadn't, Grace had come face to face with her past. With her first husband, the man whose love for her had somehow withered on a childless vine. Who had let her go when she'd said she wanted to go — a request she'd made partly to hear what it sounded like outside of her skull. A man she'd thought about ever since but had never contacted and hadn't known how. He wasn't on Facebook, a fact that did not surprise her. Grace had heard he'd moved to the country, settled down. She'd heard he moved overseas. What had become of him? Her Matthew.

Matt.

'*Fuck,*' says Harvey, toe to toe with Suze on the driveway at the front of Matt and Naomi's home. Cars are parked at odd angles all over the front lawn. The wake is in full swing. Their daughters are inside.

'I know,' says Suze. '*I know.* It's unbelievable. They were married and everything. Not for long, but still. Married.'

Harvey looks down at his feet, at Suze's feet. His head is moving side to side of its own volition. 'Fuck,' he says.

'I know.'

'*Bloody hell.*'

'I know!' Suze seems increasingly pleased that Harvey's reaction is commensurate to the size of the news and her delivery of it.

'She's mentioned him to me before,' Harvey says, finally leaving the comfort of dumbstruck obscenity. 'She said she was married, they'd tried to have a kid and couldn't, so she'd gone overseas to work as a nurse somewhere, some sad and poor place, and that was it. They'd lost touch. She didn't seem heartbroken, but maybe ... who knows. Shit.'

'Well, it would have been confronting today to see him standing up in front of everyone, effectively saving the day. To know that he's remarried and has children. No matter how you feel now, that would be difficult,' Suze says.

Harvey nods. Suze puts a hand on his shoulder and then removes it, deciding it's not Harvey who most needs comforting.

'Did Matt see her?' he asks after a long pause, during which a family he doesn't know files past them wielding things covered in alfoil.

'She said she doesn't think so,' Suze says. 'She said she hopes not.'

'Do you think I should call her?'

'Maybe,' Suze says. 'I don't really know.'

Harvey takes this to mean yes.

'Fuck,' he says.

'*I know.*'

With this, Suze throws up her arms in a flippant oh-well-must-run gesture that looks utterly unconvincing to Harvey and she strides into Matt and Naomi's home as though there is still much more interference to be run before the day is out.

Beam looks at his phone. At the sky. At the phone. At the faded 'No Junk Mail' sign on the mailbox and the kaleidoscope of catalogues bulging out of its slot.

He hadn't meant to find Grace. He hadn't *asked* to find Grace. This isn't his fault, and yet somehow he feels responsible for a woman he hardly knows, at least not in the sense of time and injury, walking tearfully out of a funeral for all the wrong reasons. He has done this, brought old worlds together via the clusterfuck of his own. Even if you walk softly through this life, you hurt others, he thinks. Probably just as well he's never bothered to.

Looks at his phone. Types: Grace, are you okay? Can we talk?

39

Wakes are the loosest of social ceremonies and the most fraught. Harvey did a whole morning of talk on this a few years ago after a wake in south-west Sydney erupted into gang war and arrests. 'Macca would be happy' was the front-page splash of the *Telegraph*, a quote from one of the deceased's brothers tendered as a statement to police in the paddy wagon.

The assumption by people about the recently deceased's send-off expectations — usually with a subtext along the lines of *He would have wanted us to get shitfaced* — makes for many unsatisfactory wakes. Listeners made the case to Beam that wakes should be abandoned altogether; they do nothing to aid grieving and are frequently hijacked by strangers looking for either a party or a cause. Others said wakes could have greater purpose with a set framework just like funerals — a run sheet and an endpoint. Others still justified the free-for-all approach — death is shitty. It deserves chaos.

Harvey remembers one call that day in particular, from a middle-aged woman who'd recently buried her mother, a stoic matriarch who, when she knew she was dying, began baking and freezing in earnest so that the wake would not be catered for with anything less than her best recipes. Everyone subsequently sat about a churchyard nibbling Nanna's famous fruitcake, four months in the deep freeze and shrouded in imminent death. *Delicious*, they said.

He is thinking about this as he wends his way through the current confusion in Naomi's house, wondering if Lionel has left a few careful instructions for the wake just as he did for the funeral. But there is too much haphazard movement in here, Beam decides, and even the venue — a house of roaming boys and hopeful furnishings — feels as though Lionel Beam might never have set foot in it.

The place is heaving with sweaty, tentative people. There's a gaggle shoring up martyrdom in the kitchen, nuking sausage rolls and relaying headcounts on the number of children gathered around the game device in the lounge room. There are people gathered in tiny circles of earnest chat, surreptitiously eyeing off other circles. There are men laughing loudly, bottles of Matt's unlabelled home-brew in their hands, beads on their brows. There are shrew-eyed women moving between everything, working it all out.

Beam wanders through as though invisible, expected at the next juncture. He heads straight out the back door and down the side yard towards Matt's shed where three men he doesn't know bundle out of the metal door in rambunctious laughter. Matt follows them, issues a hardy cheers with beer aloft and then spots Harvey.

Beam smiles at Matt but feels like someone practising at smiles. Matt puts his beer down on the uneven grass where it promptly falls over. He reaches out his arms to Harvey and pulls him roughly into a bear hug.

In one of those half-minutes that splices through time and moorings, Beam pictures Matt as his best friend. A real buddy. They're fishing on Sunday mornings, testing out a first batch of new home-brew, laughing uproariously at a shared observation, nodding sagely the next — the wisdom of brothers. He sees this all in Shorton settings, as it would need to be, and it seems odd and yet utterly plausible that the family he's kept at highways' length for so many years should finally deliver him that tricky thing: a real male friend.

He's never been able to shape this for himself in Sydney and certainly not after he and Suze broke up. She'd been the library monitor of their shared friendships, always reminding him to phone someone (usually a husband of one of her friends) because it was the anniversary of something or to organise a hit of tennis because nascent friendships die in the first few months if nothing is scheduled, apparently.

Beam has always enjoyed good associations with people at work and might justifiably call many of them his friends, but even he knows these connections fail certain tests: none of them live in his phone, he can't remember any of their kids' names, he actively avoids them on public transport. It's unlikely any of these relationships, as loud and privileged and funny as they seem within the station's walls and floors, would survive beyond work.

And I don't work there anymore, so there's that.

People want to be Harvey's friend, of course, in the way that people feel a certain ownership of public figures. They pat him on the back at his local coffee shop, address him by his first name to comment on a recent talkback topic, even wave at him on the train in a casually intimate manner. Perhaps because of this, and knowing that close family friendships had been an option he'd cut off himself, Beam has never felt lonely or obviously friendless. He's never felt the need to replace empty encounters with anything solid. If you don't look friendless, it's hard to feel it. And he's always had Suze, even now.

Pulling out of Matt's beery embrace, Harvey looks upon his brother-in-law as someone who could have been a clear contender for more substantial friend material. He is that wonderful thing: a good bloke.

A good bloke once married to Grace.

'Need some shed time?' Matt asks and doesn't wait for a reply. He ushers Beam into the tin bunker, produces two fresh beers and looks at the roof.

Harvey waits for him to say her name.

Instead, Matt says loudly, 'Here's to Lionel Beam.' And he lifts his beer above his head.

Confused but compliant, Harvey does the same.

Aping majesty, Matt continues: 'May all of his earthly opinions reach him at his new address!'

'No lost luggage,' Beam pipes in.

'May there be books!'

Harvey adds: 'That he's already read.'

'May there be non-stop FM radio talkback!' Matt says.

'Nothing but shit all day long.'

'And may you, Harvey Beam,' Matt continues, 'find peace now. Find a little bonsai.' And with this toast, Matt thrusts his beer extra skyward, causing it to shoot out foamy spray.

'Wait,' he adds with a comedic head-turn, 'you've already found a piece now, Harvey. The nurse. Here's to you, Don Juan!'

Beam makes a laughing sound. He sees that Matt couldn't possibly have seen Grace at the funeral today or is making a really bad joke. Finds himself beginning to say something, words that get lost as he moves around them, suddenly feeling the need to reinspect Matt's beloved tiny trees. He starts mumbling about leaves and hobbies and brothers and is bending up and down to get a closer look at each shelf. Eventually, he hopes, he will arrive at what he needs to say.

And then Harvey spots it. In the very corner of the lowest shelf in the shed, overwhelmed by larger plants and the layering of shadows, a small bonsai with a neat handwritten: *Amazing Grace.*

'What's that one about?' Beam asks, heart in his cheeks, pointing at the little plant and then recoiling his arm to spin and point at something else, which happens to be a watering can requiring little explanation.

'That one,' says Matt, taking a long swig of his beer, 'is the one that got away.'

'Yes,' Harvey says. 'Yes.' He looks to his beer bottle for the next line. Can barely focus.

'And this?' he says at last. 'What do you call this particular home-brew, Matt?'

'That's just home-brew, Harvey.'

'No special flavour?'

'None that I can recall.'

'Well, I think you've nailed it with this one, Matt. Really, really nailed it.' Beam eyes the bottle at ridiculously close range lest it reveal a secret ingredient.

'You okay, Harvey?'

'Yeah,' Beam says, and wipes the beer across his forehead as though just back from auxiliary firefighting duty. 'It's just been a big day.'

'Sure has,' Matt says. 'Although it didn't go as badly as I thought it would.'

'Fuck, really?'

Beam feels for the shape of his phone in his suit jacket, which is presently holding in an olfactory tsunami of sweat and terror.

Matt says: 'No, I really thought Naomi and Penny would go hammer and tongs today — it's been building up again like the mother of all afternoon storms. But I think Bryan's efforts took the wind out of that.'

'Is he here?' Harvey says.

'I doubt it. Not sure I'd be opening him a beer if he did turn up.'

'Look, Matt,' Harvey says and looks at him squarely. 'I really can't thank you enough for what you did today. I mean, I just. I can't, I didn't ... there's ... it was, I don't know. You know. So many. What do you do?'

Matt grins. 'You should work in radio, Harvey.'

Beam laughs. 'I used to. Now I wouldn't even get a job hosting late-night love song dedications.'

The two men step out of the shed and walk slowly back to the house.

Falling into step behind Matt, his head full of things unsaid, Harvey stares hard at his funeral shoes and wonders if he's just failed the first and only test of friendship.

40

The hours lose shape after the sun sets. People go and people still come. No-one arriving now seems remotely post-funereal. Lynn makes an abortive attempt to put Naomi's boys to sleep, an act unnoticed by Naomi who is sitting on a dark-corner divan with Penny. They are ensconced in a conversation that, from Harvey's furtive glance, seems almost affectionate. It is, incredibly, the least strange thing he's observed today.

Conversations grow louder and Grace still hasn't answered his text. Beam considers phoning her, the liquid-courage call that is always the best and worst idea, but soon enough finds himself sat at Naomi's dining table with Suze, Cate and Jayne. Harvey signals to Suze that he might like a glass of that red she's having, to which his ex-wife rolls her eyes and takes a deep sip.

Cate looks up from her phone and says to no-one in particular, 'You know what's weird?'

'Twins,' replies Jayne.

'Weirder,' Cate says.

'I don't know,' says Suze.

'Tonight,' Cate says, 'was so much more fun than I thought it would be. It should have been depressing or lame, but it wasn't. Is that bad?'

'Evolution,' says Harvey.

His daughters reply in unison: 'What?'

'Humans developed laughter in the face of grief because we can't process all that sadness,' he says. 'It'd kill us.'

'That's bullshit, Harvey,' Suze says. 'Is that bullshit?'

'No, I think that's been studied,' he says. 'It's an academic theory.'

'I'll google it,' Jayne says.

'Oh,' Harvey says, now feeling the need to show that the sadness of which he speaks is not his own. '*Normal* Google won't have it, Jayne,' he says. '*Mere mortal* Google won't have it. You'll have to access the Google reserved for *academics*.'

Jayne looks at her sister quizzically. Beam's tone has ventured into his comfort zone of the uncomfortable.

'Someone *academic* came up with it,' he continues. 'Devoted an *entire life* to stumping up a case for it, referenced all sorts of boring arseholes and died an ironically miserable death celebrated by neighbourhood strangers with home-brew.'

Suze looks at the ceiling.

'Jesus, Dad,' says Cate. 'Issues.'

'Shots fired,' says Jayne.

'Harvey, can we have a word?' Suze says. She stands up, pushes in her chair and gestures to the next room or somewhere beyond.

Beam follows but not before giving the girls a playful thumbs up.

His route through the lounge room is happily interrupted by Finn's demand for Uncle Harvey to take the corner shot in the FIFA contest being played out on Matt and Naomi's large flat-screen. Beam obliges and somehow manages to switch off the Xbox and turn on the ducted vacuum with the push of two buttons.

He finds Suze in one of the children's darkened bedrooms, a child's night light soft-focusing one corner.

'Suze?' he says, finding his way to the sentry in the opposite corner. 'Are you angry with me? Should I stay in Shorton? Are we going to kiss for old times' sake?'

'You idiot,' she says and slaps him on the shoulder. 'I just wanted to know if Matt knows about Grace. What did he say?'

'I don't think he knows,' Beam says. 'I honestly don't.'

'Well,' Suze says, brushing the shoulder she's just slapped. 'What are you going to do?'

'I don't know,' Beam says. 'Call for back-up?'

'*Harvey.*'

'I don't *know*, Suze. It'll be okay.'

Even in the semi-dark, his ex-wife finds something exasperating to look at directly above her. 'Harvey,' she says finally, 'you know not everything takes care of itself. You can't run away from everything.'

Beam thinks he doesn't know this at all; is about to say so when the room lights up out of his jacket pocket.

Beam pulls out his phone, sees Grace's name. He kisses Suze on the cheek and calls a taxi.

41

ON AIR

'A wise man once said, or quite possibly a woman — in fact, I'd pay good money on it being a woman — that betrayal is its own punishment. If that's true, then we should all get off Wayne Carey's case now because the size and scope of that man's betrayal should buy him a lifetime in purgatory. Of course that's not me saying that, listeners — let he who is without sin and all that — but that's what you would have read in the weekend's papers. That's certainly what I read all weekend, ingesting it all in one hit like a bad airport novel. Speaking of bad airport novels, Kelly, have we got a prize for Caller of the Morning? We neglected to give one away yesterday and I haven't heard the end of it.'

Kelly, a commerce graduate who's lost her way, doesn't look up from her desk.

'Thanks, Kelly. Fantastic concert tickets coming up for the best call.'

Kelly looks incredulously through the glass, arms upturned: *What concert tickets?*

'But back to Wayne Carey. King Carey. Football royalty. On the field he can do no wrong and in this country that counts for a lot, if not everything. But according to reports that are now widely confirmed, the King is now at odds with his own club due to an indiscretion at a recent social gathering. That's how the ABC is describing this tawdry situation, folks, but I can put a finer point on it. Wayne Carey had an affair with his teammate's missus. The *missus*. Of his *teammate*. In the very same act, he ultimately betrayed his own wife in a very public and humiliating way. Folks, we could talk all morning about what sort of guy does this to his wife, about the long-term repercussions of a very short-term act. And I'm happy to take those calls. I'm always happy to take your calls. But I'm also very keen to explore the other dimension to this and in many ways it's the part that enrages us most, whether or not we care to admit it. It's what I'm calling the no-go zone. It's that place not bounded by contracts or rules; nothing is written down about the no-go zone. It's shaped by human expectations, dangerously implicit and often only ratified after the zone has been breached.'

Beam looks over at Kelly, who is reading the *Sydney Morning Herald* with her feet on the desk.

'Wayne Carey didn't just have adulterous sex with anyone. He had it with his teammate's wife. That's a no-go zone. We've called it. Polite society has called it. And it lifts the act from linear betrayal to something far more complicated and socially unforgivable. Or does it? Are we only having this discussion because the centrepiece is Wayne Carey? Maybe Wayne Carey doesn't think the no-go zone applies to him *because* he's Wayne Carey? Maybe elite sport occupies a rarefied atmosphere that exists beyond normal society?'

Beam spins the biro at his fingertips. Today's topic hits on *everything*. God he loves this job. 'Maybe,' he posits, setting up his call to arms, 'King Carey and Anthony Stevens will be able to sort this out over a little kick-to-kick?'

He looks through the glass at his utterly disengaged producer just as the phones light up and her arms flail across the desk, causing an eruption of broadsheet chaos.

It's going to be a magic morning, Beam thinks. A huge ratings week. *Thank you Wayne Carey and your kingly dick.*

And it is. It's talkback gold, bar a couple of suitably twisted ex-wives who argue vehemently that all zones that aren't the home-zone are no-go zones. After the last couple of dry, politics-heavy days of talk, Beam knows the suits on level eight are being reminded today of his power to get people talking.

He hears a litany of betrayal yarns, some choked out in rage, others eked through sniffly recollections. Always the common denominator is a betrayal made infinitely more painful by the choice of target; by the breaking of a rule that shouldn't have to be written down. Some are clear-cut — the guy who hooks up with his best mate's ex-wife, the woman who sleeps with her sister's husband — yet others are beautifully divisive dinner-party fodder, panoplies of ethical conundrums and moral ambiguities. It's sad and dark and wonderful.

Bookending it all are two calls from self-confessed breachers of no-go zones, both women, both now married to their best friend's ex-husbands, who argue that the zone is redundant if permission from the otherwise aggrieved third party is granted.

'Indeed,' Harvey says, rounding out three hours of talkback manna that felt like twenty wild minutes, 'it's generally easier to ask for permission than forgiveness. But how many of us would grant it?'

42

Harvey stands at Grace's unopened front door, abruptly weary and uncertain. He experiences an unbidden rush of self-awareness — it's been happening a lot lately — that merely serves to illuminate how confused he is. Having never coveted clarity, Beam is underwhelmed by its staccato arrival in middle age.

He's about to knock when the door opens and Grace stands before him. She is wearing a thin white dress, no shoes, her hair splayed around her shoulders. *Oh God*, Beam thinks. He instinctively bends down to remove a shoe because his dick is getting very hard, very quickly. *For fuck's sake, Harvey.*

In the cab he had prepared himself for a night of talking, for the revelations about Grace's marriage to Matt that she'd always glossed over. For hours about sliding doors and missed opportunities, regret and resolve. For an inevitable ending.

But Grace only wants Beam, for now at least, to make love to her. She tells him this as she roughly takes Harvey's hand and leads him along the dark hallway to her bedroom. The bed is unmade, awash with sheets and cushions, and Grace climbs into the middle of it and waits for Harvey to remove a suit that might as well be a straitjacket secured with magician's padlocks so frenzied are his movements to escape it.

Not for the first time, perhaps for the thirtieth or fortieth, Beam finds himself feeling utterly grateful and unworthy of this woman's body. Of her unlikely presence in his life.

He's grateful too that he hadn't had the conversation with

Matt tonight that might stop all this. To hell with courage.

If this is the last time he gets to make love to Grace, Beam is going to ensure its preservation in both their memories. He is acutely present, slow and deliberate, addressing every contour, every hollow, every part of her that might never have been kissed. He returns to her mouth again and again, makes it about them, about her. When he is deepest, Beam holds himself deathly still inside her, rejecting every compulsion to rush. He grasps the small of her back as she comes and tells Grace he loves her over and over.

Everything that is wrong with the world can be fixed, he thinks.

In the morning, Beam awakes to Grace's fingers playing with the hairs on his chest, disappointingly grey and wiry in the unforgiving early sunlight.

'You know what's weird, Harvey,' she says at last.

Beam improves his arm's cradling of Grace's head, looks up at the ceiling fan and smiles to himself. 'Twins?'

Grace laughs loudly and Harvey inwardly thanks his funny daughters. An image of Suze snaps into his vision and he blinks to flick the channel.

Finally Grace says, 'No, what's weird is that you came back here for closure, but I'm the one who found it.'

And Beam nods, though he isn't entirely sure why.

43

Beam takes the aisle seat and realises he's on the wrong side of the plane to wave goodbye. He hopes someone on the other side makes sufficient hand movements in one of the tiny windows to give his family something to aim for.

It had been an overly long morning of farewells at any rate — a two-hour flight delay that neither Penny nor Naomi was going to yield to. Little Finn had become lost in the airport at some point and Harvey had made increasingly frantic checks of the men's toilets before the boy reappeared holding a stuffed kangaroo and the hand of an elderly Chinese woman.

'Three is so much harder than two,' Naomi had said to the woman by way of thanks.

Penny had glanced at Harvey and rolled her eyes. While the sisters had seemed to make a semblance of peace at Lionel's funeral, they had quickly settled back into the bristly circling game that is their discomfort zone. To fully unpick the hurts of the past would require a laying down of arms that neither woman seemed to have the energy for.

Harvey had listened to both sides of their stories in recent months, countless times in myriad settings, sober and drunk, tearful and indifferent. He'd entered an echo chamber long vacated by their mother. And he believed both his sisters, in fact. Each case would win at trial. And he had rediscovered how fiercely he admired their strength to simply stay here. Maybe you had to stay angry to hold on.

Bryan had not come to the airport, not that Harvey had either expected or wanted him to. 'He sends his best wishes,' Penny had said sincerely. And they had all laughed uproariously as if it might be true.

Beam had said goodbye to his mother at Naomi's that morning. Lynn hated airports — the noise of the planes could set her tinnitus off for days. She gave Harvey a long hug and told him to come home sooner next time. 'I won't live forever,' she'd said. Patted his stomach and told him to lay off the wine for a while.

'Why don't you come and visit me, Mum?' Harvey had said. 'I've got a spare room and you'd love it. You'd love Sydney. I could take a few days off.'

'Well,' Lynn had said, nervously eyeing the tiles between their feet. 'You know the terrorism worries me. There's no need to keep building all those mosques. I worry about you crossing that bridge too. I sit here and I worry about it every single day.'

Harvey thought this seemed highly unlikely.

'But let's wait until you get a job,' she'd said, 'and we'll talk about it then.'

A job.

Beam knew his mother would never come to Sydney. He'd have to come back here to see her again — and he would. The idea no longer sat in the dark part of his brain that couldn't make a decision.

Plus Cate was staying here for now. Beam had not been able to talk her out of it, not that he'd tried hard. He could see what appealed to her about the idea — the lure of a fresh canvas. Reinvention. Roll again. She was not so different to him.

'You'll get bored,' he'd said to her the night before. 'You'll miss your mum and your sister.'

'They drive me crazy, Dad.'

'What about me?'

'They drive you crazy too.'

He'd laughed and hugged her tightly and kissed her on the

crown of her head.

And then he'd cried. In spite of himself, Beam let a single tear give way to a stream of them. He'd cried for reasons he didn't know and couldn't see yet. Not while he was still here.

He had to go.

44

Of all the take-offs Beam has experienced in his life, this is the worst. The plane idles up the runway — *idles* — as though it has another couple of kilometres to spare, which it doesn't: the route is abruptly short, truncated to allow for a new housing development, and Beam knows in his marrow and before anyone else does that it's not going fast enough. The nose will lift and then slam to the ground. Some will survive if they don't explode.

Having tied up a few loose ends in his hometown, Harvey will die today. Every story is already written.

But Grace puts a hand on Beam's arm just as the plan begins its half-hearted ascent and he breathes in sharply, then deeply, and lets his temple rest against hers.

'That's the worst part over,' Grace says. 'Easy from here.'

'Why does it have to be so *hard*?' Beam asks.

'I don't know,' she says and threads her fingers through Beam's. 'Do you want me to say something philosophical?'

'God, no.'

Grace laughs and it's easily his favourite sound these days.

Directly above them in the overhead compartment is Matt's farewell present to Harvey, carefully stowed in a box lined with damp newspaper and wrapped in a heavy-duty bin liner with small holes punched through.

He'd given it to Harvey two nights ago; said he thought the airport goodbye should be siblings only, though they both knew why he wouldn't be there.

'Your first bonsai,' Matt had said, handing Harvey the small tree. No longer *Amazing Grace*, the handwritten label now reads: *Look after me. Google it.*

And Beam had. He'd printed out instructions from Penny's computer that night.

Caring for your bonsai over time creates a deep sense of satisfaction. There is no replacement for time; it is always constant and moving forward. It is said that through the study of bonsai, one will learn more than bonsai. Apply water when the soil appears dry — never allow the soil to become completely dry.

Permission, he thinks now as the plane dips recklessly to the left, *is generally easier to seek than forgiveness.*

A final glimpse of Shorton River appears over Grace's shoulder.

Matt had made it mercifully easy. Beam knows he deserves less, but he'll take it.

45

ON AIR

'It's just gone ten pm, lovelorn folk, and I must say it's been highly enjoyable filling in tonight for your resident DJ, Dr Love. And that's his real name, apparently — it says so here on his business card. Born for the job.

'I'll keep taking those love song requests right through until midnight, after which I turn into a pumpkin and cab it home. That's what we're here for, folks. To fill each other's ears and crowd out too much thought. Keep moving forward one song at a time. "Late Night Love Notes" — it's so much cheaper than therapy.

'Thanks to Kenneth for that last request, "Tainted Love" by Soft Cell, an odd choice I'll grant you, but love isn't all roses and sexy texts, is it, Kenneth? It's a tough gig. Lots of collateral damage while you figure it out, by which time you're old and requesting eighties songs because you can't sleep.

'Goodnight, Kenneth.'

Goodnight.

ACKNOWLEDGEMENTS

Many thanks to early readers of this manuscript, each of whom gave me thoughtful and wise suggestions about everything from character names and plot devices through to the time of day people normally have sex in middle age. Monique Price, Emily Schofield-Cox, Matt Brown, Mignon Shardlow, Clint Greagen and David Cox — thank you so much.

Fremantle Press, what a great crew you are and what wonderful work you do. Georgia Richter, the understanding and warmth you extended to Harvey Beam helped me finish this book with a wellspring of confidence rather than self-doubt — manna for the first-time novelist.

A novel in progress is a game of inches, a marathon of one hundred metre sprints. It sits in the house like an extra child, often getting too much attention, sometimes getting none. The people in my house have been very good about accepting the presence of the extra house guest. Thank you Coxy, Emily, Lara, Carlton and Buddy, the under-walked dog.

Finally, thank you collectively to those family and friends who have supported my creative writing endeavours, even when they suspected I was mining their lives. This is not my story and not my family's story; it is many people's stories, real and imagined.

It is what it is.

First published 2018 by
FREMANTLE PRESS
25 Quarry Street, Fremantle WA 6160
(PO Box 158, North Fremantle WA 6159)
www.fremantlepress.com.au

Cover image: Shutterstock (background); Nemida; Tetra Images / Alamy Stock
Photo A5KN0P; LAMB / Alamy Stock Photo LAMB / Alamy Stock Photo
Printed by McPherson's, Australia

National Library of Australia
Cataloguing-in-Publication entry:
Cox, Carrie, author
Harvey Beam / Carrie Cox
ISBN 9781925591088 (paperback)

Cox, Carrie, 1972– author.
Harvey beam / Carrie Cox.
ISBN: 9781925591088 (paperback)
Dysfunctional families—Fiction.
Conduct of life—Fiction.
Suspense fiction.

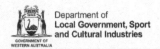

Fremantle Press is supported by the State Government through the Department
of Local Government, Sport and Cultural Industries.

Publication of this title was assisted by the Commonwealth Government through
the Australia Council, its arts funding and advisory body.